CHRONOSYNC

SCIENCE OF THE SOUL

By

Neil Perry Gordon

ISBN: **979-8-9875632-6-7**

To my late brother, Craig,
This novel is for you—a tribute to your enduring spirit and the countless ways
you inspired me. May your soul continue its heavenly journey toward rebirth,
guided by the same boundless wonder you carried throughout your life.

Contents

CHAPTER ONE
THE INTERVIEW

The silence was absolute, as if the entire world had paused, holding its collective breath for the answer about to be delivered—the answer that would change everything.

"Dr. Wallace," I began, my voice carrying the gravity of the question, "we find ourselves at a pivotal moment in human understanding. Is the soul eternal? Has ChronoSync truly provided evidence that we live beyond one lifetime?"

Dr. Adrienne Wallace met my gaze, her brown eyes reflecting years of research and discovery. "Marcus, ChronoSync has pierced the veil of humanity's greatest mystery. Our findings indicate that the memories and experiences often attributed to the soul do not perish with our physical form but are carried forward, encoded within our DNA."

She paused, allowing her words to resonate. "Labeling the soul as 'eternal' crosses into philosophical and theological territory. Nevertheless, what ChronoSync offers is scientific evidence of a consciousness that endures. Our research has documented cases where individuals encounter remarkably detailed memories that align with historical records—memories that don't belong to their current lifespan."

My heart raced with excitement and awe. "Dr. Wallace, you're addressing one of humanity's deepest enigmas."

Adrienne met my gaze, her expression serious yet serene. "Indeed! ChronoSync offers compelling evidence that the soul is reborn. The patterns we've discovered in the DNA tell a coherent story of experiences and memories that transcend an individual's current lifetime. These are fragments and chapters of a continuous journey beyond the here and now."

I leaned back, absorbing the impact of her words. "Please forgive my need for absolute clarity, but what you are saying is that there is incontrovertible evidence to suggest the soul's journey continues beyond our present life?"

She pushed back a strand of her golden-brown hair and nodded. "That's precisely what I'm saying, Marcus. The evidence we've gathered and analyzed points to a journey—a continuity of the self that extends far beyond what we once understood. This isn't mere speculation; it's a conclusion drawn from rigorous scientific study and observation."

Reflecting the monumental nature of this acknowledgment, I continued, "And what you're suggesting here today, on this global stage, is that an afterlife and reincarnation isn't just a religious or spiritual belief but a fundamental truth of our existence?"

"Correct," Adrienne replied. "ChronoSync doesn't just hint at the possibility of reincarnation—it provides a window into its reality. With every session and life we unveil, we gather more evidence that what we call the 'soul' does not cease with death but is an ongoing presence throughout the ages, carrying with it the wisdom and experiences of many lives."

I absorbed the gravity of her declaration, hesitating before adding my thoughts. "This revelation isn't just a scientific milestone; it's a philosophical lantern illuminating paths in our minds previously shadowed by doubt."

Adrienne smiled. "ChronoSync has opened doors to understanding the soul's journey. While this is proof, I also see it as an invitation to explore the boundless potential of human consciousness. This technology challenges us to reconsider the very nature of our existence, prompting us to reflect on how we live our lives, how we treat each other, and how we approach the profound mysteries of life and death."

I exhaled, the weight of the interview settling over me. "Your revelations today—they'll resonate far beyond the walls of this studio.

They'll stir debates everywhere—in homes, universities, and especially in places of worship."

She nodded, a solemn affirmation of the truth I had spoken.

"We're on the cusp of a new historical epoch," I continued, the realization dawning on me and everyone behind the scenes. "The kind that future generations of scholars, theologians, and philosophers will honor and pay tribute to."

Adrienne interjected softly, "I hope that's the case."

"And ChronoSync," I went on, the story unfolding before me, "has fundamentally altered our grasp of humanity and has dared to answer the life-altering questions about our existence."

"Indeed, it will open many doors," Adrienne acknowledged.

I offered a thoughtful nod. "Your work has invited us to explore further, to question more, and to consider a future filled with possibilities that were once pure speculation or faith. The discourse on the soul's perpetuity is only just beginning."

Adrienne met my gaze, unflinching, her voice steady. "Our research into the human genome has uncovered markers suggesting the persistence of the soul's journey. These markers carry complex information beyond genetic inheritance—echoing past experiences."

I pressed on. "But how does this scientifically prove reincarnation?"

Adrienne responded thoughtfully. "In a scientific framework, 'proof' requires observable, repeatable outcomes. ChronoSync offers such compelling evidence. The consistency of past-life memories across diverse populations is remarkable and suggests a pattern that only the concept of reincarnation could explain."

I rubbed the back of my neck, furrowing my brow in contemplation. "But where are these soulful memories stored?"

Adrienne paused, thoughtfully considering my question. "The storage of memories, particularly those spanning multiple lifetimes, is a complex and fascinating phenomenon," she began, her tone reflective. "Our research suggests that memories are encoded within the very fabric of our being, woven into the tapestry of our DNA and cellular structure."

She continued, her explanation gaining momentum. "ChronoSync employs AI to identify and interpret these memories, drawing upon a sophisticated algorithm that analyzes genetic sequences and neural patterns. By mapping the intricate connections between past-life experiences and present-day individuals, ChronoSync unlocks the latent memories stored within our biological framework, providing a window into the rich tapestry of our consciousness."

Adrienne's words resonated with me, sparking a newfound understanding of the groundbreaking work in past-life research. As I absorbed her insights, I couldn't help but marvel at the profound implications of ChronoSync's ability to illuminate the hidden depths of human experience, transcending the limitations of time and space in the quest for truth and understanding.

"So you're saying it's possible that these memories, these experiences… they don't just disappear. They are, in a sense, eternal?"

"That's right. Our consciousness is the essence of who we are and carries us forward beyond our current lifetime. The implications are staggering and point to a continuity of the soul that many have long suspected but have been unable to substantiate until now."

"Dr. Wallace," I began, my voice steady. "Can you explain in detail how ChronoSync works?"

Adrienne nodded, her hands folded neatly on her lap. "Certainly, Marcus. At its core, ChronoSync deciphers the language of the human genome, searching for markers that we believe carry the memories of our past lives. These markers are more than mere genetic milestones; they are, we hypothesize, the imprints left by the experiences of what many would call the soul."

Adrienne's explanation hung in the air as I took a moment to absorb her words. I leaned in, intrigued. "So, it's a kind of DNA memory?"

"Exactly," Adrienne affirmed. "And advanced AI algorithms reconstruct these memories into a coherent narrative."

The conversation shifted as I pondered the implications. "As we know, reincarnation has been a cornerstone of various religions and beliefs. But now, you're suggesting it's a universal truth?"

Adrienne's eyes reflected the significance of her answer. "Our research indicates that reincarnation is not just a belief but a reality. Evidence shows a consistent pattern of past-life experiences across all our clients, regardless of their current faith or skepticism."

"And what will be the impact on society?"

Adrienne sighed, her words pressing into the air. "As you would imagine, the ramifications are profound. It challenges the very fabric of many societal norms and beliefs. On the one hand, it will be a source of great comfort for many, providing a sense of continuity and purpose. Conversely, it will raise complex questions about morality, identity, and the nature of consciousness itself."

I nodded. "What does this mean for personal relationships, justice, and how we perceive our lives?"

Adrienne paused, choosing her words carefully. "It's complex. On a personal level, it can strain or strengthen current relationships as people reconcile their past connections with the present. In the realm of justice, it poses questions about guilt and responsibility across lifetimes. And as for our lives"—she spread her hands slightly—"it encourages us to live with an awareness that our actions ripple beyond our current existence."

I absorbed her words, my mind swirling with the implications. The depth of ChronoSync's impact was staggering, touching on many facets of human existence. I marveled at the thought of it. The intricacy of the device and its profound capabilities fascinated me.

"Dr. Wallace," I began, my voice tinged with genuine interest, "why did you name your creation ChronoSync?"

"It's an interesting story," she said, facing me fully. "The name ChronoSync didn't come to me immediately. It evolved as the concept behind the device became clearer."

I nodded, eager to hear more.

"ChronoSync is derived from two Greek roots," Adrienne continued. "Chrono, meaning time, and Sync, short for synchronize. The essence of the device is its ability to bridge different points in time, to synchronize past lives with the present. It's not just about viewing the past; it's about creating a harmonious alignment between our former selves and who we are today."

As the interview progressed, I couldn't help but notice the meticulous array of lab equipment surrounding us. Each piece, I assumed, contributed to the complex network that allowed ChronoSync to communicate its findings. But for some reason, my eyes were drawn to an intricately designed, silver, translucent vessel that stood about ten inches tall. Its almond shape tapered gracefully at the ends, resembling a small, elegant sculpture. The surface of the device was smooth and slightly reflective, giving it an ethereal glow under the laboratory lights. Tiny, delicate engravings of intricate patterns spiraled around its body, almost like veins of a leaf, hinting at the sophisticated technology housed within. The translucent material allowed a faint, pulsating light to emanate from its core, suggesting a heartbeat-like rhythm that gave the impression of a living, breathing entity. The overall aesthetic was futuristic and organic, blending sleek modernity with a sense of ancient mysticism.

Sensing my curiosity, Adrienne gently moved her hand toward the device, her fingers lightly stroking its outer casing as if it were a beloved pet. The delicate motion was almost reverent, a subtle dance between the tangible and the mystical.

"This," Adrienne began, her voice almost a whisper, "is the brain of ChronoSync." My eyes widened as I realized the significance of the vessel before me. The room held its breath, her words settling around us like a tangible presence.

"I gave her a name," she said with a slight blush, giving the piece a gentle stroke. "She's Mira."

"Mira?" I said, offering a smile. "Why Mira?"

"Mira is derived from the Latin word mirari, meaning to wonder or to marvel. It evokes a sense of awe and mystery. Additionally, Mira is a star in the constellation Cetus, known for its dramatic variability in brightness, symbolizing the device's dynamic and transformative nature."

Adrienne's connection to the device was palpable, a bond transcending mere technology. At that moment, I wondered if ChronoSync was more than a technological marvel. Could it be a connection to the Divine? Had Dr. Wallace opened a channel to the spirit world? The thought sent a shiver down my spine, the implications both thrilling and terrifying.

My final question was one of personal curiosity. "Dr. Wallace, how has this affected you personally?" I asked with genuine wonder.

Adrienne's smile was tinged with philosophical depth. "It made me realize the preciousness of each moment and the importance of leaving a positive imprint on the fabric of eternity. We're not just living for today but for the lineage of our souls."

As the final words of our interview hung in the air, I leaned forward, an idea dawning in my expression. "Dr. Wallace, to truly convey the essence of ChronoSync to our readers, I'm inclined to ask if I might experience it firsthand. Would it be possible to waive the fee for an enquiring journalist looking to deepen his report?"

Adrienne's eyes gleamed with approval at my professional pursuit. "For the sake of thorough reporting, I think we can make an exception. We'll waive the $50,000 fee and give you and *The New York Times* a firsthand understanding of ChronoSync."

I nodded, my professional demeanor giving way to a more personal excitement. "That's an incredible opportunity, Dr. Wallace. I'm ready to dive into my past and bring that experience to life for our readers."

CHAPTER TWO
ÉTIENNE

With the cameras gone, I returned to ChronoSync's laboratory, surrounded by the soothing hum of machines and the antiseptic scent of technological progress. The team had been thorough, taking blood samples, scraping cells from my tongue, and snipping strands of my hair—each specimen a potential key to unlocking my past life. As I awaited the analysis, a technician caught my eye—a slender man in his thirties whose eyes burned with the zeal of belief in the technology he served.

Curious to hear a different version than Dr. Wallace's, I asked, "How does all this work?"

The technician, a young man named Alex, adjusted his black-framed glasses and leaned against a steel lab table, his passion for the subject evident. "ChronoSync merges the frontier of AI with our genetic legacy to decode the saga of our previous existence," he began, his hands moving animatedly. "Central to our system is a complex algorithm, an AI creation, that meticulously combs through our DNA. Our genome is a historical document, charting our physical journey and holding faint echoes of our past lives."

I nodded, encouraging the explanation.

"Contrary to traditional genetic markers linked to our inherited traits, ChronoSync targets elusive sequences within our DNA," Alex continued. "These segments, once dismissed as genomic detritus, are where ChronoSync hunts for residual patterns that match historical and genealogical records."

I grimaced. "What do you mean by 'genomic detritus'?"

Alex smiled, eyes alight with the enthusiasm of a scientist on the brink of discovery. "The term 'detritus' typically refers to debris or discarded material. In genetics, it's been used to describe parts of our DNA, once thought to be just biological leftovers without function—junk DNA, essentially. However, with ChronoSync, we've begun to see these segments not as waste but as untapped archives. They're not merely residue; they hold patterns that connect us to our ancestors in ways we never imagined possible. By targeting these sequences, ChronoSync doesn't just look at what's inherited but also at what history has silently left within us."

As I listened, Alex described how individuals who embark on the ChronoSync journey have their DNA exhaustively mapped out. "AI then sifts through this rich genetic landscape to find sequences that resonate with data we've scanned from the pages of history."

"And when it finds a match?" I inquired, my journalistic instinct piqued.

"Ah, that's where ChronoSync truly excels," Alex said with a smile. "It doesn't just locate a match. It weaves the found patterns with contextual data from the era, creating a predictive model of the individual's past life. It then renders this information into an immersive virtual reality narrative."

I imagined the vast implications, both personal and societal. "So, you're providing a window into one's history, not through stories or speculation, but through some sort of direct experience?"

"Exactly," Alex affirmed. "ChronoSync isn't just a glimpse into who we might have been—it's an expedition into the very essence of our existence, crafted by the silent stories etched in our DNA."

Gesturing to the small device pulsating before us, I asked, "And what role does this device play in all of this?"

Alex's expression grew even more animated. "The vessel, or Mira, as Dr. Wallace named her, is the brain of ChronoSync. This is not just another piece of technology; it's the key to accessing and projecting the temporal data."

I nodded as he continued, "Mira's translucent material allows a faint, pulsating light to emanate from its core, suggesting a heartbeat-like rhythm. This light is a manifestation of its compact fusion reactor, which powers the device. Furthermore, Mira is the interface between the user and the vast, untapped archives of one's genetic history. You can say it's the medium through which ChronoSync translates silent DNA sequences into living, breathing narratives."

Leaning forward, I absorbed the profound possibilities. Mira wasn't just a tool but a gateway to the past, blending the boundaries between technology and the human spirit. I sat back, contemplating the extraordinary voyage I was about to undertake—one that would take me through the annals of time, not as a passive observer but as an active participant in the history of my soul.

*

My footsteps echoed in the hushed corridors of ChronoSync's austere offices, starkly contrasting the maelstrom of thoughts whirling in my mind. Upon arriving, Alex, the same enthusiastic technician who had taken my samples the day before, greeted me. With a solemn nod, he ushered me into a sparsely furnished room.

"Mr. Vega, thank you for coming back. We have completed the analysis," Alex said, gesturing for me to sit across from him.

Settling in, my heart rate ticked upward in anticipation as Alex opened a sleek, silver file. Inside lay the findings, the narrative of a life I had once led. Alex cleared his throat and began to read aloud.

"ChronoSync Past-Life Experience Report: Marcus Vega," Alex said, glancing up at me before continuing. "In the mid-18th century, at the heart of the Enlightenment in France, you were a celebrated philosopher and publisher. Your Parisian salon was a crucible for revolutionary ideas, attracting intellectuals who debated the future of society. You published essays that championed reason, freedom of speech, and reforms, laying the groundwork for transformative societal changes."

Alex's voice gave life to the words, each sentence painting a vivid portrait of my dynamic past. "Your name was Étienne DuBois. As a publisher, your pen and press were not just tools but powerful catalysts for change, disseminating ideas that would echo through the ages."

I could almost hear the clatter of the printing press and feel the thrill of distributing radical thoughts under the cloak of night. Étienne was not just a man of words but a man of action. He understood the power of the written word and wielded it like a sword, cutting through the ignorance and tyranny of the time.

Alex scanned the report before continuing. "You were at the core of your intellectual community," he said, his voice taking on a thoughtful tone. "Your existence was interwoven with the very fabric of the Enlightenment. Spirited discussions and the covert spread of revolutionary texts marked your days." He looked up briefly as if imagining the scene himself. "In the dimly lit rooms of Paris, amidst the smoke of candles and the murmur of thoughtful conversation, you understood your purpose."

He paused, letting his words settle. "Étienne's salon," he resumed, "was more than just a gathering place; it was a battleground for ideas. The walls of your home had witnessed some of the most profound discussions of the era. Thinkers like Voltaire, Rousseau, and Diderot debated the nature of man, society, and governance within those walls. There, the old world met the new, and the seeds of revolution were sown."

Alex took a deep breath before continuing, his tone reflecting a mix of admiration and caution. "Your contributions went far beyond the printed page," he added, his voice steady. "You were known for your courage in facing the dangers of such a role. In a time when dissent was dangerous, you risked everything to ensure that the flame of Enlightenment continued to burn."

He stopped, letting the full depth of Étienne's life sink in. "Étienne DuBois's life was one of purpose and peril," Alex concluded, his gaze meeting mine. "He was a man who stood at the crossroads of history, whose efforts helped to shape the future. His commitment to the ideals of the Enlightenment—reason, liberty, and justice—left an indelible mark on the world."

But there was more. Alex's tone shifted, becoming more intimate.

"There was a woman, Lila. She fervently supported your ideas and was an ardent revolutionary. It seems she viscerally connected with you. Her presence was a spellbinding force in your life."

I blinked, taken aback. A woman? I hadn't expected that. The image of a passionate revolutionary intertwined with my past was startling and strangely familiar. My mind raced, trying to piece together the fragments of this revelation, the echoes of a connection that transcended time itself.

"But Lila was more than a companion; she was a muse and a co-conspirator. You met during a heated debate in your salon, where her fiery rhetoric and passionate beliefs captivated you. Together, you plotted and dreamed of a new world."

"Were they lovers?" I asked.

Alex nodded. "Their romance had blossomed amidst the revolutionary fervor, each encounter charged with the energy of their shared ideals. Lila's eyes saw into Étienne's soul, understanding him in ways he scarcely understood himself. But their love was not to last. During a violent uprising against the King's men, Lila was shot. In her dying breath, she promised to find Étienne again, her words etched in her writings: 'Our souls are bound for eternity.'"

Lila's pledge echoed in my mind, a haunting reminder of love transcending lifetimes. I wondered if our souls were indeed bound and if I would, in this lifetime, meet this soul again. The uncertainty gnawed at me, but the possibility filled me with a profound sense of purpose.

I added, trying to reinforce my understanding, "You know all of this because of ChronoSync's ability to pinpoint my past life by identifying my DNA, placing it at a specific time in history. If Étienne left any historical record, as he did as a prominent publisher, you can verify and bring those details to life."

Alex nodded, a hint of a smile on his face. "Exactly, Marcus. ChronoSync's AI technology cross-references your DNA with historical databases. When it identifies a match, it can pinpoint specific events, relationships, and personal achievements from your past life. In Étienne's case, his extensive records as a publisher allowed us to piece together significant moments of his—and, by extension, your—past life. This technology doesn't just tell us who you were; it helps us understand the context of your past experiences, making it all come alive in astonishing detail."

Settling into the moment, the weight of lifetimes upon me, I almost overlooked Alex's next offer, which came as a soft inquiry, nearly reverent in the face of my profound journey.

"Mr. Vega," Alex asked, his voice tinged with anticipation, "would you like to step directly into Étienne's shoes? To see his world through his eyes with our virtual reality experience?"

I took a moment to process the question, my thoughts swirling with the magnitude of the offer. Then, wide-eyed and filled with sudden eagerness, I replied, "Yes, I would. Absolutely."

Alex led me to a small room with walls lined with equipment that hummed with possibilities. The centerpiece was a sleek and futuristic virtual reality headset, waiting like a portal to another time.

I hesitated for a moment, my heart pounding with a mixture of excitement and apprehension. Alex's reassuring smile did little to quell the swirl of thoughts in my mind. I could feel the headset's weight in my hands, its surface cool and smooth, an artifact of cutting-edge technology designed to bridge the gap between reality and memory.

As I slipped it over my head, the fit was snug but comfortable, the interior padding molding gently to the contours of my skull. There was a brief moment of darkness, a silence that stretched on, amplifying the sound of my breathing. Then, with a soft melodic chime, the device activated.

A cascade of light enveloped my vision, patterns and symbols dancing before my eyes, aligning and calibrating. I could feel a subtle vibration through the helmet, like the purring of a distant engine, as the sensors adjusted to my neural patterns. The room around me began to dissolve, the familiar walls and equipment fading away, replaced by a shifting landscape of data and imagery.

Colors burst into view, coalescing into shapes and forms that gradually became clearer and more defined. I was no longer in the small room but entirely somewhere else, a new reality around me. The past and present began to blur, the boundaries of time bending to the will of the ChronoSync device.

I could hear Alex's voice, now distant and ethereal, guiding me through the transition into this alternate reality. "Remember, Marcus, focus on the objective. Your thoughts shape this world," Alex's words echoed, a reminder of the delicate balance I had to maintain.

The landscape before me solidified into a scene of a bustling marketplace in the heart of a city. The scents of fresh bread and spices filled the air, mingling with the vibrant chatter of vendors and shoppers. I marveled at the accuracy of the simulation, every detail meticulously recreated from my past-life memories.

As I navigated the streets in Étienne's shoes, I was no longer a spectator but an active participant in the daily theater of what I assumed was the intellectual heart of mid-18th century Paris. I felt the cobblestones underfoot and heard the mix of languages merging into the symphony of the melting pot.

In the salon, great thinkers from all walks of life poured in, their voices a cascade of accents, speaking fluent French. An elderly philosopher lamented the stagnation of the old regime, his words heavy with insight. At the same time, a young poet, her eyes bright with the promise of new ideas, chatted excitedly about her latest work inspired by Étienne's essays. Each shared a piece of their story, seeking the comfort of shared ideals in their discourse.

Remarkably, I understood every word, even though I didn't speak French in my present life. The language flowed naturally, a relic from my life as Étienne, connecting me to these conversations with a profound familiarity.

As Étienne, I dispensed not just publications but counsel. With every discussion, I learned of a thinker's new theory, shared my concern over a looming crackdown, and rejoiced in the news of a pamphlet's broad circulation. The salon was more than a meeting place; it was a microcosm of the community's intellectual pulse, where joys and sorrows were woven into the daily fabric of life.

Emerging from the depths of Étienne's life, I felt a seismic shift within myself. The virtual journey through time had not just been a window into a former existence; it had unveiled the profound interconnectedness of human lives across the spectrums of time and philosophy. I vividly recalled the intimate moments with Lila—how our whispered conversations and shared glances bridged the gap between our souls, our dreams and fears laid bare in the quiet corners of the salon. We stole precious moments together in a secluded garden, where I would read my poetry to her, my words weaving a tapestry of revolution and love. At the same time, she sketched my likeness, her eyes capturing every detail with love and admiration. The nights we spent under the Parisian sky, discussing the ideals that would shape the future, were not just memories; they were the most cherished echoes of that life, resonating with a depth that transcended time.

As I disconnected from Étienne's world, now back in my present-day reality, I grappled with a new understanding. I had walked in the shoes of a French philosopher and publisher of truth and lived his joys, sorrows, everyday struggles, and vibrant intellectual life. This man, Étienne, was me in every meaningful way, and I realized that my current life as a journalist was a continuation of my past life's purpose. My eternal journey now had a renewed meaning, merging the wisdom and commitment to truth from my past life with the passion and drive of my present, guiding me to uphold the same principles in the modern world.

The ramifications of ChronoSync's revelations unfurled before me like the vast expanse of a tapestry still being woven. What would it mean for humanity if everyone could experience the life they had lived? How would it reshape our understanding of identity if we could see firsthand the threads of our souls woven through different cultures, religions, and lands?

I considered the empathy such experiences could foster and the barriers they might dissolve. At the same time, I pondered the complexities and challenges that such profound knowledge could introduce to our concepts of self and others, of past and present. The resilience and adaptability I'd witnessed in Étienne's life in revolutionary Paris were traits that humanity would need as they confronted the vast, uncharted implications of ChronoSync's revelations.

Lila's promise that our souls were bound for eternity echoed in my mind, a haunting reminder of love transcending lifetimes. I wondered if our souls were truly bound. Would we meet again? In this lifetime? The uncertainty gnawed at me, but the possibility filled me with a profound sense of purpose. As a journalist, this drove me to document the unfolding human drama and the interconnectedness of all souls, hoping my work might bring me closer to finding her again.

CHAPTER THREE
LIFE AFTER DEATH – LIFE BEFORE BIRTH

The New York Times
Humanity's Greatest Mystery Solved
By Marcus Vega

NEW YORK—The riddle that has perplexed philosophers, theologians, and seekers of truth across millennia has been unraveled, not through metaphysical speculation but through the objective lens of science. ChronoSync has emerged as a technological marvel, providing palpable evidence of our existence beyond the confines of our current lives, threaded within the intricate helixes of our DNA.

Within the white walls of a lab where the threads of history are woven into the tapestry of tomorrow, my initiation into the world of ChronoSync commenced. There, amidst the symphony of advanced machinery, I took my place in a lineage spanning centuries. Although the price of this journey stands at a daunting $50,000, for the sake of journalistic discovery, this fee was generously waived for *The New York Times*. This monetary sum, currently a tollbooth on the highway of our heritage, is not a permanent fixture. With her far-reaching vision, Dr. Adrienne Wallace, founder and CEO, sets the stage for a global network of ChronoSync centers. In this unfolding scenario, the cost of unveiling one's soulful odyssey is predicted to dwindle to a figure within the reach of all, transforming what could be a privilege into a shared human right.

In the crisp air of the ChronoSync lab, under the bright clinical lights, I met Alex—the technician whose steady hands would shepherd me through the gateway of time. As he gathered my bodily samples, each a whisper from my DNA yearning to unveil its secrets, I sensed the approach of a profound revelation. The strands of my hair, the cells from my tongue, and the blood from my veins each carried stories from an epoch I never knew I had witnessed.

Alex gathered the pieces of my genetic puzzle with the precision of a historian and an archivist's care. His every move was methodical, his focus absolute, as he prepared to feed the narrative of my being into the voracious maw of the AI that lay at the heart of ChronoSync's supercharged analysis.

He spoke softly of the marvels ahead, his voice a blend of excitement and reverence for the process. "Each sample," he explained, "contains genetic markers—subtle echoes of your past that the AI will decipher." Then added, "It's like listening for the melody of your history within the symphony of humanity."

With each vital recorded and each data point secured, Alex turned to the machinery that bridged the gap between then and now. The AI hummed to life, a chorus of electronic whispers, as it began the complex dance of analysis. It sifted through the rich tapestry of my genetic code, isolating sequences, mapping traits, and cross-referencing the past with the present.

In moments that stretched endlessly, the AI weaved the threads of my DNA into a vivid historical panorama. First, as a written report, then displayed through cables into the virtual reality headset, was the Paris of the mid-18th century, where cobblestone streets echoed with the fervor of revolutionary ideas and the camaraderie of a shared quest for enlightenment.

ChronoSync has shattered the boundaries of what we previously deemed possible. Through it, I have observed the trodden paths of a man named Étienne—a philosopher and publisher during the French Enlightenment. His existence, now vividly resurrected, had faded into the annals of history.

Discovering my past life as Étienne, a luminary of intellectual and revolutionary movements, has profoundly shaken the foundations of my beliefs. The virtual reality experience provided by ChronoSync has opened both a window and a doorway into my former self. I wandered the bustling salons and streets of Paris, engaging with thinkers and radicals, each interaction enriching the canvas of this transformative era in history.

Such a profound personal journey through ChronoSync has far-reaching implications beyond individual enlightenment. As more people delve into their past lives, the ramifications will ripple through various aspects of society. This emerging technology will undoubtedly change personal perceptions and challenge established norms and scientific paradigms.

The ChronoSync phenomenon will unfurl its influence into every thread of our social fabric. The healthcare sector will ponder the implications of past-life traumas and the secrets of genetic memories on today's well-being.

Art and culture will flourish under this new paradigm, with creators drawing inspiration from lives once lived, giving birth to art, literature, and music infused with echoes from ages past. Relationships, too, have entered a renaissance of connectivity as people rediscover bonds that defy the constraints of one lifetime.

In the wake of ChronoSync's revelation, businesses will pivot to unprecedented marketing strategies that appeal not just to the contemporary palette but also to the sophisticated tastes sculpted over the span of past lifetimes. Companies will delve into history archives to tailor their products and advertisements, catering to preferences and inclinations carved through the ages.

The mental health field will explore new terrains, providing therapies to integrate past selves' experiences into the present individual's psyche. Ethicists and philosophers will debate the morality of such deep dives into our essence, raising questions about privacy and the sanctity of the soul.

Meanwhile, the technology sector will boom with innovations to enhance the ChronoSync experience, creating industries dedicated to past-life exploration while safeguarding against the exploitation of this delicate and profound knowledge.

Social services will be transformed, recognizing the influence of past lives on current societal roles and offering support systems that consider the holistic journey of the individual soul. Marriage counselors and family therapists gain a new tool, facilitating understanding and reconciliation through the lens of eternity.

Even our daily routines undergo subtle shifts as individuals seek meaning in the mundane, enlightened by the awareness of their vast, multi-era identities. Past-life skill sets lead to novel vocational training programs as people recall and harness talents from previous existences.

ChronoSync will have transformative repercussions for religions, atheists, and others who do not believe in an afterlife or reincarnation. Religions will face a paradigm shift, with some embracing the new technology as undeniable evidence of their doctrines. For them, ChronoSync will validate beliefs long held sacred, providing tangible proof of concepts like reincarnation and the eternal soul. However, other religious groups must reconcile their teachings with this new data, leading to theological crises and potential schisms within their communities. Atheists and skeptics, who have long dismissed the notion of an afterlife, will be confronted with irrefutable evidence that challenges their view, sparking profound existential and philosophical debates. The implications of these revelations will ripple through every facet of society, reshaping fundamental understandings of life, death, and the human experience.

Indeed, the light of this discovery touches every facet of our lives, challenging us to redefine progress, success, and fulfillment. Once a familiar weave, the fabric of society will be stretched and re-patterned as we grapple with the reality that identity is not a single thread but a tapestry of many lives lived. Our understanding of self, others, and the Divine is undergoing a metamorphosis as profound as it is universal.

Yet, with ChronoSync comes a dichotomy as stark as day and night. In enlightened hands, it promises an era of empathy and understanding—a world where the past empowers the present. But in the grip of malice, it holds the potential to control destinies, an omnipotent force capable of altering the very core of humanity.

As a journalist, I stand at the vanguard of this epochal shift, documenting the metamorphosis of a civilization awakening to its immortality. Dr. Wallace's invention has not only confirmed the persistence of the soul but has also invited us to envision a world where every life becomes a lesson, a legacy, and a stepping stone on the path of our collective odyssey.

ChronoSync is not just the culmination of humanity's quest to answer the eternal question of life before birth and life after death; it is the beginning of humanity's grandest exploration. It is a key to unlocking not only the secrets of our past but also the potential of our future. It is a testament to the indomitable human spirit, eternally journeying through the cosmos on an odyssey of rebirth and rediscovery.

As this groundbreaking story graces the front page, it heralds not the end but the dawn of an adventure as boundless as the universe. Through ChronoSync, our histories converge, our spirits unite, and humanity's saga unfolds as an infinite echo resonating through the corridors of time.

CHAPTER FOUR
THE POPE'S SPEECH

Amidst the buzzing nervous energy of St. Peter's Square, I was immersed in the collective anxiety of the crowd. The recent confirmation of past lives and rebirth by ChronoSync had sent shockwaves through the Catholic community, leaving the faithful to wrestle with the implications of their beliefs. I noted the distinct hush that had fallen over the square, an aberration from the usual din, as uneasy murmurs betrayed the inner turmoil of the gathered. Eyes turned toward the balcony in anticipation of the Pope's address, the importance of the moment not lost on any of the faithful present. The impending papal speech loomed, ready to reconcile the age-old doctrine with the newfound evidence of life's continuity beyond death, leading toward rebirth.

In the square's swelling silence, the air was charged with trepidation. A usually vibrant spot where the voices of countless pilgrims merge into a melody of devotion was now still. Even the typically spirited birds atop the ancient columns stood mute; their songs paused as if nature held its breath. The crowd pressed closer to the Vatican's balcony, an instinctive draw toward a beloved shepherd about to challenge millennia of doctrine.

Pope Leo stepped forward, his figure a solitary silhouette against the marble backdrop. The collective hearts of the ten thousand skipped a beat, their eyes fixed on the Pontiff, a man now bearing the weight of an inconceivable truth that demanded a reckoning of soul-deep beliefs.

When he broke the silence, his voice carried the timbre of spiritual authority and the quiver of human vulnerability. "Beloved children of God," he intoned, the words heavy with the moment's solemnity, "the world stands at a spiritual crossroads."

As the Pontiff stood before the silent crowd, his voice began to weave the threads of a speech that would be etched in history. "Science has brought evidence that challenges our understanding before us, yet it also enriches it," he began. "The Divine tapestry is far more intricate than we have known. Today, I ask you to open your hearts wider, to perceive the grandeur of God's creation in ways we have never before contemplated. We stand before a leap in understanding, a new chapter in the spiritual journey of the Church and humanity. Let us step forward with faith and courage."

The multitude listened, hanging on to every word, their beliefs a tempest of hope and confusion. He spoke of the fragility mirrored in their eyes but also of hope for an evolution toward a greater expanse of humanity—a call to embrace this new truth, not with fear, but with the courage to evolve and adapt. "Faith," the Pope proclaimed, "once an unassailable fortress, now seems as precarious as the flutter of a dove's wing."

As the speech unfolded, I scribbled furiously as a witness to this historical juncture, knowing the Pontiff's words would soon echo around the globe. This speech wasn't just a theological pivot but a call to moral arms, asking each person to reflect. Once a murmur of personal crises, the crowd stood unified in their yearning for guidance as the beloved Pope offered a beacon of light in an overwhelming sea of doubt.

He paused, letting his words settle. "The Church, confronted by ChronoSync's proof of an afterlife and rebirth, embraces the enduring journey of the soul. It is a pilgrimage through time, where judgment and repentance prepare us for spiritual evolution—a testament to our commitment to rising to a higher level of humanity."

The Pope stood in the hush of St. Peter's Square, a solitary figure against the vastness of history and faith. His voice carried across the piazza and the chasm of uncertainty. He acknowledged the seismic shift in spiritual consciousness the technology had provoked. He called for the Church to embrace reincarnation, to see it as an extension of God's tapestry, a new chapter in the Divine plan for humanity.

Standing amid the murmurs of the restless crowd, I felt an unexpected tap on my shoulder. A Vatican official, distinguished by his solemn demeanor, regarded me with an authoritative but discreet gaze. Noting my press badge emblazoned with my credentials as a *New York Times* journalist, the official leaned in, his words a hushed whisper: "Mr. Vega, His Holiness requests your presence."

Following the thin, well-dressed man, I stepped through a modest side door, leaving the echoing chants of St. Peter's Square. Each corner I turned unfurled another stretch of hallowed halls, the Vatican's opulent history etched into every sculpture and painting—a pantheon of faith now cast in a new, uncertain light.

Around me, the Vatican's interiors sprawled in all their baroque magnificence, a silent testament to centuries of unwavering belief. Opulent artwork depicted scenes of Divine ascension and mortal plight; now, these images were like relics of an obsolete narrative, their truths teetering on the precipice of the Church's newfound acceptance. As I passed sculptures poised in silent adoration, I contemplated the dichotomy of their expressions, now questioning, affirming, in the soft glow of history's turning tide.

The official's steps were sure and quiet, contrasting with my racing thoughts. This was more than a meeting; it was a passage into the heart of a faith faced with transformation, a Church reconsidering the very heavens it had preached immutable. Ahead, an encounter awaited, not just with a man but with the living symbol of a spiritual paradigm, at once disrupted and enlightened by the advent of ChronoSync.

Walking through these passages, I was acutely aware of the monumental shift. The visages of saints and angels, once harbingers of a final judgment, now appeared to gaze upon me with an air of uncertainty. Would these sacred images be replaced to reflect the new truths of a soul's continuity and rebirth? The thought lingered as I moved through the interior; the legacy of two millennia whispered from the marbled floors to the vaulted ceilings. Soon, I would sit with the Pope, contemplating what this pivot meant for the Roman Catholic Church.

In the privacy of a room that had hosted countless seekers of truth, I prepared to document a conversation that might well redefine the spiritual narrative for generations to come. Here, amidst the repository of beliefs now called into question, I was about to witness the potential birthing of new doctrine, possibly new iconography—a renaissance in its truest sense, born from the reconciliation of ancient faith with a newfound reality.

In the sanctum of the Pontiff's office, I felt the magnitude of the moment as Pope Leo welcomed me with an amiable smile. It was not the grandeur of the room but the Spanish Pope's presence—an embodiment of humility and history—that overwhelmed me. Clad in traditional papal vestments, Pope Leo wore a white cassock adorned with a simple golden cross that hung from a delicate chain around his neck. A kind of serenity marked his features, his slightly wrinkled face illuminated by the soft light filtering through the stained-glass windows. His eyes, a deep and thoughtful brown, reflected a wisdom and curiosity that belied his years. His demeanor was gentle yet commanding, an aura of tranquility enveloping him as he beckoned me to sit with the gentle gesture of a hand.

"How was it, my son, to walk in the shoes of Étienne?" the Pope inquired, a soft Spanish accent gracing his words. "To experience a life so different from your own, yet undeniably yours?"

I gathered my thoughts and memories of my virtual journey as Étienne flooded back. "It was transformative, Your Holiness," I began, my voice a blend of awe and reverence. "To feel the heartbeat of a past life, to see the world through the eyes of a philosopher and a publisher—it's a profound reminder of our shared humanity, transcending faith and time."

The Pope nodded thoughtfully, his gaze unwavering. "And what of the journey from the old world to the new? What does it tell us about rebirth, the persistence of the spirit?"

I leaned forward, taking a moment to reflect. "I believe it shows how the soul endures and adapts."

A silent understanding passed between us, two men grappling with the mysteries of existence, now laid bare by technology yet still shielded by faith. The Pope, a man whose life had touched the depths of suffering and soared to the heights of spiritual leadership, offered a smile that bridged the gap between history and hope.

"I assume you have questions for me," he said, a knowing smile creasing his face.

Though prepared for such an honor, I was propelled by the profoundness of the moment, offered a smile in return, and embarked on an inquiry into faith, time, and existence. In the sanctified stillness of Pope Leo's private office, with a view of the Vatican Gardens lending a serene backdrop, I took a deep breath and initiated the unprecedented interview.

"Your Holiness, in light of ChronoSync's discoveries, how does the Church reconcile the concept of an afterlife with the new evidence of past lives and rebirth?"

Gazing thoughtfully out the window before returning his attention to me, Pope Leo replied, "The Church has always held that life is sacred and eternal. These findings are not a contradiction but an extension of understanding. We are called to incorporate this broader view of existence into our faith."

"Your Holiness," I asked, "the Church teaches that after death, each person is judged individually by God and sent to Heaven, Hell, or Purgatory based on their earthly life. This judgment is final and does not involve a cycle of rebirth or reincarnation. The concept of reincarnation is considered incompatible with Catholic teachings on the nature of the soul, the afterlife, and salvation. Does this not challenge the core Catholic belief that the soul's destiny is determined after a single lifetime?"

The Pope nodded slightly, his expression contemplative. "It challenges us to expand our interpretation. We must now consider that the soul's journey involves many lives, many lessons."

"And what of sin, repentance, and redemption in this context?"

"Our spiritual evolution is a process. Each life is a chance for growth, for mercy to be sought and grace to be found."

I noted the Pope's hands clasping and unclasping, a physical echo of the Church grappling with new paradigms.

"How will the Church address those who feel their faith has been undermined?"

Pope Leo's eyes met mine, and there was a firm resolve within them. "We will walk with them through this. Faith is not in doctrines but in the Divine mystery. We are committed to guiding the faithful toward understanding and peace."

Sensing an opportunity, I asked, "How can you explain how one's religion, passed on through one's parents and grandparents, is now being questioned since many people are discovering that they weren't the same religion in their past life? Christians are discovering they were once Muslims, Jews, or Buddhists, and so on."

The Pope considered the question, his gaze growing distant as he pondered the implications. After a long moment, he spoke with a profound and gentle authority. "It appears that the soul's journey, less by the lineage of our ancestors, determines who we are. Each soul's path is unique and sacred, shaped by life experiences. This newfound knowledge offers us an extraordinary opportunity."

"How so?" I asked eagerly.

"It challenges us to broaden our understanding of faith, to see the Divine presence in all paths and practices. Through this revelation, humanity may understand that there is only one Almighty, seen through different lenses across different cultures and religions. This could blur the lines and diminish the animosity that has long divided us. We aim to embrace this diversity with compassion and wisdom, guiding people to find unity in the spiritual journey rather than inherited labels. In recognizing the common thread of divinity that runs through all our lives, we may finally come to a deeper, more inclusive understanding of faith."

Finally, I ventured, "How will this revelation affect the Church's teachings moving forward?"

The Pope stood and approached an intricate tapestry, his fingers tracing the weaves. "Like this tapestry, our teachings are complex and interconnected. We will weave this new knowledge into the fabric of our doctrine, with careful thought and prayer."

As the Pope spoke, his movements around the room, gentle touch on religious artifacts, and lingering gaze out the window spoke volumes. He was a leader at a crossroads, not just for the Church but for humanity, guiding his flock through a threshold of unparalleled spiritual discovery.

As our conversation drew to a close, a question lingered on my mind— deeply personal and reflective of the new age we were stepping into. I hesitated momentarily, then asked, "Your Holiness, in light of this profound connection between science and spirituality, would you ever consider submitting your DNA to Dr. Wallace for ChronoSync's interpretation of your past life?"

The Pope turned to me, his eyes soft yet contemplative. "Marcus," he said slowly, "each soul carries its own journey, its own secrets, and its own truths. Whether I would choose to unlock those mysteries is a question that speaks to the heart of faith itself. Perhaps, in time, we all may seek to understand the echoes of our past, but for now, my role is to shepherd humanity through this present moment, where the past and future converge in ways we are only beginning to grasp."

His response left me with a sense of awe and a renewed understanding of the delicate balance between faith and the thirst for knowledge. It seemed that the mysteries of the soul were just beginning to unfold.

CHAPTER FIVE
TASK FORCE

Stepping onto the platform of Union Station in Washington, DC, I couldn't shake the whirlwind of thoughts from my recent interview with the Pope and the global reaction it triggered. The revelation of ChronoSync's findings had sent shock waves through every corner of society. The confirmation of past lives and rebirth elevated the dialogue beyond the everyday discourse on the existence of the Almighty. Practitioners of Eastern philosophies, long accustomed to the mysteries of reincarnation, found their beliefs resonating with the masses. Meanwhile, agnostics and atheists were confronted with a new perspective on what it means to be human.

During my interview with the Pope, I had been forthright, my questions piercing the veil between science and spirituality. Reflecting on the Holy Father's responses, I could still feel the impact of his words, echoing the sentiments of millions. The Pope had seemingly accepted the findings of ChronoSync outright, calling for a measured approach to integrating this new understanding within established doctrines.

The reactions to the interview were as varied as they were passionate: theologians fiercely debated on news channels, spiritual leaders organized forums to discuss the implications, and scientists offered their interpretations, both skeptical and supportive. Social media platforms were ablaze with opinions, from outright rejection to ecstatic affirmation, including many unfounded conspiracy theories.

Walking through Union Station, I felt the enormity of my role as a journalist in this pivotal moment in human history. Each step resonated with the voices of those eagerly awaiting the hearing's outcomes. I realized that this committee's findings would significantly shape human consciousness's future and spiritual evolution's direction.

Ahead lay a federal hearing delving into moral and ethical realms previously uncharted by law. The air was thick with anticipation as people from all walks of life gathered, united by a common quest for understanding the complexities of past lives and their relevance in the here and now.

Stepping out into the chill of an early morning breeze, I was keenly aware that the world was watching, pondering the profound question: How does one legislate the soul's journey?

Entering the grand hall of the Dirksen Senate Office Building, I felt its historical weight. Now poised to address issues that would have been speculative spiritual drama just a few months ago, the committee's mandate was clear yet daunting: determine the societal impact of past-life actions and their legal ramifications.

Inside the hearing room, discussions were already fervent. Legal experts debated the notion of violent crimes committed in previous existences and their bearing on the present. Could someone be held accountable today for deeds done in a life lived centuries ago?

Legislators faced the Herculean task of examining existing laws and identifying the need for new legislation. Concepts like the statute of limitations were dissected with fresh urgency, given that actions from previous lives might come to light.

In the solemn atmosphere of the congressional hearing, a senator from Massachusetts asked a probing question to a philosopher about the afterlife and karmic justice: "In cases where an individual is proven to have committed a serious offense in a previous existence, should our legal system hold them accountable today?" The senator's question highlighted the deep moral complexities introduced by the acceptance of past lives.

One of the experts, who drew upon Rudolf Steiner's teachings, responded thoughtfully. "The philosophy of Anthroposophy acknowledges that the soul endures a form of penance or purification across lifetimes as part of its karmic evolution," he explained. "Steiner's philosophy posits that this intrinsic process of rebalancing and self-correction during one's journey in the afterlife might negate the need for punitive measures in the present life for past misdeeds."

Echoing this perspective, a Kabbalah scholar affirmed that a purification process exists for the soul, indicating a congruence between diverse belief systems on the transformative journey of the soul beyond death. This spiritual insight profoundly reflects how temporal laws might adapt to a new understanding of justice that extends beyond a single lifetime.

Another senator chimed in, his brow furrowed. "What of inheritance? Could an individual claim assets from a past life, disrupting present legal heirs?"

An economist offered a thoughtful perspective. "The idea that wealth could be transferred across different lifetimes is intriguing but presents practical challenges. To entertain this, rigorous mechanisms would be essential to guard against false claims of inheritance or entitlement. Furthermore, introducing historical financial claims into our present economy could disrupt the established order. Thus, if we were to consider this, we would need a robust framework that prevents the erosion of economic stability while exploring such transfers."

I took notes, each question and response painting a picture of a world on the cusp of legal reinvention, grappling with the continuity of the human soul and its deeds.

"The very notion of integrating past life offenses into today's legal frameworks presents not only logistical challenges but profound ethical questions," the senator from Ohio said, reflecting on the expert's and scholar's insights. "Would it be just to hold someone accountable for actions beyond their current memory and life experience?"

The room fell into contemplative silence as these questions loomed large over the assembly. Another expert, a philosopher specializing in ethics, took the floor. "If we entertain the idea of karmic justice, it might suggest that individuals inherently receive their due through the natural course of their spiritual journey, without external legal repercussions. Our focus could shift toward rehabilitation and moral education in this life, emphasizing growth and redemption."

As the discussions progressed, the diverse views converged on a critical consensus: applying such esoteric beliefs in legal systems would fundamentally alter the fabric of societal justice and personal responsibility. It would require a paradigm shift in how society perceives identity, continuity, and morality.

The senator, nodding thoughtfully, summarized the session's groundbreaking dialogue. "Today's discussion reveals a fascinating intersection between spirituality and law, urging us to reconsider the depths of justice and redemption. Perhaps the greatest lesson is the need for a more compassionate and understanding legal system that recognizes the complex journey of the human soul."

The hearing was adjourned, leaving all participants much to ponder about the future intersections of law, ethics, and spiritual beliefs. This signaled a new era of philosophical inquiry and legislative consideration.

I lingered in the room after most had left, my mind racing with the multitude of unresolved questions stirred up by ChronoSync. I thought about the potential implications for personal identity, accountability, and the fundamental nature of justice. How could society balance the ancient wisdom of karmic retribution with modern fairness and legal integrity principles?

As I walked out of the chamber, I understood that the day's discussion had only scratched the surface of a much deeper philosophical ocean. The idea of intertwining spiritual concepts with the law was both intriguing and daunting. It challenged traditional notions of justice and called for reimagining societal structures.

I pondered the ethical implications of such a shift: Would it lead to a more humane and enlightened society or create new forms of inequality and moral ambiguity? I knew these questions would take time to be answered, and the journey to understanding them would be long and complex.

CHAPTER SIX
THE SECOND COMING

As dusk draped the skies of France in shades of melancholy purple, I found myself in a serene corner of a Parisian café, face-to-face with Elodie, the enigmatic woman soon to be at the epicenter of global attention. She extended the ChronoSync report across the table—a document as controversial as riveting, poised for imminent disclosure in *The New York Times*. Although her demeanor was composed, her brown eyes blazed with a fervor that betrayed a profound inner conviction.

Elodie leaned forward, her voice a determined whisper that filled the quiet space around us. "From childhood, I've felt an unmistakable pull toward something far greater than myself; a destiny that has shaped every step I take," she said in French-accented English. The connection she felt with Joan of Arc wasn't merely a historical curiosity; it was a visceral, lived experience. "I've been driven by visions that directed me not toward ancient battlefields but toward a modern struggle against the world's deep-seated injustices."

She opened the contents of the report with a steady hand. "This isn't about waging war," Elodie clarified, her tone resolute. "It's about awakening—an uprising of the spirit. The world's turmoil is the arena, and my fight is to rally not soldiers but hearts and minds." Much like Joan's, her inspiration was to galvanize and stir humanity to unite and combat the despair that shrouded them with a vigor that mirrored the saintly warrior of old.

"Elodie," I said, leaning in, my curiosity piqued by the woman's profound conviction and the parallels she drew with the legendary martyr, "like Joan of Arc, do you hear the voice of the Divine guiding you?"

Elodie paused, her gaze thoughtful as she considered the depth of the question. "It's not the voice of God that I hear," she began slowly, her eyes reflecting a complex tapestry of belief and purpose. "Rather, it's the collective outcry of humanity, the silent whispers of the oppressed, and the desperate calls for help that reach my ears and compel me to act. These are the voices that drive me, that guide my actions. They are as holy to me as any words spoken by saints."

I nodded, absorbing her words. Then, with a furrowed brow and curiosity coloring my voice, I asked, "Elodie, this report you're sharing with the *Times*—does it confirm you as Joan of Arc in a past life, or is this more about channeling the essence of her spirit?"

Elodie maintained her composure as she spoke. "The ChronoSync report confirms that I am indeed the reincarnation of Joan of Arc," she stated unequivocally. "Our souls are bound by similar destinies and callings, aligning me with her spirit and essence." She gestured broadly, emphasizing the depth of their connection. "It's as if the torch of her legacy has been directly handed to me. I embody her reincarnation, a modern vessel for her indomitable spirit of courage and justice."

I absorbed this bold declaration, my mind spinning with the ramifications of such a profound spiritual lineage. The narrative was extraordinary—destined to captivate the public and provoke discussions on destiny and legacy.

Elodie clasped her hands on the table, her demeanor calm yet resolute. "In this light, I hear a Divine command—a call from the core of human compassion and justice, compelling me to advocate for those unable to defend themselves."

I nodded, my understanding deepening as Elodie elucidated her mission's spiritual and humanitarian underpinnings. Her connection to the Divine was not through mystical visions but through deep empathy and a solid commitment to societal transformation, making her a direct conduit for the legacy of resilience and justice.

"It's about embodying the virtues Joan of Arc stood for—courage, conviction, and a commitment to justice," Elodie added softly, her eyes burning with passion. "These virtues are timeless and as vital today as they were in Joan's time."

I was further drawn into the significance of Elodie's story. It transcended her experience, unfolding as an influential blueprint for global change. In her, the spirit of Joan of Arc was revived for a new era—Elodie stood as the modern incarnation of that timeless warrior, wielding not only the symbolic sword of truth but also the mantle of Joan's enduring legacy.

"This ChronoSync report," Elodie continued, her voice filled with awe and determination, "is a technological milestone. But it goes beyond identifying past-life identities to track the legacy of a soul's essence passed onto another. It's not about the historical facts of who I was but the spiritual continuity of who I am becoming."

She paused, letting the significance of her words settle. "Essentially, the report doesn't just trace lineage; it maps the journey of a soul's purpose and calling across the ages, showing how the torch of Joan's spirit has been passed to me. It's a profound recognition of soul legacy rather than mere past-life identity."

Moved by her profound insights, I expressed my concern, my voice tinged with apprehension. "Aren't you worried about being perceived as a messiah when drawing these parallels? That could be fraught with danger."

Elodie's reply was prompt, her gaze unwavering, cutting through the lingering doubts. "Joan of Arc faced threats and certain death, yet she never wavered. She embraced her path with bravery because she was steadfast in her mission. That same conviction drives me," she proclaimed. "Although I do not claim the title of a messiah, I am fully aware of the risks associated with such a transformative role. Yet, like Joan, I remain steadfast in my commitment to my purpose, regardless of the challenges I may face."

Her words resonated deeply, not just as a testament to her bravery but as an affirmation of her unwavering commitment to embody Joan of Arc's legacy in spirit and action.

I nodded, now fully grasping the complexity of Elodie's stance. "But consider the implications," I urged, my voice a mix of concern and admiration. "Being seen as a messiah could attract fervent followers and fierce opposition. It could polarize, perhaps even destabilize, depending on how your story is manipulated by others or perceived by the public."

Elodie acknowledged my point with a nod. "Indeed, the role of a perceived messiah is a magnet for controversy. It invites scrutiny and can certainly provoke opposition. The path of all transformative figures is lined with both adulation and vilification. However, the potential to inspire and effect change on a grand scale also entails the risk of becoming a symbol—sometimes a target. But this is the path I choose, fully aware of its dark and light aspects."

Our discussion underscored the dangers and profound impact of Elodie's work. She stood at a historical and innovative crossroads, reigniting the legacy of a past hero through the lens of modernity, challenging conventions, and igniting debates about the essence of leadership and heroism in the contemporary world.

I scratched my chin, my skepticism slowly morphing into intrigue and respect. "So, your mission is not just about channeling Joan but transforming that influence into practical actions that address today's societal issues?"

Elodie nodded, her expression earnest. "It's not enough to carry her legacy; I must also translate it into actions that resonate with our times. This means advocating for justice, pushing for systemic changes, and empowering the oppressed. Joan fought with armor and sword; I fight with knowledge, voice, and unwavering commitment to the cause."

I scribbled notes, my journalist instincts kicking in as I realized the depth of the story unfolding before me. Elodie's tale was not just one of spiritual reincarnation but a dynamic blueprint for modern-day heroism. "Your story is about bridging epochs," I mused aloud. "Connecting the valor of the past with the urgency of the present."

Elodie smiled, a light of determination in her eyes. "That's correct, and it's a bridge built on the foundation of timeless virtues. The challenges we face today may be different, but the essence of courage and justice remains unchanged. We need that now more than ever."

"ChronoSync can serve as a mirror, reflecting not just who we were but who we are and who we can become," Elodie added, her voice vibrant with conviction. "It offers a profound opportunity for humanity to reflect on our collective journey, celebrate our progress, and confront our failures to forge a better future."

Our conversation deepened, weaving through the philosophical implications of her claim and exploring the potential societal impacts of such a profound connection. As we spoke, the room hummed with the energy of history intermingling with the possibilities of the future, each word not just spoken but felt, a testament to the enduring power of legacies reborn.

As I contemplated Elodie's story, I reflected on my own life. I pondered my purpose and whether it explained my life path. I had always been driven by an insatiable curiosity, a trait that set me apart from my peers. My relentless pursuit of truth and deeper understanding had often put me at odds with the more conventional approaches to journalism. Yet, this trait made me the perfect person to cover ChronoSync's groundbreaking revelations. I had a knack for seeing beyond the surface, delving into the heart of the matter with a tenacity few could match.

In Elodie's words, I found a reflection of my journey—a quest for meaning transcending mere professional achievement. The notion of being reborn with a purpose resonated deeply with me, stirring a sense of kinship with the countless souls whose stories were now coming to light through ChronoSync. I realized that my role was not just to report these stories but to weave them into the larger tapestry of human experience, highlighting the interconnectedness of all lives across time.

This realization reaffirmed my belief in the power of storytelling to shape understanding and inspire change. As I prepared to write my next article, I felt a renewed sense of mission. I understood that my purpose went beyond journalism; it was about illuminating the paths of the past to guide the future, ensuring that the lessons of history were not just remembered but actively used to build a better world.

CHAPTER SEVEN
RESET

As I strolled through the bustling corridors of New York-Presbyterian Hospital, my mind reeled from the reports I'd seen earlier in the day. Suicide rates had skyrocketed to levels a hundred times higher than what was considered normal. The impact of ChronoSync technology on society's view of life and death was more profound and disturbing than I had ever anticipated.

I arrived at the office of Dr. Helen Ramirez, a leading figure in mental health and a pivotal voice in the current crisis. The medical community and the media eagerly sought her insights to understand this unprecedented shift in human behavior.

"Marcus, thank you for coming," Dr. Ramirez greeted me as I followed her into her cluttered but cozy office. She gestured toward a chair, and as I sat, she leaned back against her desk, her expression grave.

"As you might have guessed, we're facing a true crisis," she began, her voice steady despite the chaos unfolding around us. "ChronoSync has given people undeniable proof of an afterlife, drastically altering how they perceive death."

I nodded, my brow furrowed in concern. "I've witnessed and written about the psychological comfort it brings to some, knowing that life's struggles are just temporary hurdles, or even necessary for spiritual growth."

"Yes, that's one side of it," Dr. Ramirez agreed, her hands clasped tightly. "For some, this knowledge is a balm, reducing their fear of death. It helps them cope with suffering, knowing there's continuity beyond this life. But there's a darker side to this coin."

Dr. Ramirez's expression reflected the seriousness of the situation as she continued to unpack the implications of this dangerous misconception surrounding suicide.

"Consider this," she said, her voice steady yet filled with palpable urgency. "We now view suicide as a mere pause rather than a permanent cessation of life."

She walked over to a whiteboard, sketching a simple cycle diagram. "Here"—she pointed—"people now see life as a loop rather than a linear journey. They mistakenly believe that ending their current life will allow them to escape to a new existence without facing the long-term consequences of their actions or the unresolved issues they leave behind."

Dr. Ramirez paused, her gaze still firmly on me. "Now, I must be clear," she said with a note of caution in her voice. "I am not a theologian, nor am I an expert on what happens in the afterlife, and certainly not on the intricate workings of reincarnation. My expertise lies in mental health and the psychological impacts of our beliefs on behavior."

She emphasized, "However, even without delving into the specifics of spiritual doctrines, we can observe the tangible effects these beliefs have on our society and individual behaviors. The idea of suicide as a 'reset button' is a dangerous misinterpretation that not only threatens individual well-being but also the fabric of our community."

"From a psychological perspective," Dr. Ramirez elaborated, "the belief in a direct and simplistic causality between actions in this life and outcomes in any potential next life overlooks the complex nature of human experiences and spiritual growth. It's essential to approach these issues with a nuanced understanding, recognizing the broader implications and responsibilities that come with them."

I looked up from my notes, offering Dr. Ramirez a nod before she continued.

"Thus, while I don't claim to know the metaphysical truths of the afterlife," she said, "I firmly believe in addressing the psychological and societal impacts of our beliefs about it. We must ensure that our understanding promotes health, resilience, and ethical responsibility, rather than escapism or harm."

Leaning on the table, Dr. Ramirez locked eyes with me. "This is more than just an existential crisis. It's a societal one. When individuals start viewing suicide as a viable option to dismiss their hardships—whether these are financial troubles, relationship issues, or even chronic illnesses—they undermine the fundamental value of facing and overcoming life's challenges."

She sighed, a sound of deep concern rather than exhaustion. "It's vital to grasp that this perspective warps the natural progression of human learning and maturation through adversity. Each existence, with its distinct challenges, offers a chance for growth and evolution. Avoiding these lessons might bypass critical stages necessary for the soul's advancement," she noted thoughtfully. "Although I cannot claim expertise on the experiences a soul endures after death during its rebirth journey, I can only surmise that escaping life's difficulties could negatively impact the soul's development. Moreover, if we consider the philosophical or spiritual implications according to the teachings of many world religions and spiritual philosophies, actions taken in one life can have consequences in the next. If suicide is seen as an escape mechanism, it could potentially lead to negative repercussions in subsequent lives, complicating the soul's journey rather than simplifying it."

Dr. Ramirez highlighted another critical aspect: "There's also a significant impact on those left behind. Families, friends, and communities suffer immense grief and confusion. The ripple effects of a single suicide can be devastating on a larger scale, leading to more mental health issues among the bereaved."

Dr. Ramirez paused, letting her words sink in. "Our challenge, then, is to address these misconceptions clinically and educate the public on the holistic implications of their choices—not just for themselves but for society at large. We need a comprehensive strategy that combines mental health support, spiritual counseling, and public education to combat this trend effectively."

I nodded, my gaze fixed intently on Dr. Ramirez. "So, they view life like a computer that they can effortlessly reboot whenever it bogs down?"

"That's right," she confirmed with a nod. "And this belief is spreading faster than we can counter it. Our traditional methods of suicide prevention are becoming ineffective. People aren't afraid of dying anymore because they see it as a chance to begin again."

The implications were chilling, and I felt a cold dread settle in my stomach. "What can be done to combat this trend? How do we restore the sanctity of life when death is no longer feared?"

Dr. Ramirez sighed, a look of determination lighting her eyes. "We must focus on the value of the experiences in this life and the importance of facing and overcoming challenges rather than escaping them. And perhaps most importantly, we need to educate people about the potential consequences in the afterlife of choosing suicide—a topic that's still largely unexplored even with ChronoSync's revelations."

My mind raced with the importance of the situation. "It sounds like we're not just fighting a medical or psychological battle, but a philosophical and spiritual one."

"Yes," Dr. Ramirez agreed, her gaze firm. "And it's a battle we cannot afford to lose. The very essence of what it means to be human is at stake."

I closed my notebook, Dr. Ramirez's words resonating deeply. I glanced around the busy hospital ward, feeling the pulse of human life and struggle around me.

I felt inspired as I considered the unique angle my column could take. Turning back to Dr. Ramirez, I articulated my thoughts more clearly, aiming to convey the potential public benefit of my work.

"Dr. Ramirez, I'm not just looking to understand this crisis from a clinical perspective," I explained, my voice earnest. "I'm hoping to share these stories and insights through my column. My goal is to bring the human aspect of this issue to a broader audience and illuminate the profound impacts ChronoSync is having on individuals and society."

Dr. Ramirez hesitated momentarily, her professional instincts balancing the ethical considerations. Finally, she nodded. "I think I understand your aim. There's a patient who might be willing to share his story with you. He's been particularly affected by the issues we've discussed."

Dr. Ramirez led me through a quiet corridor, her footsteps barely audible on the polished floor. We stopped at a room at the end of the hall. Inside, a man lay in a hospital bed, his gaze fixed on the ceiling, lost in thought. His features were gaunt, etched with the signs of inner struggle. Dr. Ramirez paused at the door, offering a brief introduction. "Marcus, this is Charles. Charles, this is Marcus Vega from *The New York Times*. I'll leave you two to talk," she said softly before closing the door behind her.

I approached the bed and gently pulled up a chair, easing into the delicate conversation. "Thank you for speaking with me, Charles," I began, calm and reassuring. "As Dr. Ramirez mentioned, my name is Marcus Vega. I'm a journalist, and I'm trying to understand how ChronoSync has impacted people's lives."

The man turned his head slowly to face me. His voice was low, filled with a resigned bitterness. "Yeah, I'll talk. What's the point of keeping it all in anymore?"

He began sharing his story, explaining how he had become obsessed with resetting his miserable circumstances. "I thought if I could just start over, maybe I'd get it right next time," he confessed.

"So I tried to end it all. I thought I'd be free of this life's pain, free to try again. But my brother saved me," he said, a trace of anger lacing his words. "And here I am, supposed to be grateful for it."

I listened intently, my pen barely keeping up. "You're planning to try again?" I asked cautiously.

The man nodded, his expression hardening. "I don't see why I should be forced to continue suffering in this life when I know there's another chance waiting for me. They say it's a gift to live, but what kind of gift forces me to suffer?"

His words sank in. This interview revealed the dark side of what might happen when existential beliefs shift so radically. The conversation continued, and I probed gently, weaving through the philosophical minefields laid bare by the advent of technology that could peer into the soul's journey through time.

I leaned in slightly, my journalist instincts piqued by the perspective contrast. "Did you ever go through the ChronoSync analysis yourself? Learn about your past life?" I asked, curious to understand the man's convictions.

The man scoffed, a bitter smile flickering across his face. "For $50,000? Look at me." He gestured around the stark hospital room, his tone mocking yet laced with resignation. "I live hand to mouth. There's no way I can afford it."

He paused, his eyes meeting mine. "But I've read your columns, you know. I see what ChronoSync has proven. That's enough for me to believe. Even without my analysis, the idea that there's something beyond this… It's enough to make me want to hit reset."

His words hung in the air, each dripping with a sorrow that clung to me. This conversation revealed the darker implications of what happens when existential beliefs are upended so drastically. As we continued, I carefully navigated through the philosophical challenges and emotional turmoil brought about by a technology that could unravel the soul's journey through time.

"Does knowing that others can confirm their past lives while you're still searching for yours affect you?" I asked gently, my voice soft, as I tried to explore the complex emotions and ethical dilemmas this disparity might create.

"Yeah, it does," the man admitted, his voice dropping to a murmur. "It feels unfair. I'm locked out of understanding myself deeply because I can't afford it. But then again, just knowing it's possible changes everything. It makes life here seem less permanent—like a bad chapter in a never-ending book."

I found the man's analogy striking. I nodded, deeply moved by the metaphor's resonance in the sterile hospital room.

"This idea of life as just one chapter of a larger story is a profound understanding," I said thoughtfully, my voice low. "It's a powerful image that captures the essence of what many feel when faced with the possibility of reincarnation."

I continued to reflect on the man's words, realizing they highlighted a profound layer of irony and injustice—how socioeconomic barriers prevented access to life-altering insights offered by ChronoSync. I knew these insights would shape my understanding and significantly influence how I presented this narrative to my readers, underlining the broader social and ethical challenges posed by such groundbreaking technology. This interaction reinforced the urgency and importance of addressing these disparities, ensuring that the benefits of such advancements could be accessible to all, not just a privileged few.

CHAPTER EIGHT
SAMURAI WIFE

In the luxurious, sunlit living room of Michael and Elizabeth Ashton's Malibu home, I set up my recording equipment, acutely aware of the palpable tension between them. Known as Hollywood's golden couple, their seemingly perfect union had recently experienced the seismic tremors of ChronoSync technology, revealing deep secrets from their past lives.

"Can you tell me more about your experience as an artist in Florence during the Renaissance? How do you think that has shaped who you are today?" I asked Michael, aiming to delve deeper into his psyche.

Michael leaned back, his eyes distant as he gathered his thoughts. "From what I could understand, I was quite the struggling artist, never quite achieving the recognition I thought I deserved. It was a lifetime of creating and striving, yet I always overlooked it. There was a profound loneliness in that existence, a sense of not fully being seen or appreciated."

He paused, his gaze returning to the present, to the comfort of his luxurious twenty-thousand square foot ocean-front mansion and the apparent success surrounding his current life. "It's intriguing to think about that past life now," he continued, his tone contemplative. "I believe I've carried forward some of that artistic passion and perhaps the resilience I had to develop. But, the frustrations from that life, the constant struggles for acknowledgment, don't seem to burden me as much now."

Michael's expression shifted to one of introspection. "I understand the soul evolves through each new birth, learning and adapting from past experiences. If so, perhaps the lessons from my time as a Renaissance artist have helped mold me into who I am today, more than just an artist, but someone who appreciates recognition yet doesn't depend on it for validation."

He glanced at Elizabeth, a small smile forming. "I've found success, love, and family in this life. It's more than I could have ever hoped for. Perhaps the hardships of my past life were the fire needed to forge the strength and perspective I enjoy now."

I hung on to every word, recognizing the depth of Michael's reflections. The story of a man who lived two very different lives, one marked by unrecognized toil and one filled with success and love, provided a compelling narrative about personal growth and the possible evolution of the soul across lifetimes.

Turning to Elizabeth, I probed gently, "I understand you learned you were once a slave trader's wife from Charleston, South Carolina, before the Civil War. Can you share more about that life and how it's influencing your current feelings and relationships?"

Elizabeth's eyes mirrored a blend of distant memories and current insights. "In that life, my name was Catherine," she began, her voice imbued with softness and quiet strength. "I was married to John, a man who ran the slave market in Charles Town, as it was called back then. Our relationship was complex, bound by the societal norms and harsh realities of that time. I was a supporting wife, totally fine with selling human beings as slaves."

She paused, her gaze drifting across the room as she continued, "Learning about Catherine has brought many emotions and questions. I'm struggling to reconcile how I, a progressive liberal in this life, could have been so cruel in my past life. It's not about finding John or connecting to him in this life. It's about understanding how I could have been that person. This revelation has been deeply troubling."

Her voice trembled slightly as she added, "I've been having trouble sleeping and dealing with everyday things. The contrast between my past self and who I am now is haunting."

I nodded, capturing every nuance of her struggle. "These revelations have illuminated aspects of yourself and introduced complexities to your present life. Can you share more about life as a wife to a slave trader?"

Elizabeth took a deep breath. "Living at that time was to abide by spoken and unspoken codes. My life was governed by duty and obedience, virtues esteemed above all else in society. The household was a microcosm of the rigid hierarchies that ruled our lives, and as a woman, my role was circumscribed by the expectations to be subservient and supportive."

She paused, her eyes reflecting the harshness of that era. "The discipline was severe. Every action reflected my husband and, by extension, his business and social standing. Missteps were not merely personal failures but breaches of family honor. Society was rigid, the roles predefined, and the personal desires of a wife were suppressed in favor of societal duties."

Her hands clasped tightly together, she continued, "Imagine a life where your movements, words, and thoughts are dictated by an external set of rules that value compliance and honor above individual happiness. It was a life of beauty and order but also silence and shadows. I was completely complicit in the cruelty and inhumanity of the slave trade, which is so hard for me to accept now."

I leaned forward. "It must be challenging to reconcile that disciplined past with the freedoms you enjoy today."

Elizabeth nodded, a melancholy smile touching her lips. "It is. I suppose that life from long ago taught me strength and resilience, qualities I carry with me. But it also left a yearning for something beyond duty, a deeper connection to humanity I completely missed back then."

As she shared her story, the vivid descriptions of her past life painted a stark picture of the cultural and personal dichotomies women of her time faced, highlighting the transformative journey of her soul.

Elizabeth sighed, a thoughtful frown creasing her brow. "While it's enriched my understanding of who I might be beyond the confines of this current life, it's also posed profound questions about identity, morality, and personal growth. How do I reconcile who I was with who I am now? It's a question that I grapple with every day."

As the interview progressed, Elizabeth's insights provided a deeper understanding of the emotional and existential challenges posed by ChronoSync's revelations, highlighting the intricate web of past-life experiences and their impact on present identities.

Elizabeth shook her head, the weight of centuries bearing down on her. "It's complex. A part of me feels an intense bond with my past, and it's hard not to feel torn. I am committed to my principles and beliefs in this life, but this has forced me to confront aspects of my past that are deeply disturbing."

I noted the subtle shifts in her body language and how she braced for discomfort. "Has this knowledge changed how you see your future?"

She shared a look with a newfound understanding crossing her face. "I've started seeing a therapist specializing in post-ChronoSync dynamics. It's not just me—many are struggling with these revelations."

Elizabeth added, "It's about learning that even though our souls may have experienced countless lives, the choices we make in this one are what truly matter. I've chosen to confront this past, learn from it, and grow stronger."

Capturing every nuance for my piece, I understood her story was more than just a tale of personal strain under the shadow of past lives. It was a testament to human resilience and the capacity to grow beyond the confines of time and history.

"The impact of ChronoSync on individuals has been profound," I concluded, my voice thoughtful. "Many people struggle with the identities revealed from past lives, but stories like yours, where individuals choose to confront and embrace these challenges, are powerful. They show that growth isn't just about the past or destiny. It's about choice, here and now."

As the interview wrapped up, Elizabeth was more at ease; her story was laid bare, but her commitment to personal growth was renewed. Her journey, symbolic of a new era in human understanding, highlighted the complexities of identity in a world where the past was as present as the future.

But as I turned off the recorder and began to pack away my notes, I couldn't shake the sense that this was more than another story. Elizabeth's determination seemed to echo in the quiet room, her words lingering like the final notes of a symphony.

The world outside was moving at its usual pace, indifferent to the revelations we had just shared. But in this small, quiet space, something had shifted. Elizabeth wasn't just a subject in my article; she had become a symbol of the silent battle so many were fighting—a struggle not against external forces but within themselves. Against the weight of history, the ghosts of past lives, and the tyranny of destiny.

As I rose to leave, her eyes met mine with a look that spoke volumes. It was the look of someone who had faced her demons and come out the other side, not unscathed, but stronger, tempered like steel in the fire of her past.

For in a world where the past can now be relived, remembered, and, for some, reconciled, the true power lies not in the memories themselves but in what we choose to do with them. Elizabeth had decided to grow, to rise above the burden of her past lives. And in that choice, she had found a freedom transcending time.

CHAPTER NINE
THE PAST LIVES CRIME ACT

In the wake of ChronoSync's revelations, the world navigated a novel and complex legal landscape. Initially designed as a cutting-edge method to explore past lives through DNA memory encoding, the process had unearthed more than just personal histories—it had exposed unsolved crimes, some dating back centuries. The global outcry was immediate and loud, compelling lawmakers worldwide to grapple with a question that once belonged solely to science fiction: should individuals be held accountable for actions committed in past incarnations?

In response, an international summit was convened, establishing the Past Lives Crime Act (PLCA). Under this groundbreaking legislation, ChronoSync administrators were required to register with government bodies and report any evidence of serious crimes discovered during sessions with their clients. These reports would then trigger investigations, potentially leading to the prosecution of individuals for deeds committed by their former selves.

The enforcement of PLCA introduced a slew of legal, moral, and philosophical debates. In Washington, DC, a special judicial panel, the Historical Crimes Tribunal (HCT), was established to oversee these cases. The Tribunal, a blend of modern judicial practices and historical research, was staffed with legal scholars, historians, and forensic anthropologists.

The newly inaugurated HCT headquarters buzzed with activity. Judge Maria Alvez, recently appointed to lead the Tribunal, reviewed each case with a sense of gravity and unease. One of the first cases on her docket was particularly contentious: a prominent politician, now accused of being a warlord during the Taiping Rebellion in China between the years of 1850 and 1864 and responsible for numerous atrocities.

The air was thick with tension and media clamor as the courtroom filled. Cameras flashed as the accused, Senator John Grayson, took his seat, his expression stoic. His defense was spearheaded by the renowned lawyer Helen Cartwright, who argued vehemently against what she termed "the absurdity of prosecuting centuries-old crimes based on genetic memories."

In the courtroom's back row, I sat among a cluster of journalists, my pen and notebook ready. As a sharp observer, I meticulously noted every development of the unfolding trial, aware that my report could significantly influence public opinion on this unique case. Renowned as the leading journalistic authority on the ChronoSync phenomenon, I had become a regular on cable news, revered for my expertise that could influence public sentiment and academic perspectives.

After years of covering high-stakes stories, I honed my instincts, which made me respected and feared by those in power. My colleagues admired my unwavering commitment to the truth, even when it put me at odds with influential figures.

From the outset of the case, I had been tracking the ethical complexities involved. My attention alternated between Senator Grayson, whose calm composure starkly contrasted with the passionate arguments of his defense attorney, Ms. Cartwright. Observing the jury and the crowded courtroom, I interpreted each reaction, weaving them into my analysis. My forthcoming article would explore the trial's intricate details and consider how its outcomes might redefine societal understandings of justice and moral accountability through different lifetimes.

As Prosecutor Samuel Leeds rose to his feet for his opening argument, I scribbled notes, my mind racing with the implications of the historical precedent this case could set.

"Ladies and gentlemen of the jury," Leeds began, his voice resonating through the courtroom. With a solemn expression, he paced before the jury, his footsteps echoing in the hushed room. As he spoke, he reached out to a table, picking up a copy of the ChronoSync report bound in dark blue leather. With deliberate care, he held it aloft. "Today, we stand before you to address a matter unprecedented in the annals of justice." He gestured toward the senator, his gaze unwavering. "We are here to discuss not only the actions of the man before you, United States Senator John Grayson, but those of a persona from centuries past, tied to him by the unbroken thread of the soul." His fingers brushed across the report as he set it back down. "As we have learned through the scientific breakthrough of ChronoSync," he continued, his tone gaining intensity, "the essence of a person, their soul, is continuous and unchanging." With a deliberate motion, he placed the report down, his eyes fixed on the jury. "Given the extraordinary capabilities of this technology, which has unveiled these past transgressions," he insisted, his voice unwavering, "we must now confront our moral obligations."

The jury responded with a collective murmur, their heads nodding in unison.

"As we delve into these matters, I implore you not to be swayed solely by the philosophical and spiritual implications of reincarnation but to focus also on the tangible, the very real atrocities committed by the senator's past self—a warlord in medieval Europe whose reign was marked by ruthless suppression and expansion. This was a man whose authority knew no bounds and whose hands were stained with the blood of the innocent," Leeds argued vehemently. As he spoke, a collective shudder passed through the jury. Several members exchanged uneasy glances, their eyes widening slightly in horror, reflecting a visceral reaction to the gravity of the accusations.

"Imagine, if you will, entire villages engulfed in flames, their inhabitants driven to despair and death under his command. Historical records, corroborated by ChronoSync's findings, reveal a campaign of terror—mass executions, forced displacements, and unspeakable acts of cruelty. Consider the siege where wells were poisoned, the winter crops burned to instigate starvation, and the horrific decree to execute children in rebellious towns to crush future uprisings."

I noticed a palpable tension among the jurors as the prosecutor paused, allowing his words to linger. Their expressions ranged from shock to disbelief, and their gazes were fixed intently on the attorney. A silent understanding passed among them as if they were collectively grappling with the weight of the revelations.

"These acts were not merely aggressive war tactics but calculated, deliberate actions intended to terrorize and dominate. The scars left by these atrocities lingered in communities, resonating through the years to reach us here in this courtroom," Leeds said, turning to look at the accused.

"Thus, we are compelled to ask: Does the passage of time erode the need for justice? Should these grievous acts go unanswered simply because they are distant in history? Or do we, as guardians of justice, have a duty to uphold the rights of those long gone, ensuring that such crimes are addressed, irrespective of the era in which they were committed?" Leeds paused, allowing the questions to hang heavy in the air, a silent challenge to the jurors.

"The severity of these crimes demands accountability, transcending the boundaries of time and the cycles of rebirth. We cannot, in good conscience, allow the temporal distance of these actions to diminish their gravity. Our moral duty to honor the victims and to seek justice for their suffering obliges us to act not just for the past but for the ethical foundations of our future. Therefore, I ask you to consider all the evidence, reflect on the continuity of the soul and the unending quest for justice, and render a verdict that speaks to our highest principles of morality and humanity."

As Leeds concluded his opening statement, the weight of centuries bore down upon the jurors, tasked with reconciling the stark brutality of ancient crimes with the sad figure of Senator Grayson and determining how justice should be served in such an extraordinary context. The air in the courtroom seemed heavy with history, each juror carrying the burden of the past as they prepared to deliberate the fate of a man tied to deeds long forgotten by time. With a solemn nod from the judge, the attorney for the defense—Ms. Cartwright rose to offer her perspective, her voice steady yet filled with conviction as she addressed the court.

"Your Honor, members of the jury," she began, her voice resonating with confidence and deliberation, "Today, we are asked to embrace a precedent that could forever alter the fabric of our justice system. This law compels us to extend the arm of justice across centuries, to prosecute a man for deeds committed in a past life—a life separate from the one he leads today, where he has served his community and country with honor and integrity."

Pausing to let her words sink in, Cartwright scanned the room, making eye contact with each of the jurors as she continued, "We are here to discuss not just the fate of Senator John Grayson but to debate the very principles upon which our legal system is built. The prosecution has presented a narrative of historical crimes, crimes so distant in time and context that they are more suited to a history book than a courtroom in modern America."

I noticed that, like a crosswind rushing through a room when a window was opened, the jury shifted, agreeing with the attorney's words.

"With all due respect to the pains of history," she added, her tone turning persuasive, "we must ask ourselves—what is the essence of justice? Is it justice to hold a man accountable for actions committed centuries ago under moral and societal norms vastly different from today? Actions he has no memory of, no connection to, other than a genetic link revealed by a technology that, while impressive, should not be mistaken for a moral compass."

Cartwright moved slightly closer to the jury, her expression earnest. "Senator Grayson stands before you today, having led a life of public service devoid of crime. Yet, we are asked to see him not as he is but as someone he might have been in another era, another world almost. If we accept this premise, where do we draw the line?"

She paused again, allowing her questions to permeate the courtroom. "This case," she concluded, "is not only about whether Senator Grayson committed these acts in a past life. It's about whether punishing him today, in this life, serves the cause of true justice. It's about whether we, as a society, decide to honor the principles of personal responsibility, of moral and legal accountability rooted in the present, not the distant shadows of the past."

As Cartwright returned to her seat, the courtroom contemplated the profound legal and ethical questions her statement had raised. The stage was set for a trial that would explore the facts of the case and the boundaries of justice and identity.

As the courtroom settled into a focused silence, the prosecution called Dr. Adrienne Wallace to the stand as its first witness. Adrienne approached with measured steps, exuding an aura of professionalism and authority. Her hair, neatly pulled back into a sleek bun, framed her determined expression, while her attire—a tailored suit in charcoal gray—reflected her status as the founder and CEO of ChronoSync. Every detail, from the crisp lines of her dress to the confident stride in her step, spoke of her expertise and command of the subject matter.

Taking her seat, Adrienne wasted no time in asserting her authority. With a clear and commanding voice, she elucidated the workings of ChronoSync, delving into the intricate mechanisms that allowed the technology to decode genetic memories. With precision, she explained the scientific principles behind the process, emphasizing the rigorous methodology employed to ensure the accuracy of the information retrieved. As she spoke, each sentence reinforced the importance of ChronoSync in uncovering the truths hidden within the depths of human DNA.

However, Cartwright, the defense attorney, was prepared to challenge her on these points. Rising with a composed yet critical demeanor, Cartwright initiated a sharp cross-examination.

"Dr. Wallace," Cartwright started, her tone probing, "while ChronoSync may reveal details about a past life, can you assure this court that the interpretations of these memories are entirely objective and free from analytical bias?"

Adrienne admitted the potential for some level of interpretation but was quick to reinforce her point. "While interpretation does play a role, the fundamental events and actions revealed by ChronoSync are supported by rigorous validation processes, including cross-referencing with historical records, which significantly bolsters their credibility."

Cartwright navigated deeper into ethical complexities, challenging Adrienne: "Considering the concept of soul rebirth, how can we hold someone accountable for crimes in a previous life?"

The courtroom tightened with anticipation as Adrienne carefully weighed her response, recognizing the depth of the philosophical and legal implications. "You raise a pivotal point," she replied thoughtfully, her composure intact despite the gravity of the discourse. "ChronoSync was designed to uncover historical truths, not as a prosecutorial tool. However, when our technology uncovers severe crimes like murder or mass murder, ChronoSync is legally required to report these violent crimes to the authorities, creating a complex web of ethical and legal dilemmas."

She elaborated further, capturing the courtroom's rapt attention. "The idea that the soul persists across lifetimes challenges us to rethink traditional legal boundaries. For minor offenses, perhaps the statute of limitations could still apply, acknowledging that past lives should not indefinitely burden the present. Yet, for grave offenses, where time traditionally does not absolve liability, there might be a moral and ethical imperative to seek justice beyond the conventional constraints of time."

She paused, allowing her words to resonate in the charged atmosphere. "If we accept the soul's continuity, we must ask ourselves—Are we merely bodies hosting a continuum of past consciousness, or are we entirely new beings entitled to start afresh?"

Adrienne's remarks sparked a murmur among the spectators as the courtroom grappled with the philosophical conundrum of balancing historical justice against the integrity of the present individual's moral agency. Her testimony highlighted a critical frontier in law and ethics, suggesting that the pursuit of justice might extend beyond the temporal boundaries of a single lifetime, yet questioning whether it should.

Cartwright continued as the jurors settled back into a charged silence following Adrienne's testimony. Her strategy was clear: introducing a spiritual dimension that might sway the philosophical debate about justice for past-life crimes.

"Dr. Wallace," she began, her voice calm yet piercing, "let's consider the spiritual aspects of rebirth. Many world religions, in tune with ChronoSync's findings, suggest that the soul undergoes a form of purification between incarnations. If this is the case, why would a soul—purged of its past sins—need to be punished once more in one's new life?"

The question hung in the air, casting a ripple of contemplation across the room. Adrienne paused, considering her response carefully. "It's a compelling argument," she admitted. "The notion of spiritual purification does suggest that the soul is cleansed of past wrongs. This would imply that the essence of the individual standing trial today may not bear the moral culpability of actions from a past life."

Cartwright nodded, pressing on with her point: "So if we accept the possibility of such spiritual processes, doesn't this challenge the ethical foundation of prosecuting someone based on past-life actions? Could this purification process render our attempts at justice redundant or even unjust?"

The jurors leaned in, captivated by the unfolding dialogue that now treads the delicate lines between law, science, and spirituality. Adrienne responded, her tone reflective. "Yes, that is the dilemma. If we believe the journey toward rebirth cleanses the soul, applying temporal justice might seem unnecessary or inappropriate. However, the challenge remains in proving the existence and efficacy of such spiritual processes to a legal standard, which is currently beyond our scientific capability."

Cartwright concluded her questioning with a pointed remark. "Therefore, it appears we are in uncharted waters, attempting to anchor our laws in theories that challenge our legal precedents and delve into religious and spiritual beliefs that are inherently subjective and beyond empirical verification."

As she sat, the room buzzed with the intensity of the questions she had raised. Overseeing the proceedings, Judge Alvez recognized the depth of the philosophical issues. She understood that the decisions made here would resonate far beyond the confines of the courtroom, challenging how society understands justice, morality, and the essence of human identity across lifetimes.

I sat in the back row, my pen poised over my notebook, reflecting on the monumental verdict that had just been delivered. The jury found Senator Grayson guilty, a decision reverberating through the courtroom and beyond. My mind raced as I considered the implications of this landmark case. In many ways, the conviction would set a precedent echoing through the corridors of justice, science, and ethics.

As the room began to empty, I stood up. I filed out while considering how the jury's decision underscored the complex interplay between legal accountability and the philosophical questions raised by ChronoSync's technology. The concept of being judged for actions committed in a past life had always been abstract, almost theoretical, until now. This trial had brought those abstract ideas into stark reality, challenging conventional notions of justice and personal responsibility.

The guilty verdict left me with a sense of profound contemplation. While it asserted that individuals could be held accountable for crimes committed in previous incarnations, it also raised numerous questions about the nature of justice and moral culpability across lifetimes. How would society balance the need for historical accountability with the rights of individuals in the present? As I closed my notebook and prepared to leave, I knew that my next article would delve into these issues, exploring the broader implications of the jury's decision and what it meant for the future of justice in an age where the past could no longer be buried.

The trial tested not only the boundaries of the legal system but also my understanding of my place in the world. There was a renewed sense of purpose, a drive to continue questioning and exploring the hidden truths beneath the surface. As I stepped out of the courthouse into the bustling city streets, I realized that my journey, much like the unfolding story of ChronoSync, was beginning.

CHAPTER TEN
INHERITANCE

The New York Times
Unraveling the Inheritance Conundrum in the Era of
ChronoSync
By Marcus Vega

The recent landmark ruling finding Senator John Grayson guilty of murder has drastically altered our country's legal framework. Further complicating the legal system is the effect of ChronoSync technology on the already complex world of inheritance law. This revolutionary technology, which uncovers past-life identities, challenges conventional understandings of individuality and continuity and redefines the fabric of legal norms concerning inheritance and property rights.

ChronoSync's ability to authenticate and reveal previous incarnations offers unprecedented insights into the lives people once lived, potentially reshaping how assets, land, and even cultural artifacts are claimed and adjudicated today. As courts grapple with the implications of individuals claiming assets based on past-life connections, a new legal landscape is emerging, filled with lucrative opportunities and profound challenges.

This seismic shift in legal practice confronts established principles of inheritance, pushing the boundaries of how justice is conceived and delivered. It forces lawmakers, jurists, and the public to navigate a complex maze of ethical, moral, and practical questions: Can and should a past-life identity impact the legal rights and obligations of the present? How do we balance historical grievances with contemporary legal standards?

As the integration of ChronoSync technology into global legal systems redefines our established notions of identity, ownership, and rights, its broad implications compel us to reassess the technicalities of law and the essence of societal structure and individual rights across different eras. The ripple effects of this groundbreaking technology are found most acutely in inheritance law, where conventional protocols are being challenged by the profound questions and scenarios that ChronoSync introduces.

Wills: At the forefront of these challenges are disputed wills, which have traditionally been straightforward legal documents. Wills are meant to ensure a clear transition of assets following a person's death. Yet, ChronoSync's unveiling of past-life identities has blurred these clear transitions significantly. For instance, a high-profile case in California involves a contested will of a deceased real estate agent. This will is now the center of a legal battle involving claimants who assert they are his children from a previous life. This scenario forces the courts to navigate uncharted waters, integrating metaphysical claims with traditional legal adjudication. The courtroom has thus transformed into a complex arena where philosophical debates about the essence of personhood and continuity intersect with legal principles, marking a significant departure from conventional legal practices.

Estates: Intestate succession, or the process by which assets are distributed without a will, is similarly affected. The usual priority given to biological relatives is being questioned in the wake of past-life revelations. In Florida, a contentious battle over an estate showcases this shift. Multiple parties have emerged, each asserting inheritance rights based on supposed past-life connections to the deceased. This situation forces legal systems to redefine what constitutes a "family" in inheritance disputes, challenging deeply entrenched legal and societal norms.

Ownership of Historical Artifacts: The impact of ChronoSync extends into the realm of cultural heritage and property. Claims to historical artifacts based on past-life identities are increasingly common, leading to legal and ethical dilemmas. For example, in New York, a court case involves a woman claiming ownership of a 15th-century painting by asserting she is the reincarnation of the original artist. This claim challenges the museum currently housing the painting and raises profound questions about the ownership of cultural and artistic works—blurring the lines between past and present ownership.

Corporate Succession: Corporate governance and succession planning are also transforming. A notable case within a Fortune 500 company features a junior executive who alleges he is the reincarnation of the company's founder. He claims a substantial stake in the company and a leadership role based on these past-life affiliations. This claim disrupts traditional corporate succession planning and introduces a unique challenge to corporate law by verifying and valuing past-life experiences in modern corporate governance.

Land Rights and Property Ownership: Land and property disputes have become more complex, with claimants citing past-life relationships to assert ownership rights. In Australia, a significant legal dispute involves a group claiming ancestral rights over a profitable mining area, arguing they were the land's original owners centuries ago. These claims pit current legal landowners against those who invoke historical ownership, forcing courts to navigate a labyrinth of historical, legal, and ethical questions.

Inheritance Taxation: Taxing assets inherited through past-life connections presents new challenges for tax authorities. A debate is underway in the UK regarding the classification and taxation of such inheritances. Lawmakers grapple with the implications of taxing assets "inherited" from individuals who lived centuries ago, raising questions about the continuity of property rights and the appropriate methods for valuing such properties for tax purposes.

Conclusion: ChronoSync technology is reshaping our understanding of identity and inheritance, and legal systems worldwide are scrambling to adapt. Governments are at the epicenter of this legal upheaval, tasked with developing regulations that can accommodate the fast-paced changes brought on by technological advances. Legal scholars and estate attorneys are being pushed to the limits of their traditional expertise, and the more astute among them are quickly establishing specialized estate planning services. These services promise to navigate clients through the complexities of ChronoSync-related legal issues and offer the prospect of significant financial gain for law firms willing to pioneer in this new legal frontier.

As ChronoSync's implications unfold, the legal community, governments, and financial institutions must work together to develop a legal framework that respects historical identities and contemporary legal principles. The journey is fraught with challenges but also ripe with opportunities for those who can creatively and effectively respond to the evolving landscape. The quest for a balanced and equitable legal system in the era of ChronoSync is not just a necessity but an imperative, driving the legal profession into a new era of jurisprudence and innovation.

CHAPTER ELEVEN
A BREACH

We were shown a table at a café in Tribeca, the clamor of the bustling city just a muffled backdrop to my growing concerns. My eyes, usually calm and observing, now flickered with a storm's intensity as I processed the sheer volume of complications unfolding from ChronoSync and its aftermath. Across from me sat Harlan, a fellow journalist and longtime confidant, whose keen interest was evident in his focused gaze and the quick, attentive nods he gave as I spoke. Harlan, known for his sharp analytical skills and deep understanding of technological impacts, was the perfect sounding board for the cascade of issues I was about to unload.

The café, with its warm ambient lighting, soft clink of coffee cups, and the constant hum of conversations, provided a stark contrast to the gravity of our discussion as I delved into the unexpected repercussions I'd been learning about from a myriad of sources—academic journals, insider interviews, and confidential leaks—all painting a complex picture of ChronoSync's ripple effects across society.

"Let's start with the artifact issue," I began, my fingers absentmindedly tracing the rim of my coffee cup as I delved into the topic. "Reports from ChronoSync have pinpointed sites with artifacts that have eluded archaeologists for decades. But the problem is, it's not the academics or museums that are first on the scene; it's been treasure hunters."

I leaned forward, my voice dropping to underscore my point. "For instance, there was a case where a man used his ChronoSync report to locate and excavate a Saxon burial site in England. The relics he found were worth millions and ended up in private collections before anyone could verify the site's historical significance."

Harlan, frowning, interjected, "So, they're looting history for profit?"

"Exactly," I replied. "While some argue they're saving these artifacts from obscurity, they're bypassing all legal and ethical guidelines."

Harlan nodded, absorbing my words.

"We're seeing a clash between modern technology and ancient rights, private gain and public good. And with ChronoSync enabling access to these hidden treasures, the line between archaeological research and high-stakes looting is getting dangerously thin."

I paused, noting my friend's intrigued expression. "Then there's the natural resources angle. ChronoSync reports have pinpointed spots brimming with untapped resources—minerals, oil, and precious metals. It's led to a gold rush of sorts. Individuals and companies scramble to acquire mining rights or invest in exploration ventures. It's a potential economic boon but rife with ethical dilemmas."

"Take this Mongolia incident, for instance. A ChronoSync report has revealed a massive deposit of rare earth minerals. A woman named Dr. Elara Zhao, who learned she had been a farmer in Mongolia, made this groundbreaking discovery. Her vivid memories from her previous life led her to the exact location of the mineral deposits. Within weeks, the area was swarmed by unauthorized miners, stripping the land, disrupting local communities, and violating international law, all without a thought for environmental repercussions."

"And the government's response?" Harlan asked.

"They're overwhelmed but starting to react. Legal battles are underway, but the damage is significant," I explained.

Shifting in my seat, I then touched on another sensitive topic. "Now, historical land claims—this is where it gets messy. There's this town in New England where ChronoSync unearthed a colonial-era will that contradicted the current land ownership records. It's set neighbor against neighbor, with some residents facing eviction as new claimants backed by wealthy investors push to take over."

Harlan shook his head. "It's like opening Pandora's box. What about historical accuracy in media? You mentioned some issues there."

I nodded. "Oh, that's another arena of abuse. With access to detailed, previously unknown historical data, some creators are churning out heavily biased or outright false content, aiming to sensationalize rather than educate. It stirs up controversy, misleads the public, and often distorts our understanding of history."

"And predictive historical analysis?" Harlan queried, clearly intrigued.

I tapped on the table. "It's being used to forecast economic trends, market crises, and even political events. But imagine the potential for manipulation if this information falls into the wrong hands. It's like insider trading, but with historical events."

Harlan leaned back, absorbing the scope of the issues. "So, what's being done about all this?"

I looked hopeful for the first time. "Well, the government is doing its best to step up. They plan to establish a new regulatory agency to manage ChronoSync's consequences. They're holding a press conference soon to lay out the details."

Skeptical as ever, Harlan interjected, "Sure, but can they enforce it? We've seen regulations fail before. This technology is unprecedented, and the stakes are incredibly high."

I shrugged. "They'll have the authority to regulate its use, ensure compliance with laws, and impose penalties for misuse. It's crucial to reign in these abuses and make sure ChronoSync benefits the public good, not just private interests," I concluded, a sense of relief in my tone.

Harlan nodded thoughtfully. "That could be a game-changer. Proper oversight might help balance the scales."

As we finished our coffees, the weight of our discussion lingered, blending into the ambient noises of the café. We both recognized that while the road ahead was fraught with challenges, the forthcoming agency might pave the way for responsible innovation with ChronoSync.

Just as we were wrapping up our discussion on ChronoSync's unintended consequences, Harlan's phone vibrated, breaking the contemplative silence that had settled between us. As he glanced at the screen, his eyebrows shot up in surprise, and he quickly unlocked the device to read more.

"Marcus, you won't believe this," Harlan said, turning his phone so I could see the screen. The headline blazed across the top of a major news outlet's website: "Massive Data Breach Exposes Private Histories of ChronoSync Users."

The article detailed how hackers had infiltrated ChronoSync's database, stealing vast amounts of sensitive data that included detailed historical analyses of individuals' past lives. These analyses, which were meant to be private, allowed users to explore their histories and personal past-life events through ChronoSync's time-viewing technology. The leaked information was already appearing on various internet forums, exposing secrets and private family histories to the public.

"The breach has exposed everything from family secrets and old legal disputes to intimate personal details that were never meant to be public," I read aloud, my voice laced with disbelief.

"This is catastrophic," Harlan said, shaking his head. "It's not just a violation of privacy; it's like ripping open someone's diary for the whole world to see."

My mind raced as I considered the implications. "Think about the potential fallout. People could face public embarrassment, or worse—blackmail and threats. Families could be torn apart by resurfaced old conflicts and secrets."

Harlan was already typing rapidly on his phone, likely jotting down notes for a story. "I need to cover this from all angles," he said, looking up at me. "The technical aspect of the breach, the impact on individuals, the response from ChronoSync, and what this means for past-life privacy laws going forward."

I nodded, already pulling out my notebook. "I should look into who might be behind this hack. Was it just for chaos, or is there something more targeted at play here?"

We quickly settled our tab and stood up, each ready to dive into this new lead. As we left the café, the consequences of the situation were palpable between us. This breach was a massive invasion of privacy and a stark reminder of the vulnerabilities inherent in handling such deeply personal data. It underscored the dangers of the ChronoSync, where the past could be just as vulnerable as any other data when digitized.

CHAPTER TWELVE
FALLOUT

I hurried through the bustling streets, my mind racing with the potential fallout of such a breach. The news of the hack sent shock waves through the elite circles that could afford ChronoSync's services, and I knew this story had long legs to run. The situation gnawed at me as I entered ChronoSync's Astoria, Queens headquarters, my heart pounding urgently.

The receptionist, sensing the importance of my visit, quickly ushered me to Adrienne's office. As the founder and CEO, Adrienne had always appreciated the honest coverage she received from me and my articles in *The New York Times*. Today, however, the usually poised leader was a picture of distress. She looked up as I walked in, offering a weary smile that barely masked her anxiety.

"Adrienne, this is a mess," I said, sitting across from her. "Can you tell me what happened?"

She sighed deeply, running a hand through her hair, streaked with stress-induced silver. "Hackers got into our most secure databases. They exposed personal sessions, Marcus. It's a complete breach of privacy."

She paused, her gaze falling to her lap as if everything was pressing her down. "I don't know who else to turn to," she whispered, her voice cracking. "My PR team is in overdrive trying to contain this, but they can't keep up. Every minute, more damage is done. I thought we were prepared for anything—everything—but not this. Not an attack like this."

Her hands clenched tightly in her lap as if bracing herself. "I need your help, Marcus. I didn't know where else to go."

I could see the exhaustion in her eyes, the sharp edge of panic beneath the surface. This wasn't the composed, confident Adrienne I was used to.

She was unraveling, the pressure mounting faster than she could handle. And now it was on me to help pick up the pieces.

I stroked my chin, my journalist instincts kicking in despite my empathy for my friend. "How could this happen? You've always been so confident in your security measures."

Adrienne shook her head, disbelief still evident in her eyes. "Security has always been one of our top priorities. We invested heavily in the best technology and experts. I thought it was impossible. How they managed to bypass everything we had in place is mind-boggling."

I could see the turmoil in her eyes but pressed on. "What are some of the worst cases?"

Adrienne hesitated, then took a deep breath. "I'll share some with you, but only off the record."

I nodded, appreciating her trust. "Of course."

Adrienne took a deep breath, the revelations pressing down on her. "Michael Weiss. His sessions revealed he was a ruthless warlord in a past life. Now, his reputation as a philanthropic real estate mogul is in tatters. Business partners are fleeing, and his once-loyal employees are beginning to question their allegiance. He's being painted as a villain reborn. Investors are pulling out, and his company's stock is plummeting. Weiss's carefully curated image of benevolence has crumbled, exposing a darker side that no one could have anticipated. The fallout is unprecedented, and the empire he built is on the brink of collapse."

I winced. "That's brutal. Are there others?"

Adrienne nodded grimly. "There's this woman, Victoria Mitchell. She's a prominent cable newswoman, and her past-life report revealed she was a courtesan in the royal courts of Europe. The network is dropping her show. Her public image is in shambles, with former colleagues distancing themselves to avoid the fallout. Her once-loyal viewers are now divided. Victoria's carefully crafted persona of elegance and professionalism has been irreparably tarnished, and the world she knew is unraveling at an alarming pace."

I shook my head, feeling each story's weight like a physical burden. "The outrage, the lawsuits—how are you handling this?"

Adrienne's voice wavered with emotion. "We're enhancing our security and setting up a compensation fund. We're fully cooperating with authorities to catch the hackers. But, to be honest, it's been a nightmare."

I reached across the desk, my hand finding hers, the warmth of her skin soft beneath my fingers. When our hands connected, something shifted between us—a current of understanding I did not expect. Adrienne's eyes met mine, and I saw a flicker of something unspoken, a shared vulnerability in them. Her fingers tightened slightly around mine, acknowledging the silent exchange. "Can ChronoSync survive this?" I asked, my voice low, almost a whisper, as the solemnity of our situation hung between us.

"I don't know, Marcus. We have to rebuild trust," she said with a sigh, her voice tinged with determination and weariness. "This technology can do so much good, and I hope this will not define us. But I'm afraid it will be a long, hard road."

The room was thick with unspoken words. I could see the toll this was taking on her, not just as a CEO but as a person deeply committed to the vision. Her shoulders were slightly slumped, and the toll of recent events dimmed the usual spark in her eyes. I wanted to offer more than just professional support; I wanted to be there for her as a friend, someone she could lean on.

As I prepared to leave, Adrienne looked up, a hint of vulnerability in her eyes that I had never seen before. "Marcus, would you like to have dinner tonight? Just as friends—not as a journalist."

I paused, sensing the unspoken importance behind the invitation. I knew this was more than just a casual dinner; it was a reaching out, a plea for connection in a time of crisis. "I'd like that, Adrienne. I really would."

Our eyes locked, and for a moment, the chaos of the outside world faded away, leaving just the two of us in a shared understanding and unspoken bond.

*

We met later that evening at a cozy restaurant in Chelsea. The ambiance was warm, with soft lighting casting a gentle glow on the rustic wooden tables. Adrienne and I were seated in a corner booth, providing a semblance of privacy amidst the bustling dinner crowd.

As we settled in, the conversation began to flow more easily. Adrienne opened up about her life and the loneliness of being so devoted to her work. "I'm forty, divorced, and my two boys, Joshua and Robert, live with their father. I thought dedicating myself to ChronoSync would be worth it, but now I regret missing out on so much of their lives."

I looked at her with genuine concern. "That must be incredibly hard. Do you get to see them often?"

Adrienne shook her head, her eyes glistening with unshed tears. "Not as much as I'd like. Their father and I have an amicable arrangement, but they're with him most of the time. I missed birthdays, school plays, and just… being there."

I reached out, my hand gently covering hers. As my skin touched hers, a rush of emotions surged through me. It was as if the simple gesture bridged a chasm of time and distance that had kept us apart for so long. Why I felt this way, I had no clue. The inexplicable connection left me bewildered yet comforted, stirring a profound sense of familiarity and longing that defied explanation.

Adrienne looked at me, her eyes searching mine. "But what about you, Marcus? Are you married, divorced, or have a girlfriend or maybe a boyfriend? What's your story?"

I chuckled nervously, scratching the back of my neck. "Uh, definitely not married. And no, no boyfriend. I'm… I'm pretty sure I like girls."

Adrienne laughed, the tension easing between us. "Pretty sure, huh?"

I shrugged, my cheeks flushing slightly. "Okay, I'm very sure. I'm thirty-five and have never been married. I had a serious romance a few years back, but we broke up because my life, like yours, revolves around work. Sometimes, I wonder if I've missed my chance at something more meaningful."

Adrienne tilted her head, her gaze softening. "Do you ever regret it? Not finding someone to share your life with?"

I sighed, feeling a bit more at ease. "There are moments when I see friends with their families, and I wonder what it would be like. But I've focused on chasing stories and making a difference in my career. It's hard to balance it all."

Adrienne nodded in understanding. "It's a lonely road. Being so driven, so focused on something that consumes you."

I smiled wryly. "Yeah, it is. But I've always hoped that one day, I'd find a way to have both—a fulfilling career and someone to share it with."

Adrienne smiled softly. "Maybe there's still time for us to find that balance."

We talked for hours, sharing stories of our lonely lives, aspirations, and fears. The food was delicious, but the conversation nourished us both as the brick-by-brick walls we had built around ourselves began to crumble.

By the time we left the restaurant, the night was well underway. We walked together through the quiet streets, the air cool and crisp. As we reached Adrienne's apartment, we had an unspoken understanding.

"Would you like to come up for a drink?" Adrienne asked softly, her eyes searching mine.

I nodded, my heart pounding with anticipation. "I'd like that."

Inside her apartment, the atmosphere was charged with a new energy. We talked some more, but the words soon gave way to a deeper, unspoken connection. The touch of our hands, the gentle brush of our fingers, and the proximity of our bodies led us toward an inevitable conclusion.

As we moved through the apartment, each step closer to the privacy of her bedroom, the anticipation between us became almost palpable. My hand grazed Adrienne's cheek, and she responded with a soft sigh, leaning into my touch. Our eyes locked, conveying everything that words couldn't. Slowly, our lips met in a tender kiss, hesitant at first but growing bolder with each passing second.

Our hands explored each other, tracing paths over clothes that quickly became unnecessary barriers. We revealed our bodies, vulnerabilities, and desires with each piece of clothing that fell away. The final defenses were shed, leaving us exposed yet more connected than ever.

We came together tender yet passionate in the dim light of the bedroom. It was a dance of shared loneliness and newfound intimacy, every movement a testament to our discovered connection. For a moment, the world outside ceased to exist, and all that mattered was the rhythm of our hearts beating in unison.

As we lay entwined, the aftermath of our passion lingering in the air, Adrienne whispered, "Thank you for being here, Marcus."

I held her close, my arms a protective cocoon around her. "I wouldn't want to be anywhere else," I replied, feeling a sense of completeness I hadn't known before. At that moment, I realized that I had found something irreplaceable in Adrienne, a bond that went beyond words and touched the very core of my being. I wondered if Adrienne felt the same.

CHAPTER THIRTEEN
REVELATION

I paused beyond the doorway of Adrienne's apartment, the soft click of the latch still resonating in the silence. The warmth of her skin, the intoxicating blend of her scent and sweat, lingered on me like a ghost. This encounter had been unexpected, a wild divergence from my meticulously charted path. But as I walked down the dimly lit hallway, a sense of clarity washed over me. I had never thought of myself as someone who sought deep connections, but now, the threads of my fate weaved seamlessly with Adrienne's. Perhaps I was meant for this, meant to intertwine with her in a profound, almost predestined way.

The world outside was in chaos. ChronoSync, the revolutionary company that had unlocked the secrets of past lives, was under siege. Reports of breaches and sensitive information leaking into the public sphere dominated the airwaves. The once-revered institution now teetered on the brink of collapse, its downfall imminent. No more readings, no more peering into the enigmatic tapestry of reincarnation. The doors to the past were closing, sealing off the revelations that had only begun to surface.

Yet, amidst this turmoil, humanity buzzed with new energy. The scientific proof of an afterlife and reincarnation had shattered the old paradigms, sending ripples through every facet of society. Philosophers debated, theologians reeled, and ordinary people grappled with the implications of a reality beyond death. Always the observer and the documentarian, I stood at the forefront of this seismic shift.

My mind raced as I descended the stairwell, the urgency of my mission propelling me forward. I had to capture this moment to chronicle the drama and history unfolding in real time. The world was changing quickly, and I was determined not to let it slip through my fingers. Each interaction and revelation was a piece of the puzzle I was driven to assemble.

As I stepped into the cool night air, my pulse quickened, caught between the sharp chill and the dark unknown ahead. The city around me hummed with an eerie vibrancy, the neon lights casting a dream-like glow on the rain-slicked streets. I pulled my coat tighter around me, my thoughts lingering on Adrienne. There was something about her, something that transcended the physical connection we had shared. I had glimpsed a reflection of my soul in her eyes, a recognition beyond mere coincidence.

I pulled out my phone and checked the latest updates as I walked. Headlines blared about the ChronoSync debacle, and speculation about what would come next ran rampant. But beyond sensationalism were stories of ordinary people grappling with the extraordinary. Tales of lives rediscovered, of past loves and ancient grudges resurfacing. Humanity was in the throes of an existential renaissance, and I was at the epicenter.

I paused at a crosswalk, waiting for the light to change, and allowed myself a moment of introspection. The world shifted beneath my feet, catching me in the undertow of my thoughts. I felt a sense of purpose for the first time in a long while. My connection with Adrienne had opened a door within me, revealing that life was more than just a series of moments to be recorded. It was meant to be lived, experienced with all its highs and lows, joys and sorrows.

As I stood there, the sound of city life swirling around me, I began to ponder the more profound implications of my newfound purpose. The trial and its ramifications had already stirred a maelstrom of thoughts, but my connection with Adrienne added another layer to my contemplation. It wasn't just about uncovering the truth for the public; it was about understanding my journey and the people who crossed my path.

My mind wandered back to my ChronoSync session, where I had delved into my past life and discovered my connection with a woman named Lila. The experience had been surreal, revealing a history I never knew existed. I had seen myself as Étienne, a man deeply in love with Lila, whose life was intertwined with mine in ways I could scarcely comprehend. The memories were vivid—walking through the cobbled streets of Paris, sharing whispered secrets under the moonlight, and Lila's promise to find me again, her dying words echoing in my mind: "Our souls are bound for eternity."

The details documented in my ChronoSync report were not just facts but fragments of life as real as my current one. The session left me both awed and unsettled, challenging my perceptions of reality and destiny. I spent countless hours analyzing the implications, but one thought remained clear—there was the existence of a bond that transcended time.

As I stood there, the thought struck me like a lightning bolt: Could Adrienne be the reincarnation of Lila? The possibility sent a shiver down my spine. Our connection felt so profound, so familiar. I remembered the ease of our conversations, the unspoken understanding bridging our interactions.

My heart raced with the realization. Could this be the fulfillment of Lila's promise? The notion seemed fantastical, yet ChronoSync had already upended my understanding of reality. The light turned green, but I lingered for a moment longer. If Adrienne indeed was Lila reborn, what did that mean for me? For us? I had a renewed determination as I crossed the street.

The thought consumed me as I walked through the city. I knew I had to learn the truth. If Adrienne were indeed Lila, our souls would be bound in a way that defied rational explanation, a cosmic love story that would span our lifetimes. I realized there was a way to confirm my suspicions. As CEO and founder of ChronoSync, Adrienne would have certainly used the device on herself. If she was indeed Lila, she would know about her past life.

Once again, the light turned green, and I stepped forward, each stride a declaration of intent. I was ready to embrace the uncertainty, to dive headfirst into the chaos. With Adrienne by my side, anything was possible.

We were bound together by something greater than ourselves, a cosmic thread that defied explanation.

Walking through the bustling city, I couldn't help but smile. The world was on the brink of a new era, and I was determined to be a part of it. Documenting the past, living in the present, and shaping the future were all interconnected, a tapestry of existence that I was eager to explore.

My thoughts remained on Adrienne. I needed to talk to her. The idea that she could be the reincarnation of Lila filled me with a renewed sense of purpose. I would approach her carefully, explaining my revelations and their profound impact on me. I was confident that she, of all people, would understand the significance of our shared history.

And with Adrienne, I knew that the journey would be anything but ordinary. If she was Lila, our love was destined, eternal, a story transcending time. The prospect of rediscovering our connection in this lifetime filled me with hope and excitement. I felt a sense of urgency to see her, confirm my suspicions, and embark on this extraordinary journey together.

I hurried back to Adrienne's apartment, my heart pounding with anticipation. I envisioned our conversation, the moment she would confirm my suspicions and the shared realization that we had found each other again after centuries. But as I approached the building, a sense of unease crept over me.

As I entered the lobby, Tommy, the doorman, met me with a troubled expression. "Mr. Vega," Tommy said, his voice tinged with worry. "Something happened while you were gone."

A chill ran down my spine. "What do you mean? Is Adrienne okay?"

Tommy shook his head, his eyes reflecting his concern. "She was taken. Two men came and forced her from the lobby," he said, gesturing before him. "They took Dr. Wallace away in a black SUV. I tried to stop them, but they were too strong."

Panic surged through me. "Taken? By who? Did you see their faces? Did they say anything?"

Tommy bit his lower lip, clearly distressed. "I couldn't get a good look at their faces, and they didn't say much. It all happened so fast. I'm sorry."

My mind raced. Who would want to take Adrienne? And why? This was no doubt connected to ChronoSync and its recent turmoil. Adrienne was the CEO and founder, and with the company's recent troubles, it made sense that she might be a target.

I took a deep breath, trying to steady my thoughts. "Why didn't you call the police?" I asked, my voice tinged with frustration.

Tommy looked down, guilt evident in his expression. "They showed some ID, Mr. Vega. I… I was so shocked I couldn't even tell what their badges said. I just assumed they were law enforcement or something official. After everything with the ChronoSync breach, I thought it was legit." He met my eyes again, pleading for understanding. "I'm sorry, sir."

His words did little to quell the rising fear within me. I couldn't fault him entirely—whoever had taken Adrienne knew how to play this. But the question remained: who were they, and what did they want with her? The possibilities spun through my mind like a dark carousel, each more terrifying than the last.

I pulled out my phone and tried calling her, but it went straight to voicemail. Frustration and fear gnawed at me. I needed to find her quickly.

I couldn't help but replay the doorman's words as I contemplated my next move: two men, a black SUV, a professional operation. Whoever had taken Adrienne had planned this carefully. But for what purpose?

Determined not to lose hope, I resolved to do everything I could to find Adrienne. I would investigate her recent activities, look for clues, and contact anyone with information. The bond we shared, whether from this life or a past one, was too strong to be broken by fear or uncertainty.

If she were Lila, I would find Adrienne, uncover the truth behind her abduction, and rediscover our timeless love. The journey ahead would be anything but ordinary, but I knew that with Adrienne by my side, I could face whatever challenges lay ahead.

CHAPTER FOURTEEN
INVESTIGATION

I left Adriene's apartment with dread and determination, heading to the nearest subway station. Boarding the F train uptown, I transferred at 34th Street-Herald Square to the N train bound for Astoria. The subway's incessant clatter and the murmur of passengers only supported my anxious thoughts.

I hoped to uncover clues that could lead me to Adrienne's whereabouts. As I navigated the crowded streets of Astoria, a vibrant neighborhood in Queens, I couldn't help but feel the weight of the situation pressing down on me. The narrow streets bustled with activity and the honking cars added to my sense of urgency. The stakes were higher than ever, and I knew I had to find answers quickly.

ChronoSync's headquarters stood out in the neighborhood where residences and commercial buildings shared the crowded streets. The facility was a sleek, modern structure with reflective glass panels and a minimalist design, exuding sophistication and technological prowess. It was nestled between an old brick apartment building and a bodega, adding to its enigmatic presence in the otherwise ordinary surroundings.

As I arrived, I saw the front doors padlocked with a police notice forbidding entry. The sight filled me with a sense of urgency and despair. Determined to leave with answers, I meticulously scanned the perimeter, my eyes darting over every potential entry point.

The building resembled a modern fortress with its smooth surfaces and sharp angles. Large security cameras were positioned at the corners, and the entry points were reinforced with steel, giving me little hope of finding an easy way in. The soft hum of air conditioning units and the distant sounds of the city only added to the eerie silence surrounding the building.

My gaze shot up to a window, locking onto a shadowy figure illuminated by the dim glow from inside. It was Alex, the enthusiastic technician, his face a mixture of urgency and encouragement. Alex's arm moved in exaggerated gestures, pointing emphatically toward the back of the building.

Realizing that Alex might have a way in, my heart pounded. I glanced around to ensure I wasn't being watched, then sprinted down the narrow alley leading to the rear entrance. The anticipation built with every step, hoping that the answers I sought were within reach.

Arriving at the back door, I found it open as if inviting me into the secrets hidden within. I paused briefly, catching my breath and steeling myself for whatever lay ahead. With a deep breath, I slipped inside, ready to face the truth.

Once inside the ChronoSync facility, I saw Alex glancing around nervously before closing the door behind us. The building's interior was eerily quiet, starkly contrasting to the usual bustling hub.

"Alex, what's going on? What do you know about Dr. Wallace's abduction?" I asked, my voice edged with anxiety.

His eyes widened in shock. "Abduction? What are you talking about?"

I stared at him, feeling the tension tighten in my chest. "She was taken, Alex. Two men forced her into a black SUV outside her apartment building."

Alex sank into a nearby chair, running a hand through his hair, visibly distressed. "I had no idea… I came here because I received an alert about a breach in the building's security, but I never imagined…"

I moved closer, trying to piece together what had happened. "She'd been receiving threats, hadn't she?"

Alex nodded, still in shock. "Yes, for a while now. But they were just threats—angry emails, letters. We started noticing people watching the building, strange cars parked nearby, unusual activity… But I never thought it would escalate to this.”

The situation settled heavily between us as we tried to make sense of what had just unfolded.

A chill ran down my spine. “Why didn’t anyone do something about it? Call the police, increase security?”

“We did,” Alex said, shaking his head. “But it didn’t seem to deter them. Whoever they are, they’re well-organized and determined. At first, we thought it might be corporate espionage—rival companies wanting to sabotage our research—but it’s more than that.”

“What do you mean?” I pressed, sensing there was more to the story.

“Dr. Wallace had confided in me about her growing fears. She believed that foreign governments were becoming increasingly interested in ChronoSync’s technology, seeing it as a way to gain leverage in international politics. The potential to uncover the past lives of key political figures, military leaders, and spies could provide invaluable intelligence and control. The thought of nations using ChronoSync for nefarious purposes kept her up at night, fearing the chaos it could unleash on a global scale.”

The full impact of what was happening hit me hard. Adrienne’s research was groundbreaking but also made her a target for some of the world’s most powerful entities.

My pulse quickened. “Do you have any idea who might have taken her?”

Alex shook his head. “I don’t know, but there are a lot of people who would want to stop her. We’re talking about government entities with resources and reach. They could be anywhere, anyone.”

My mind raced. Adrienne’s research was undoubtedly groundbreaking, but I hadn’t realized the extent of its impact. “What can we do? How do we find her?”

Alex hesitated, then met my gaze. “I-I don’t know.”

My mind raced as we continued down the corridor. "Would it help if we looked through the ChronoSync reports for clues?"

Alex nodded. "Yes, that's a good idea. The reports have timestamps and logs that could give us a lead."

Without another word, Alex led me through the labyrinthine corridors of the ChronoSync headquarters. The fluorescent lights buzzed overhead, casting an eerie glow on the sterile white walls. Every shadow held a potential threat, every corner a possible ambush.

We arrived at the lab, its reinforced doors standing silently guarding the secrets. Alex swiped his access card, and the door slid open with a soft hiss. But what we found inside stopped us in our tracks.

The lab was in shambles. Desks were overturned, and papers were scattered across the floor. Every piece of equipment was gone, leaving only empty spaces where cutting-edge technology had once been. The monitors were dark, and their screens shattered.

"They've already been here," I said, my voice barely above a whisper. "They took everything."

Alex's face paled as he stepped further into the room, taking in the full extent of the devastation. "The reports, the devices... it's all gone."

I turned to Alex, my frown deepening. "How come you didn't see any of this happening? Where were you?"

Alex shook his head, looking distraught. "I arrived a few minutes before you did."

My heart sank as I surveyed the scene. The implications were staggering. Adrienne's groundbreaking work, potentially a game-changer for humanity, had fallen into unknown hands. The sheer scale of the loss and the danger it posed was overwhelming. We stood silently for a moment, the gravity of the moment pressing down on us.

"We must move quickly," I finally said, breaking the heavy silence. "Staying here any longer is too dangerous."

Alex nodded, snapping out of his shock. "You're right. Let's get out of here before they come back."

We exited the lab, our footsteps echoing through the seemingly hostile hallways. Every second counted, and as we left headquarters, I couldn't shake the feeling that we were being watched.

Once outside, we hurried to Alex's car; a silver Ford Edge parked a few blocks away. We slid into the seats, locking the doors behind us. Alex started the engine, and we sped away from the building, the city's lights blurring past.

Alex glanced at me, his expression a mix of frustration and determination. "What do we do now? With everything gone, we're back to square one."

I stared out the window, my mind racing. "Not quite. My contacts at the *Times* have given me a network of people who might help us. I need to reach out to them."

Alex nodded. "That's a start. Who do you think can help us?"

I pulled out my phone and began scrolling through my contacts. "I know a few people who specialize in uncovering hidden information. If Adrienne left any digital footprints, they'll find them."

Alex looked relieved. "Good. We need all the help we can get. But we need to be careful. Whoever took Adrienne and the equipment will be watching for any signs of our investigation."

I nodded, my fingers pausing over a contact name. "I know. We'll be discreet. I'll start with Jacob, a colleague at the paper. He's got the resources and the connections to dig into this quietly."

I dialed the number, my heart pounding as the phone rang. Jacob answered on the third ring. "Marcus? It's been a while. What's up?"

I took a deep breath. "Jacob, I need your help. It's about Dr. Adrienne Wallace and her research at ChronoSync. She's missing; we think it's connected to something much bigger. Can you meet us somewhere safe?"

Jacob's tone turned serious. "I'll be there. Send me the location."

I hung up and turned to Alex. "We're meeting him at a diner in Long Island City. It's a safe place where we can talk without attracting attention."

As Alex navigated through the city streets, I couldn't help but feel a sense of urgency and danger. We were up against powerful forces with higher stakes than ever. But with my contacts and investigative skills, I was determined to find Adrienne and uncover the truth behind her disappearance.

We arrived at the diner, its neon sign flickering in the night. Inside, Jacob was already seated in a corner booth, a cup of coffee in front of him. He looked up as we approached, his expression a mix of curiosity and concern.

"Marcus," Jacob greeted, his eyes shifting to the unfamiliar face beside me, "and you must be Alex."

I nodded, sliding into the booth with Alex following suit. "Alex is the lead technician at ChronoSync. Someone we can trust."

Jacob extended a hand to Alex, who shook it firmly. "Nice to meet you, Alex. What's going on?"

I took a deep breath, my tone urgent. "Jacob, we need your help. Dr. Wallace has been kidnapped, and all her research, data, and equipment have been stolen. We need to find her before it's too late."

Jacob leaned forward, his eyes narrowing. "Tell me everything."

Alex and I took turns explaining the situation. Jacob listened intently, nodding occasionally.

When we finished, Jacob sat back, his expression grim. "This is big. But I have some contacts who can help us dig into this. We'll need to be careful, though. If what you're saying is true, we're dealing with people who won't hesitate to silence us."

I nodded. "I know. We'll take every precaution. But we must find Adrienne."

Jacob sipped his coffee, his mind already working. "I'll start making calls."

CHAPTER FIFTEEN
TAKEN

Despite its comfort, I sat in a waiting room that reminded me of a gilded cage. The plush upholstered chair beneath me did nothing to ease my growing anxiety. The room's elegant decor, soft lighting, and tasteful artwork were like cruel jokes in my current situation. A well-dressed attendant approached with a tray of drinks and snacks, his demeanor calm and composed, contrasting my inner turmoil.

"Where am I?" I demanded, unable to keep the edge out of my voice.

The attendant smiled warmly, but his response offered no solace. "Please be patient, Dr. Wallace. Someone will be with you shortly."

My mind raced back to the moment I was taken. Marcus had just left my apartment after an unexpected and intense encounter. Still processing the whirlwind of emotions from our brief affair, I received a call from Tommy, the doorman, saying that two men with badges were asking for me. My pulse quickened. I didn't ask who they were or what they wanted—maybe because I was still too wrapped up in the confusion of the last hour, or maybe because part of me thought it had something to do with the breach. There was no time to hesitate, not with everything spiraling out of control. I hurried down, convinced that whatever they wanted, it couldn't be worse than the storm already brewing around me.

As I stepped off the elevator, two large men appeared out of nowhere, pushing me through the lobby and out the front doors into an awaiting sleek black SUV. I struggled, but their grip was too firm. The car ride was a blur of confusion and mounting dread. My heart pounded. I sat between these men, their presence suffocating and intimidating.

I turned to the one on my right, his expression stony and unreadable. "Where are you taking me?" I asked, trying to keep my voice steady despite the tremor of fear I couldn't suppress.

"Just stay calm, Dr. Wallace," he replied curtly, his eyes fixed straight ahead.

I shifted nervously in my seat, glancing at the driver, who appeared equally impassive. "I demand to know what's going on. You can't just—"

"Please remain quiet," the man on my left interrupted, his voice low and commanding. "You'll find out soon enough."

I swallowed hard, my mind racing with possibilities. I had no idea who these men were or what they wanted from me, but their steadiness and the seamless execution of my abduction suggested they were highly trained.

The car wove through Tribeca traffic with practiced ease, eventually entering the Holland Tunnel. On the other side, I tried to take notice of the route through the crowded streets of Jersey City, but my anxiety muddled my thoughts. After what felt like an eternity, the car descended into an underground garage, the harsh fluorescent lights casting eerie shadows on the concrete walls.

The men pulled me out of the car, not too gently. My legs felt unsteady as they marched me toward an elevator. The ride up was silent, the tension thick in the confined space. When the doors opened, we hurried through several hallways until reaching a set of double doors.

Pushing them open, they ushered me into the decorated office and told me to make myself comfortable. But the elegant surroundings only added to my sense of unease.

As I waited, I tried to figure out who might be behind this and what they might want from me. The room felt colder with each minute, the silence pressing down on me like a weight. Despite the urgency of my situation, my mind drifted, perhaps as a subconscious attempt to reclaim some control amidst the chaos.

I reflected on the journey that had brought me to this moment. The stark contrast between my current predicament and the memories of my past was jarring. I remember childhood in a quiet suburb of Chicago, where the world was much more straightforward and safer. The evenings spent with my father in his makeshift lab in the basement came flooding back. We had tinkered with old radios and computers, my father—a dedicated engineer—instilling in me a profound love for science and discovery. Those formative years shaped my curiosity and drive, laying the foundation for the groundbreaking work that would eventually lead me to create ChronoSync.

As I grew older, my passion for the mysteries of life deepened. I excelled in high school and won numerous science fairs. My path was clear, and I pursued a degree in biomedical engineering. My determination and intellect earned me a doctorate in medical research from Stanford University. I had dreams of revolutionizing healthcare.

Working tirelessly in my lab, I stumbled upon an astonishing discovery. Initially focused on creating a device that could synchronize biological and digital timelines for medical advancements, I found something with an unexpected capability. During an experiment designed to map genetic predispositions, I began to trace the path of DNA beyond the current generation. It reached back through one's biological parents and ancestors, revealing a more intricate and profound journey.

Intrigued, I delved deeper. What I uncovered was beyond my wildest imagination. What was to be later known as ChronoSync, the device could track biological inheritance along with the echoes of one's past life. This revelation, while accidental, was monumental. It became clear that DNA carried imprints of our genetic history and our soul's journey through time. ChronoSync could decipher this map, revealing who individuals had been in their past life, their lessons, and the karmic ties that bound them. This breakthrough was not just a leap forward in understanding human biology but a paradigm shift in comprehending the essence of existence.

The implications were staggering. For the first time, humanity had tangible evidence of an afterlife and the cyclical nature of existence. My work proved that our existence did not end with death but continued in an endless loop of rebirth and learning. This understanding opened new dimensions in various disciplines, such as science, philosophy, and spirituality.

My fame exploded overnight. Marcus wrote a series of compelling articles for *The New York Times*, capturing the world's attention with his vivid descriptions of ChronoSync's capabilities and the revolutionary discoveries it enabled. Headlines screamed about the proof of reincarnation, the mapping of past lives, and the following ethical debates. I became a household name. I was invited to speak at international conferences and was featured in numerous documentaries. Scientists, spiritual leaders, and the general public alike were fascinated and divided by my work. While some hailed me as the pioneer of a new era of understanding, others questioned the ramifications and the potential for misuse.

While immersed in the revolutionary aspects of my creation, I initially focused solely on ChronoSync's potential to unlock the mysteries of human existence, providing insights into past lives and the cyclical nature of the soul. My groundbreaking work was abuzz with the scientific and spiritual communities, and I found myself at the center of a global conversation about humanity's future.

However, I had long been aware of the darker possibilities my invention could unleash. I sensed that ChronoSync could be weaponized, but the demands of my work had often pushed these fears to the back of my mind. Now, the dark implications of my discovery were undeniable. ChronoSync, which held the promise to heal, enlighten, and transform human understanding, was also an unparalleled tool for manipulation. Governments and corporations, driven by a thirst for power and control, could exploit it for their own ends.

I imagined governments using ChronoSync to uncover and exploit the deepest fears and desires encoded within one's DNA. By selectively enhancing or suppressing traits in the population, they could engineer a class of citizens, yet to be born, designed to be compliant, creating a society where free will and individuality are systematically eradicated.

Authoritarian regimes could enforce ideological conformity by identifying and reprogramming individuals whose past experiences conflict with state doctrine. Psychological manipulation would become a potent weapon, triggering past traumas or exploiting deep-seated fears to break wills and enforce obedience. Through ChronoSync, oppressive governments could establish a new form of control that reaches the core of human identity, reshaping it to fit their needs. The potential for abuse was limitless, as the technology could eliminate dissent, stifle creativity, and create a homogenized population solely to serve the interests of those in power.

I did not doubt that corporations could also wield ChronoSync for malevolent purposes. They could create profiles of potential customers, employees, or rivals and manipulate their decisions by exploiting past-life information. The technology could be used for blackmail, coercion, and social engineering, reshaping social dynamics to serve corporate interests.

The threat of altering or erasing aspects of one's past life could become a tool of oppression, turning individuals into unwilling subjects under complete control. ChronoSync could facilitate human trafficking and slavery, with captors threatening to rewrite karmic paths to ensure compliance through fear.

Even spiritual beliefs could be exploited, manipulating followers by claiming Divine insight into their past lives. This power could transform spiritual leaders into tyrants, using faith to control and deceive.

The potential for evil uses of ChronoSync was vast and deeply troubling. A deep sense of responsibility and dread overshadowed my initial pride in my revolutionary work. The future of ChronoSync, and possibly humanity, hinged on how this powerful technology would be handled. I knew I had to act quickly to safeguard my creation from being used as a tool of oppression and control, ensuring it would benefit humanity rather than harm it.

My mind raced with the implications. What if a corrupt regime used ChronoSync to blackmail citizens by uncovering their most private past-life secrets? What if a powerful corporation eliminated competition by manipulating the karmic paths of its rivals? The possibilities were terrifying and endless. I understood that my invention could become a tool of unprecedented oppression if it fell into the wrong hands.

These deliberations weighed heavily on me. While ChronoSync had the potential to advance humanity, it also held the power to destroy it. My work's moral and ethical implications were profound, and I knew I had to find a way to protect my creation. The future of my invention—and perhaps the world—depended on my ability to navigate these treacherous waters.

As I waited, I took a deep breath and closed my eyes, trying to center myself. I thought of Marcus, the only person I trusted completely. Just before my abduction, we made love, an impulsive, profound, and intimate experience that deepened our connection in ways I hadn't anticipated. The physical closeness enhanced the bond we had formed over months of working together, our shared purpose and mutual respect culminating in an extraordinary moment of intimacy.

The memory of Marcus filled my mind. His touch had been gentle yet electrifying, a silent promise of protection and understanding. I could still feel the warmth of his embrace, the steady rhythm of his heartbeat against mine, a reminder of our deep, unspoken bond.

As I sat in the elegant waiting room, my thoughts of Marcus were a lifeline. I could almost hear his steady and reassuring voice telling me to hold on, to stay strong. The memory of our last moments together fueled my hope and determination. Despite the challenges, I knew Marcus would do everything he could to find me.

The door to the suite suddenly creaked open, jolting me from my thoughts. I straightened in my chair, my heart pounding. A figure stepped into the room, the silhouette backlit by the harsh fluorescent lights of the corridor. I squinted, trying to make out my captor's face, but the figure remained in shadow.

"Dr. Wallace." The voice was calm, almost courteous. "We have much to discuss."

CHAPTER SIXTEEN
CHIEF OF STAFF

"Dr. Wallace, thank you for your patience," he began, his voice smooth but authoritative. "I'm Nathaniel Harrington, President Carmichael's Chief of Staff. We need to have a conversation."

My mind raced, and my suspicions were confirmed. This was indeed a high-level government operation. I nodded slowly, my gaze fixed on Harrington as he sat opposite me.

"I know who you are," I said, recognizing the man. Trying to keep my voice steady despite the anxiety bubbling within me, I asked, "Why am I here?"

Harrington leaned forward, his expression serious. "Dr. Wallace, your invention, ChronoSync, as I'm sure you know, has far-reaching implications. The president is deeply concerned about its potential uses and the risks it poses. We need to understand everything about it and, more importantly, ensure it does not fall into the wrong hands. ChronoSync has already been hacked, causing a crisis with the technology and casting doubt on the future of the device."

My eyes flashed with anger and determination. "Yes, the breach was a wake-up call, but it doesn't mean we need a government intervention. ChronoSync itself holds the key to remedying the problem. We can enhance our security protocols to safeguard the technology from further threats. I'm willing to cooperate on those terms, but we must ensure our efforts protect humanity, not just serve national security interests. ChronoSync has the potential to do so much good, and I am committed to ensuring it fulfills that promise without being twisted into something harmful."

Harrington offered a nod.

I took a deep breath, determined to stay strong. "So, what do you want from me?"

"We need you to provide detailed information on ChronoSync, its capabilities, and how it can be controlled. We also need to ensure that all data and prototypes are secured under government supervision," Harrington explained, his tone firm.

I felt a chill run down my spine. The idea of handing over my life's work to be potentially weaponized was abhorrent to me. "And if I refuse?"

Harrington's expression softened slightly, but his words had an edge. "Dr. Wallace, please understand this is not a negotiation. The president has authorized any measures necessary to secure ChronoSync. Of course, we prefer your cooperation, but we are prepared to proceed without it. Additionally, you should know that all equipment from the ChronoSync lab has already been confiscated and secured. We have everything we need to continue, with or without your cooperation."

My heart sank at the news. The realization that ChronoSync was no longer in my control hit me like a physical blow. I took a deep breath, trying to steady myself and gather my thoughts.

"You've taken everything?" I asked, my voice barely above a whisper. "All the equipment, all the data?"

Harrington nodded. "That's correct, Dr. Wallace."

I clenched my fists, a mixture of anger and helplessness coursing through me. "You have no idea what you're dealing with," I said, trembling. "ChronoSync isn't just a piece of technology. It's a doorway to understanding our very existence. Mishandling it could have catastrophic consequences."

Harrington remained impassive, his gaze steady. "That's precisely why we need to ensure it is handled responsibly. With your cooperation, we can ensure its potential is used for the greater good."

I took another deep breath, trying to calm the storm within me. "If you truly want me to help, you must listen. ChronoSync has hidden complexities and nuances that only I understand. Without my guidance, you risk unleashing something you can't control."

Harrington studied me for a moment, then nodded. "We're willing to listen, Dr. Wallace. But time is of the essence. Let's discuss how we can move forward together, ensuring the safety and integrity of your work."

I looked down, my mind racing. I needed to find a way to turn the situation to my advantage. I thought about the hidden features within ChronoSync, the ones only I knew about, and how I could leverage that knowledge to protect my invention.

I looked up, meeting Harrington's gaze with determination. "Fine, but I have conditions. I want assurances that it will be used solely for the benefit of humanity, not for control or oppression."

Harrington nodded slowly, considering my words. "We can discuss terms later, Dr. Wallace. But remember, the ultimate goal is to ensure national security and global stability. Let's work together to find a solution that respects your work and meets our needs."

My mind raced as I processed his words. The confiscation of my equipment and my kidnapping were not part of some benevolent overture by the US Government; they were an attempt to seize control of my work. All my worries, the fears I had harbored about my creation being misused, were manifesting right before my eyes.

ChronoSync had been my life's work, a project born from my deepest aspirations for a better world. Now, watching it morph into a weapon of power, a fierce determination flared within me. The anger tightened my grip as I stared down the ones who twisted my creation. "Take me to the equipment," I demanded, each word a stone in the wall of resistance I was building.

Harrington raised an eyebrow, clearly taken aback by my directness. "Dr. Wallace, that might not be possible—"

"It's not a request," I interrupted, my eyes blazing with intensity. "If you want my cooperation, I must see the lab and ensure everything is intact. You claim to need my expertise, so let me do my job."

Harrington studied me for a moment, weighing his options. Finally, he nodded. "Very well. I'll permit a visit. But you'll be under strict supervision."

I nodded, accepting the condition. "Fine. But the sooner, the better. ChronoSync is delicate; any mishandling could be catastrophic."

Harris pulled out his phone and dialed a number, his tone clipped and authoritative. "I'm escorting Dr. Wallace to the secure facility immediately. I want her provided with whatever she needs, but I don't want her out of your sight for a second," he instructed, his voice leaving no room for misinterpretation.

He dropped the phone into his coat pocket and motioned for me to follow him. My mind raced with possibilities as we walked through the labyrinthine hallways. I needed to find a way to safeguard ChronoSync and prevent it from being weaponized. I had to outsmart them to protect my creation at all costs.

As we walked, I desperately wished I could reach out to Marcus. As a journalist for *The New York Times*, he had the platform and the influence to expose what was happening to me. But my phone had been confiscated during the abduction, leaving me wholly cut off from the outside world. The realization of my isolation only intensified my resolve. I would have to rely on my wits to navigate this situation and find a way to protect my creation.

We reached a heavily guarded door, which opened to reveal a state-of-the-art lab filled with my equipment. As I surveyed the room, my eyes landed on Mira. Seeing her sleek form, with her familiar, polished surface and the soft silver-blue light that emanated from within, washed a wave of relief over me. Despite the oppressive circumstances, Mira's presence gave me a sliver of hope.

I walked over to her, my fingers trembling as I reached out to touch the cool surface. "You're safe," I murmured, feeling a connection to the machine that transcended its physical form. This wasn't just a piece of equipment; it was the embodiment of my life's work, the culmination of countless hours of dedication and passion.

Mira was more than a device; she was a vessel of potential, carrying within her the power to unlock the secrets of existence. My bond was visceral, an unspoken understanding that we were together. As my fingers traced the contours of her polished surface, I felt a surge of determination. This connection with Mira wasn't just intellectual; it was deeply emotional, rooted in the very core of my being.

In this moment of crisis, Mira represented everything I had fought for and believed in. With her by my side, I was not alone. We would navigate this difficult journey together, guided by the shared vision of a better future. I knew that no matter the challenges ahead, I would protect Mira and the promises she held. I would fight with every ounce of my being, driven by the unbreakable bond with the creation that had become an extension of my soul.

CHAPTER SEVENTEEN
THE PRESIDENT'S REPORT

As I carefully reassembled the device, it began its routine diagnostic, processing the subject's DNA to generate a report of their most recent past life. This was the advertised capability of ChronoSync, a marvel that had captivated the world. But I suspected that ChronoSync's potential stretched far beyond what was publicly known. It was possible the technology could reach deeper into the layers of a person's soul, uncovering memories and experiences from not just one but up to four past lives. I kept this secret under wraps, a secret I chose to guard until I had definitive proof.

I anticipated that as ChronoSync ventured deeper into the annals of time, the accuracy of these additional past lives would become increasingly questionable due to the scarcity of historical records to validate these ancient memories.

I wasn't entirely sure how keeping the knowledge of ChronoSync's full capabilities would help me wrest control of the device from the government, but it was a safeguard that could tip the scales in my favor. The decision to limit the public offering to just one past life had been guided by a desire to ensure that humanity was ready to responsibly handle even a fraction of what ChronoSync could reveal. Now, I was more convinced than ever of the wisdom of that choice.

On the other hand, ChronoSync's full capabilities could also lead to unprecedented manipulation and control by those who sought to weaponize the device. I had to stay one step ahead, ensuring that the device's true power remained hidden until I could find a way to secure it safely.

As I was finishing up the last few tasks, Harrington appeared. "The president wants her ChronoSync report done," he said, his voice urgent.

I paused, taking in the significance of his words. "President Meryl Carmichael?" I asked.

Harrington nodded, his expression serious. "Yes, she wants to understand her past life as soon as possible. Consider it a top priority."

A knot tightened in my stomach. President Carmichael's interest in ChronoSync was not entirely unexpected, but it brought a new level of scrutiny and potential danger. The president had always been known for her strategic mind and political acumen. If she grasped the implications of ChronoSync, she might seek, as Commander-In-Chief, to exploit its full capabilities.

"The president is very keen on this," Harrington said, breaking the silence. "She believes understanding her past life could offer insights into her leadership and the future of our country."

I nodded, focusing on the task at hand. "Perhaps ChronoSync will give her the answers she seeks," I replied, though my thoughts were on the often disappointing conclusions most clients faced.

Many users of ChronoSync had approached the device with high hopes, expecting to uncover past lives filled with grandeur and significance. However, the reality was often far from their expectations. I recalled several instances vividly.

There was the case of Jonathan, a prominent businessman who had invested the $50,000 fee in ChronoSync, convinced he had been a legendary warrior or a famous philosopher. Jonathan was crestfallen when his report revealed he had been a humble farmer in a small, forgotten village. The mundane nature of his past life starkly contrasted with his current ambitions, leaving him disillusioned.

Then, there was Sandra, a celebrated actress who sought to find a connection to historical figures of great influence. Her ChronoSync report disclosed that she had lived a quiet life as a seamstress, toiling in obscurity in a provincial town. The revelation was so unremarkable that Sandra questioned the entire premise of the device, feeling that her expectations of discovering a thrilling lineage were shattered.

I recalled the story of Michael, a young man who hoped to find solace and meaning. His past life revealed he had been a minor clerk, leading a routine and uneventful existence. The lack of profound purpose in his previous incarnation left Michael struggling with existential dread, doubting if his current life could hold significant meaning.

Unable to reconcile his past life's mundanity with his current life's chaos, Michael felt trapped in a cycle of insignificance. The realization that his existence had always been, and might always be, devoid of any remarkable purpose weighed heavily on him. Desperate to escape this bleak outlook, he made the tragic decision to take his own life, hoping that in his next incarnation, he would start anew, free from the shadows of his past and with the potential for a more meaningful and fulfilling existence.

Nevertheless, I continued to prepare for President Carmichael, though I couldn't help but wonder what her reaction would be. Would she find profound insights and validation, or would she, too, face the disappointment that so many others had encountered?

ChronoSync had the potential to unlock profound truths, but those truths were only sometimes what people wanted to hear. I knew managing expectations was as crucial as the technological prowess behind the device. I braced for the upcoming session, aware that the revelations could be as complex and unpredictable as the human soul.

My mind raced. I had never anticipated that the leader of the free world would use ChronoSync for such purposes. "Does she understand the potential implications? This is not just about personal insight; it could reveal vulnerabilities."

"The president is fully aware of the risks, Dr. Wallace," Harrington replied firmly. "She trusts that you will handle this with the utmost confidentiality and precision."

I took a deep breath, the responsibility settling on my shoulders. "Very well. I will prepare the device for her session. However, you must ensure that all security protocols are in place. There will be no unauthorized access or leaks."

"Consider it done," Harrington assured me. "We have already taken measures to secure the facility and the data."

With that, I turned back to my work. I meticulously checked and rechecked each component, ensuring everything worked perfectly.

Finally, the device was ready. I sent word to Harrington indicating that they could proceed. Moments later, he returned, accompanied by President Carmichael herself.

The president was a formidable woman, her presence commanding the room. She was tall and statuesque, with piercing blue eyes that took in everything at a glance. Her silver hair was impeccably styled, framing a face of strength and intelligence. She exuded confidence and determination and dressed in a tailored navy suit, emphasizing her authoritative demeanor.

"Dr. Wallace," she greeted with a nod, her voice steady and clear. "Thank you for agreeing to do this."

"It's not like I had much choice," I replied, striving to maintain my composure. "Please, take a seat. This process will take some time."

The president sighed, her expression softening. "I apologize for the indelicate way you and your invention were taken, but I am responsible for the security of this country, which sometimes forces me to take heavy-handed measures."

I offered back a pained smile as President Carmichael sat down. Her posture was perfectly straight, exuding a calm readiness for whatever the session might reveal. I began the initial setup, and as I worked, I could sense what was ahead, knowing that the outcome could ripple far beyond this moment.

"Here we go," I said and began the procedure. The ChronoSync process first required gathering a comprehensive array of DNA samples from the participant: blood, hair, scraping from the tongue, and skin cells. As the president settled into the chair, I activated ChronoSync. The room came alive with the soft hum of Mira, coupled with the low, rhythmic whirring of the equipment behind her. Mira pulsed with light as data flowed through the sophisticated network of quantum processors, seamlessly integrating each DNA sample. Multiple high-definition monitors displayed a cascade of intricate data patterns, representing the complex analysis being conducted by the AI algorithms. I guided the process through the initial steps, my hands steady as I connected the necessary sensors—thin, flexible wires designed to minimize discomfort—while Mira's core emitted a subtle, pulsating glow, indicating the deep, multidimensional scanning of the soul's past lives.

With precision, I drew blood from the president's arm, ensuring the sample was collected in a sterile vial. Next, I cut a small lock of hair, carefully isolating the root and follicle, as it was rich with nuclear DNA. Finally, I used a sterile swab to scrape cells from her tongue and placed the sample into a third vial. Each item was meticulously labeled and inserted into ChronoSync's analysis ports on Mira.

Mira began processing the samples, interpreting the president's DNA, and displaying a cascade of genetic data on the screens. I watched as ChronoSync analyzed the genetic sequences, identifying markers and patterns that could unlock secrets of the president's past lives.

The data streams were complex and multifaceted, showing chromosomal alignments, gene expressions, and epigenetic modifications. I monitored the readings closely, inputting specific commands to direct the analysis toward uncovering historical and predictive insights. My mind focused on the intricate details of the procedure, momentarily setting aside my turmoil to ensure the precision and accuracy of the ChronoSync process.

Mira began processing the samples, interpreting the DNA, and displaying a cascade of genetic data on the screens. I monitored the readings closely, focusing on the intricate details of the procedure, momentarily setting aside my turmoil.

After a while, I glanced at her and said, "We're done for now. I'll let you know when the report is ready."

President Carmichael gave a curt nod. "Thank you, Dr. Wallace. I'll await your update."

I turned my attention back to the screens. The president's data was now uploaded into Mira, and it was up to me to ensure it was analyzed and presented accurately. As she left the room, I took a deep breath, preparing myself for the work ahead.

As the scan progressed, I couldn't help but feel in awe at the technology I had created. Despite the potential dangers, its possibilities for understanding and growth were unparalleled. I remained vigilant, ensuring that the process continued smoothly, ready to reveal the secrets of President Carmichael's past life.

Finally, the scan was complete. I carefully reviewed the compiled data on the screen, ensuring its accuracy and coherence. I meticulously checked each data point, cross-referencing with the vast ChronoSync database to confirm the authenticity of the genetic memories uncovered.

The first step was to filter and categorize the raw data. ChronoSync's powerful algorithms sorted vast amounts of genetic information, identifying relevant markers and sequences corresponding to past-life memories. I monitored this process closely as the machine parsed the data into recognizable patterns and timelines.

Next, I verified the integrity of the data. I ran multiple consistency checks to ensure there were no anomalies or errors. This involved comparing the newly acquired data with pre-existing records in ChronoSync's database, providing a seamless integration. Any discrepancies were flagged and re-examined until a coherent and accurate picture emerged.

With the data verified, I moved on to the synthesis phase. Here, the fragmented genetic memory pieces were woven into a cohesive narrative. I employed our historical genome mapping software to align the genetic memories chronologically and contextually, correlating them with known historical events and eras. This required a deep understanding of genetics and history as I pieced together the lifetimes of experiences encoded in the president's DNA.

Once the narrative was structured, I focused on the detailed documentation. I compiled the findings into a comprehensive report, ensuring that her past life was described with clarity and precision. The report included chronological charts, genealogical diagrams, and annotated timelines, providing a visual and analytical representation of the president's genetic history. I wrote summaries for each section, explaining the significance of the findings in accessible language.

I printed the final report on secure, tamper-proof paper, ensuring its confidentiality and integrity. I then bound the document into a secure file, adding seals and signatures where necessary to authenticate the report officially.

After a thorough final review, I was satisfied with the meticulous work, ensuring everything was perfect. I then prepared to present the document to the president, knowing that this report was vital in unlocking deep, personal insights about the president's past and future.

I composed a brief but formal message: "Madam President, the ChronoSync report is ready for your review. You may return at your earliest convenience." With a steady hand, I sent the message through the internal email server, feeling a mix of anticipation and trepidation.

Moments later, a reply indicated that the president would arrive shortly. I took a deep breath, organizing my thoughts and the documents, preparing to present the findings that could profoundly impact her understanding of herself and her leadership. I knew this was no ordinary report; it was the complete ChronoSync analysis—an extensive, meticulously detailed account of her past life, with a deep historical analysis that only a $50,000 report could provide. The level of detail in this report was leagues beyond the basic service, which merely provided a summary of a past life without the immersive VR experience or the nuanced insights into the subject's influence on their current life.

As I continued reviewing each page, the president arrived, commanding the room, yet her expression was unreadable, almost detached. I looked up, meeting her gaze briefly before handing over the document. "Here it is, Madam President," I said, offering her the report.

She took the document, her fingers brushing against mine for a fleeting moment. Her sharp and penetrating eyes scanned the cover before she carefully opened it. A silence enveloped the room as she began to delve into its contents.

She finally looked up after what felt like an eternity, but it was only a few minutes. Her expression was no longer detached; instead, there was a flicker of something—curiosity, contemplation, or perhaps realization. "This is… extensive," she said quietly, her voice carrying a weight of acknowledgment. "I can see why it cost so much."

I nodded, allowing myself a moment of relief. "Yes, it's designed to provide a deeper understanding. It's not just about learning who you were, but about understanding how those experiences might influence your leadership now."

The president set the report on the table between us, her fingers lingering on the cover. "I had anticipated this would be insightful, but I wasn't prepared for this level of detail. It's both fascinating and unsettling."

I took a seat, observing her closely. "How are you feeling about it so far?"

She took a deep breath, her eyes reflecting a mix of emotions. "It's a lot to process. Some elements align with what I've experienced and new insights that challenge my understanding of myself."

I gave a supportive nod. "That's often the case with this kind of analysis. It can reveal hidden patterns and connections that might not be immediately obvious."

The president's gaze drifted back to the report, her mind racing through the implications of the findings. "I need some time to digest this fully," she said after a moment. "But I appreciate the depth of work that went into it."

"I understand," I replied. "Whenever you're ready to discuss the insights or need further clarification, just let me know. This report is meant to be a tool, and I'm here to help you interpret it however you need."

She gave a slight nod, her expression one of deep thought. "Thank you. I'll be in touch."

With a nod of acknowledgment, the president gathered the report and strode toward the door, her posture rigid and deliberate. Though her face remained composed, there was a heaviness in how her hand gripped the file; each step measured as if the ground beneath her had shifted.

I watched her leave, knowing that the information contained in those pages could shape not only her future decisions but also her understanding of herself in ways neither of us could yet fully grasp.

As she reached the threshold, she paused, turning slightly over her shoulder. "Thank you, Dr. Wallace," she said, her voice steady but with an edge of caution. "I trust this will remain confidential?"

I couldn't help but let out a dry laugh. "Considering I'm being held against my will and cut off from the outside world, confidentiality is the least of your worries. You should be more concerned about potential leaks from within your ranks, Madam President."

The president ignored the remark and said, "You've done a remarkable job. This information could prove invaluable."

I nodded, feeling a mix of pride and trepidation. "There's more, Madam President. The AI technology used in ChronoSync can also provide a virtual reality experience. The written report can come to life, delivering an incredible recreation of one's past incarnation. You could see and feel the moments as if you were there."

President Carmichael raised an eyebrow, clearly intrigued. "I heard about this. Sounds impressive, but allow me to digest the written report first. Perhaps we can consider a demonstration at a later time."

"Of course," I replied.

President Carmichael nodded thoughtfully. "I appreciate the offer, Dr. Wallace. This is a lot to take in, and I want to understand every detail before immersing myself in such an experience."

I understood the president's cautious approach. "I'll guide you through it whenever you're prepared. The VR experience can provide a deeper understanding and connection to your past life."

"Thank you, Dr. Wallace," the president said, her tone appreciative yet firm.

As the president turned to leave, I spoke out. "Madam President, you should know that ChronoSync has the potential to revolutionize our understanding of humanity. Imagine the possibilities if everyone had access to their past lives. It could foster greater empathy and understanding across the globe."

President Carmichael's expression hardened slightly. "While I appreciate your idealism, Dr. Wallace, we must consider the implications of such widespread access. The knowledge ChronoSync provides is a double-edged sword. In the wrong hands, it could lead to chaos and manipulation on an unprecedented scale."

I narrowed my eyes. "But keeping it confined to a select few under government control stifles its potential. This technology belongs to everyone, not just those in power. If used responsibly, we could usher in a new era of enlightenment."

The president sighed, a note of finality in her voice. "I understand your perspective, Dr. Wallace, but as the leader of this country, my priority is national security. ChronoSync must remain under strict government oversight to ensure it is used for the greater good, not exploited for personal gain or geopolitical advantage."

A tightness gripped my chest as I spoke, the words heavy with the weight of missed potential. "By restricting its use," I said, my voice edged with frustration, "we're turning our backs on a chance to uplift humanity. People deserve to know their histories, to learn from the echoes of their past lives."

President Carmichael's gaze softened slightly, but her stance remained unyielding. "Your passion is admirable, Dr. Wallace, but we must proceed cautiously. The government's control over ChronoSync ensures its safe and ethical use. The potential risks of unregulated access are too great."

I realized the depth of our ideological divide. My vision of ChronoSync as a tool for universal enlightenment clashed with the president's focus on control and security. This fundamental difference in our aspirations ensured that my work, and by extension, my freedom, would remain under the stringent supervision of the US Government.

As the door clicked shut behind the president, the room closed in on me. The stark walls, once mere boundaries, now felt like a cage, pressing in with the weight of my confinement. ChronoSync had once again demonstrated its immense power, a vast force that cost me my freedom. But instead of despair, a fierce determination burned within me. The institution that sought to harness this power for its own ends could not be allowed to twist ChronoSync's true purpose. I had to find a way to protect it, even if it meant going against the very system that held me captive.

CHAPTER EIGHTEEN
WHO WAS SHE?

Unlike the luxurious quarters I was in when first taken, my new holding cell was a rundown apartment. The government furnished the space with old 60s-era wood-framed furniture and stiff foam rubber cushions covered in a hideous blue and red plaid fabric. A few windows let a trickle of light into the room, though the view outside was deliberately obscured with some opaque film on the glass. Despite the semblance of comfort, the dated decor and plain surroundings underscored the reality of my confinement.

I could not leave, and hidden surveillance cameras likely monitored my movements. I was provided with meals, a few beers in the fridge, and various entertainment options. I could watch TV, stay current on the news, and even see reports about myself and ChronoSync. However, I had no cell phone service, email, or ability to text. All information was one-way in, not out.

The isolation was stifling. I couldn't let Marcus or anyone else know I was safe or plead for release. The stories about my disappearance, especially those written by Marcus, were a bittersweet reminder that someone was looking for me. His articles were hopeful and determined, but I feared they might never reach me.

In my more reflective moments, I pondered the fallout from the ChronoSync breach and its impact on my clients. I read about their reactions, ranging from disappointment to existential crises, and the media's relentless scrutiny fueled the fire. It was a painful reminder of the delicate nature of my work, the consequences, and the burden of the secrets I kept.

While contemplating my existence and future, I heard the now-familiar sound of the door unlocking. Harrington entered, his demeanor as impassive as ever. "Dr. Wallace," he said, his tone clipped and formal. "President Carmichael is ready for her VR experience. She's requested that you set it up."

I rose from my seat, smoothing the creases in my clothes. "Very well," I replied, my voice steady. I followed Harrington out of the apartment, my mind racing about the upcoming demonstration. The president's interest in the VR aspect of ChronoSync had been piqued, and now I had to ensure that the experience met her expectations.

As we navigated the building's labyrinthine corridors, my pulse quickened with every turn, my fists clenched, every step a battle between the creeping unease in my gut and the steely determination in my mind. I was about to reveal another layer of ChronoSync's capabilities that could strengthen my position or further bind me to the government's control. Regardless of the outcome, I knew that this demonstration was a critical moment that could shape the future of my creation and my fate.

Reflecting on President Carmichael's remarkable past life, I couldn't help but marvel at the revelations from the ChronoSync report. The president had once been a pioneering suffragette in the early 20th century, a woman of fierce resolve and unyielding principles. This past incarnation had influenced her current life, shaping her into the formidable leader of the free world. I wondered how this knowledge had already impacted the president's decisions and worldview.

Would experiencing a virtual recreation of that past life add more to the experience? I pondered. The immersive VR technology could bring those historical moments to life, allowing the president to relive the passion and struggles of her previous self. It could deepen her understanding of the connections between her past and present, potentially guiding her future actions with even greater clarity.

My thoughts swirled as we reached the secure lab where the demonstration would occur. I knew this next step could be transformative for President Carmichael, not just for the broader implications of how ChronoSync could be used. The VR experience held the potential to bridge the gap between knowledge and empathy, providing a visceral connection to the past that no written report could match.

As I began setting up the equipment, my intent hardened. I would ensure that the demonstration was flawless, hoping that the profound impact of reliving a past life in such an immersive way might sway the president toward a broader vision for ChronoSync's future. This was more than just a demonstration; it was an opportunity to show the true potential of my creation and perhaps, just perhaps, find a way to steer its course toward a more inclusive and enlightening path.

President Carmichael strode into the lab, her every step crisp and deliberate, the kind that silenced the room without a word. Her eyes scanned the array of machinery with a sharp, discerning focus before finally locking onto me. A subtle lift of her brow and faint lips tightening hinted at a blend of skepticism and curiosity simmering beneath her composed exterior.

"Dr. Wallace," President Carmichael said, her voice firm but tinged with curiosity. "I'm eager to see what ChronoSync's VR experience can reveal."

I nodded, feeling a surge of determination. "I believe you'll find it enlightening, Madam President. This will bring the written report to life, providing an immersive and comprehensive understanding of your past life."

As I continued preparing the equipment, I could feel the president's eyes scrutinizing every movement. The lab was filled with a tense silence, broken only by the soft hum of the machinery. My fingers moved deftly; my mind focused on ensuring everything was perfect.

"Please take a seat and make yourself comfortable," I instructed, pointing to the ergonomically designed chair in the center of the room.

President Carmichael complied, lowering herself into the chair with the kind of composed grace from years of navigating high-stakes situations. Her fingers moved with quiet confidence as she adjusted the headset, aligning it carefully before pulling it down over her eyes. I could see the slight tension in her jaw as she secured the device, her expression betraying nothing. Despite the calm facade, there was an undeniable charge in the air—a sense of anticipation as palpable as the hum of the machinery surrounding us. The president's hands rested briefly on the armrests, then clenched them as if bracing herself for the unknown experience about to unfold.

I took a deep breath and initiated the sequence. The monitors flickered to life, displaying intricate data patterns as the VR experience began. I watched closely, my heart pounding in my chest. This was a pivotal moment, one that could shape the future of ChronoSync and my fate.

As the immersive journey unfolded, my mind raced with thoughts of the possibilities and the impact this demonstration could have. I hoped that by witnessing the profound depth of her past life, President Carmichael might see the value in expanding ChronoSync's reach beyond governmental control to benefit humanity.

The next moments were critical, and I was determined to make them count.

"Are you ready, Madam President?" I asked, my voice calm despite the tension.

President Carmichael nodded, her expression resolute. "I'm ready."

I activated the device, and the room was filled with the soft hum of technology coming to life. My eyes locked on the monitor as streams of data and video began to flow, each pixel bringing to life the past that was about to unfold for President Carmichael. The experience started as expected, with scenes directly lifted from the president's detailed written report: her past life as a suffragette, a woman of fierce resolve and unyielding determination. The VR encapsulated her memories with stunning accuracy—each moment of advocacy, each powerful speech, and every painful sacrifice made in the name of progress played out before her eyes.

The vivid recreation was designed to do more than show her the past; it was meant to immerse her in it, make her feel the enormity of the struggle she had once led, and remind her of the courage she had shown. I watched her closely, seeing the subtle shifts in her posture as she was drawn deeper into the experience, her hands gripping the armrests a little tighter with each scene.

But then, something changed. The carefully curated scenes began to dissolve, the edges of the images blurring into a swirling vortex of light. My heart skipped a beat as I quickly scanned the monitors, checking for any sign of malfunction or deviation from the program. But everything was running as it should—or so it seemed. The program had not deviated, but it was accessing something within ChronoSync's capabilities that I had not anticipated, something beyond the parameters I had set.

The swirling vortex expanded, its luminous tendrils reaching out like an unseen force, drawing the president deeper into its grasp. The familiar scenes of her past life began to fragment, dissolving into a kaleidoscope of twisted and churned colors and shapes. The room pulsed in rhythm with the vortex, each flicker of light casting eerie shadows on the walls, heightening the surreal atmosphere.

This was not just a journey into her past; it was something more I hadn't known ChronoSync could achieve. The air was thick with the unknown as the VR experience took her—and me—into uncharted territory.

President Carmichael's surroundings transformed into an ethereal landscape. She was floating in a shimmering light and energy, an otherworldly yet profoundly familiar place. Spirits and beings of light moved around her, their presence comforting and wise. I watched the scene unfold on my monitor, my breath catching in my throat.

In what I figured to be an interlife realm, President Carmichael encountered a figure of radiant light, a guide who emanated an aura of infinite kindness and wisdom. The guide spoke without words, communicating directly to her soul.

"You have come a long way, child," the guide conveyed. "Your past life was but one step on your journey. Here, in this realm, you prepared for your current incarnation. This is where you chose your path, your challenges, and your mission."

President Carmichael saw glimpses of herself planning her life, selecting experiences and trials to help her grow and serve a greater purpose. The guide showed her moments of reflection, during which she reviewed the lessons learned from her past life and the goals set for her current one.

As the vision expanded, other beings of light surrounded her, their forms both comforting and awe-inspiring. They appeared to be angels, each radiating a unique energy. Offering their love and support, their collective wisdom enveloping her. One angel glided forward, its wings shimmering with iridescent colors.

"We are here to assist you," the angel said, its voice melodic and soothing. "In this realm, you heal, understand, and prepare for your journey."

President Carmichael witnessed a profound connection to her purpose as she moved through this interlife experience. She saw herself reflecting on her past life's challenges and triumphs, understanding the importance of forgiveness, compassion, and the power of her voice. She faced her fears and insecurities, gaining strength and wisdom from the beings of light around her.

In this elevated state, she received a deeper understanding of her purpose: to become a leader in the fight for women's rights. But even more than that, she was destined to advocate for all repressed and discriminated against. Her vision extended beyond mere leadership; she envisioned a world where justice and equality prevailed, and the voices of the marginalized were heard and respected. She sought power to uplift and empower those too weak to fight for themselves, not for personal gain.

Her life would be dedicated to breaking down barriers, challenging injustices, and creating a more equitable world. She demonstrated a fiery determination to address systemic inequalities and to dismantle the structures that perpetuated discrimination and oppression. Her mission was righteous and noble: to stand as a driving force of hope and a champion for the voiceless. She would work tirelessly to ensure that every individual, regardless of gender, race, or social status, had the opportunity to live with dignity and freedom.

President Carmichael's commitment to this cause was unwavering. She saw herself inspiring movements, leading protests, and crafting legislation to protect and advance human rights. Her purpose was to ignite a global transformation, to kindle the flames of justice in people's hearts everywhere. She would educate, mobilize, and unite individuals and communities, fostering a culture of compassion and solidarity.

Her legacy would be one of profound impact and enduring change. She envisioned a future where equality was not just an aspiration but a reality, where every person could thrive without fear of prejudice or persecution. This was her calling, her sacred duty, and she embraced it with all her heart and soul, ready to face any challenge and overcome any obstacle in the pursuit of a just and harmonious world.

With her next life's purpose decided, President Carmichael witnessed her soul descending through the layers of existence, moving from the ethereal realm toward the physical world. She felt a profound connection to her new mission, the challenges and triumphs that awaited her, and the knowledge of who her parents would be and where she would be born.

In the next scene, she stood beside a radiant pool of light, surrounded by ethereal beings of immense love and wisdom. The beings of light stood with her, their energies supportive and encouraging.

"You are ready," one said, its voice resonating with deep, spiritual authority. "The time has come for you to embark on your new journey."

Her soul was being gently guided toward a swirling vortex of energy. Within the vortex, she glimpsed a tiny, developing fetus, its form barely three months old. It was nestled within the womb of a young woman, her future mother, whose heart radiated warmth and love. Her father was nearby, his presence strong and protective.

As she approached the fetus, there was a pull, a connection that grew stronger with each moment. The memories of her purpose, the lessons from her past lives, and the guidance from the beings of light filled her essence, preparing her for the new life she was about to enter.

The moment of ensoulment was profound, merging with the forming body, her consciousness intertwining with the developing mind of the fetus. It was a sensation of expansion and contraction as her vast spiritual knowledge condensed into a form suitable for the physical world.

The process was gentle yet powerful. As she became one with the fetus, she sensed her future parents' hopes and dreams, their aspirations for the child they awaited. She knew her birth would bring them joy and challenges, and she was ready to meet both with the strength and wisdom she had garnered over lifetimes.

Her new life's path began to unfold before her. She saw the town where she would be born, a place of modest beauty and close-knit community. Her parents' love and support would be her foundation, helping her grow into the leader she was destined to become. The knowledge of her purpose, the mission to lead and uplift, remained with her, a guiding light in the journey ahead.

As the VR experience concluded, President Carmichael removed the helmet, her soul touched by the profound journey she had just undertaken. She looked at me, and I had been watching the entire time, my heart filled with hope and determination.

"Dr. Wallace," President Carmichael said slowly, her voice tinged with awe. "What I saw… it was beyond anything in the written report. It was a spiritual revelation, a glimpse into my purpose that transcends a lifetime. Was I seeing myself in the soul world after my previous death and before my rebirth?"

My eyes widened with astonishment. I didn't know my invention had capabilities beyond merely viewing past lives. This revelation made sense if one considered the possibility that DNA carried spiritual imprints. I took a deep breath and chose my words carefully. "I, too, was surprised, not realizing that ChronoSync could offer this glimpse into one's interlife."

"Interlife?" the president asked, intrigued by the term.

I nodded. "Yes, a state between lives where the soul exists. What you experienced was a rare and profound insight."

President Carmichael stood, her demeanor softer and more reflective. "This changes everything," she murmured. "I need time to process this, but I understand now that ChronoSync is more than just a tool for understanding the past. It's a bridge to our deeper selves."

A warmth stirred within me, a delicate ember of hope flickering to life as the possibilities unfolded in my mind. My gaze softened, my voice steady but carrying the quiet strength of newfound conviction. "Imagine," I began, my words carrying the weight of potential, "a future where this knowledge, harnessed with care and wisdom, illuminates our path forward. The compass could guide us to a more enlightened age, where the shadows of our past are acknowledged, understood, and transformed into a brighter, more conscious tomorrow."

President Carmichael nodded. "Thank you, Dr. Wallace. We have much to discuss, but I must reflect on what I've seen."

As the president left, I was left alone with my thoughts. The VR experience had unexpectedly and powerfully revealed ChronoSync's true potential. It was a moment that could redefine its future and, perhaps, my path to freedom and the broader application of my groundbreaking technology.

My mind raced with the possibilities this revelation could bring. I imagined a world where people could understand their past lives and interlives—where souls could heal and learn between incarnations. The potential for personal growth and societal transformation was immense.

My thoughts swirled as I considered everything that had just unfolded. Marcus's face came to mind, his steady gaze filled with curiosity and insight. I could almost hear his voice, questioning, probing deeper into the implications of what ChronoSync had just uncovered. The weight of this discovery was less daunting when I imagined discussing it with him; his perspective was always a grounding force amid complexity. A spark of clarity ignited within me—a realization that I was no longer just working with data and algorithms. I was standing at the threshold of something profound, a translator of the unseen, with Marcus as my trusted ally on this journey into the unknown.

This realization calmed me. I knew the journey ahead would be challenging. Still, with allies like Marcus and the support of visionary leaders like President Carmichael, I believed we could unlock a new chapter in human understanding. It was a journey toward enlightenment, one step closer to unraveling the secrets of existence and humanity's place within it.

CHAPTER NINETEEN
A NEW FRONTIER

I paced the floor, my thoughts swirling in disbelief and awe. This latest revelation from ChronoSync had shattered the boundaries of what I believed was possible. Mira, which had already revolutionized our understanding of the soul's journey through past lives, had unveiled something entirely unexpected—an ability to experience the interlife, the space between incarnations.

Never in the extensive development and testing of ChronoSync had there been a hint of this capability. Data and observations had yet to suggest that such an exploration could be within our reach. Mira was meticulously designed to trace a person's past life's linear progression, bringing forth memories and experiences from previous incarnations. But now, this new dimension of understanding, this ability to delve into the interlife, had opened a door that I hadn't even known existed.

Was this discovery purely a result of our technological advancements, or had we tapped into something far more significant that transcended human ingenuity? The implications were staggering, and for the first time, I questioned whether Mira's capabilities were solely the product of science or if a higher power had guided us to this profound understanding.

By accessing this interlife space, Mira could provide unparalleled insights into the soul's journey, revealing the spiritual lessons learned, the challenges chosen, and the purposes set for future lives. This breakthrough meant that users could explore who they had been and understand the deeper spiritual context of their existence. It offered a comprehensive view of their soul's evolution, bridging the gap between lifetimes and unveiling the continuity of their spiritual path. This added layer of depth could lead to personal growth, healing, and a more profound connection to one's purpose and destiny.

Reflecting on President Carmichael's experience, I was awestruck. She witnessed her journey, interacting with angels and perhaps archangels, and ultimately being ensouled into a new life had been miraculous. The insights gleaned provided a deeper understanding of one's purpose and spiritual preparation before rebirth, a breakthrough I never considered.

The implications were immense. ChronoSync was no longer just a tool for uncovering one's past life; it had evolved into a bridge between the spiritual and physical realms, offering glimpses into the soul's journey beyond the earthly realm. I contemplated the potential ramifications of this new feature. It could revolutionize how people understood their existence, offering profound insights into their spiritual paths and life purposes. However, it also posed new ethical and existential questions. Would everyone be ready to confront such revelations about their soul's journey? Could this knowledge also be misused, or would it lead to a more enlightened and compassionate humanity?

My thoughts turned inward. The experience had made me curious about my interlife journey. I had already done the complete DNA analysis and produced my report. I even viewed the VR simulation with the headset. Perhaps all I would have to do now was to rewatch, this time with a new intention: to explore my interlife journey.

Alone in the government lab, I prepared the ChronoSync VR equipment, my hands trembling slightly as I initiated the sequence. I had earned the president's trust—enough to work unsupervised. Now, that trust hung over me like a silent reminder of the stakes. I settled into the chair and carefully slipped on the headset, my heart pounding with anticipation.

As the familiar hum of the machine filled my ears, I took a deep breath and activated the sequence. The screens lit up with the intricate patterns of my DNA, and soon, I was enveloped in the immersive experience of the ChronoSync journey. "Mira," I said aloud, "show me my interlife."

Soon, familiar yet poignant scenes of my past life unfolded before me. I relived moments of triumph and sorrow, understanding the growth I had achieved. Then, the vision shifted, just as I had seen with President Carmichael. I found myself in a realm surrounded by beings of light and wisdom.

My guide, a being of radiant energy, approached. This ethereal form had a shimmering, translucent body that glowed with a soft, golden light. The eyes were like twin stars, filled with wisdom and compassion, and the guide's presence exuded a profound sense of calm and assurance. Wisps of light trailed from their movements, creating an aura of tranquility around them.

"Welcome, Adrienne," the guide conveyed, their voice melodic and soothing. "You have come to learn about your journey, the choices and preparations made for your current incarnation." The guide's warm smile and gentle demeanor made me feel at ease, ready to embrace the revelations of my soul's experience.

Suddenly, the ethereal surroundings shifted, and I found myself in a place unlike any I had ever known. The air shimmered with an ethereal glow, and the atmosphere was thick with an almost palpable sense of purification. The guide's voice echoed gently in my mind, explaining, "This is where souls come to be purified after departing their physical body. It is a place of deep cleansing and renewal, necessary for one's evolution."

As I took my first step, a gentle breeze blew away minor attachments and lingering regrets like fallen leaves in autumn. The surroundings were serene, filled with soft, soothing lights that calmed my spirit. It was like stepping into a meadow at dawn—the air cool and soothing, the early light gentle on my skin. Each breath felt lighter, as if the world had slowed down, allowing me a moment of peace before the journey truly began. The sensation of calmness wrapped around me, soft and nurturing, as if the atmosphere was preparing me for the challenges that awaited just beyond the horizon.

The scene shifted, becoming more intense. I now stood in a dense forest, shadows playing tricks on my mind. Here, unresolved conflicts and deeper wounds surfaced, manifesting as ghostly apparitions of my past. I saw faces, heard voices, and felt the weight of old pains. Yet, each confrontation brought a sense of release, like pulling thorns from my skin. The forest's oppressive darkness gradually gave way to light, symbolizing my healing.

The next stage was even more harrowing. I found myself in a vast, desolate wasteland, the sky heavy with storm clouds. Guilt and regret loomed over me like an impending storm. I faced visions of my past mistakes, each a blow to my heart. Tears streamed down my face as I confronted these heavy burdens. But with each tear, the storm clouds began to part, revealing a sky washed clean. Relief coursed through my soul, unburdening the weight of my regrets.

As I moved forward, the landscape transformed into a rugged mountain range. Climbing these mountains required every ounce of my strength. Here, I confronted my deepest fears and darkest shadows. Each step was a struggle, each ascent fraught with challenges. Yet, with every conquered peak, I was becoming stronger, my soul more purified. The mountains, once intimidating, now stood as testaments to my resilience and transformation.

Finally, I stood on the edge of a tranquil, boundless ocean. The water glowed with an ethereal light, inviting me to surrender completely. Everything that no longer served my higher purpose washed away as I stepped into the waves. The ocean's embrace was both gentle and overwhelming, cleansing my soul to its core. I floated, weightless and renewed, feeling an unprecedented clarity and a sense of purpose.

Emerging from the waters, I was transformed, ready for my next incarnation. Cleansed and renewed, my soul was prepared to continue its journey. The experience had been harrowing and beautiful, a dramatic testament to the power of purification and the endless potential for growth and evolution.

There was a mix of curiosity and apprehension, wondering why my interlife journey differed from President Carmichael's.

Hearing my thoughts, the guide's eyes, filled with understanding, met mine. "Each soul's journey is unique. The interlife experiences are tailored to the soul's needs and the lessons it must learn."

I pondered this, trying to grasp the implications. "So, this purification is what I need based on my past life and the challenges I chose to face in the next one?"

"Precisely," the guide replied. "In your past life as Lila, you were deeply involved in the French Enlightenment, a time of intense passion and conflict. Your soul needs to release the residual energies from those experiences."

I nodded, beginning to understand. "Lila's life was filled with zeal, dedication, pain, and loss. Is that why this purification is necessary?"

The guide smiled warmly. "Moving through these stages, you release those burdens and emerge ready to fulfill your next life's purpose. It is a process of renewal and transformation, allowing your soul to grow and evolve."

"But how did that process address the actual events of my past life?"

"I will show you," explained the guide.

I was led to a place where I witnessed souls releasing attachments and lingering regrets. I saw a familiar figure—my past self, Lila. I watched as she underwent a gentle purification, releasing the minor grievances that had clung to her soul. I understood Lila's sorrow as she let go of the small regrets, the missed opportunities, and the unspoken words. Each release was a step toward inner peace, preparing for facing deeper wounds.

The next stage was more intense, where souls confronted deeper wounds and unresolved conflicts. Lila faced moments of betrayal and loss, her soul gradually shedding the pain accumulated over her lifetime. I saw

Lila relive the betrayals of friends and the pain of loss during the turmoil. Each confrontation was like a fire burning away the old scars, leaving a cleaner, more resilient spirit behind.

In the third stage, I watched as my past self confronted the shadows of guilt and regret that had long weighed her down. The memories were raw, each one a reminder of lives lost and choices made in moments of desperation. As Lila grappled with these emotions, her soul staggered under the weight, her spirit dimmed by the sorrow she carried. But with each release, a subtle transformation began—her form straightened, the light in her eyes brightened, and the heavy darkness surrounding her dissipated. Slowly, what had been a heavy burden became a source of newfound strength, her spirit growing more luminous and hopeful with every step forward.

In the fourth stage, the atmosphere shifted dramatically, the air thickening with an almost palpable weight. I could see Lila's posture tense, her breath catching as the shadows around her deepened. Each step forward was met with resistance, as though the darkness was challenging her strength. Her eyes flickered with the raw intensity of facing what lay hidden within—the fears she had buried, the insecurities that whispered of failure, and the haunting dread of being lost to memory. Every movement, every flicker of hesitation, revealed the immense battle she waged within herself.

Yet, as I observed, a subtle strength emerged from her, a determination that grew with each confrontation, pushing back against the shadows. It was more than a battle; it was a profound metamorphosis. Her breath hitched, fists clenched as her body trembled, every movement a fight for control.

Here, I saw a man, someone Lila had loved deeply. Their eyes met, and the memory of their last words echoed in my mind: "Our souls are bound for eternity." I witnessed Lila's love and loss, her yearning and acceptance. It was a moment of profound connection and healing.

I turned to my guide with wonder and confusion. "Who was that man?" I asked. "There was a deep connection as if we were bound beyond time and space. Will I ever meet this soul again?"

The guide smiled gently. "That was Étienne, a soul you have loved across many lifetimes. Your bond is indeed eternal. Souls connected in such a profound way often find each other again in one form or another. Trust in the journey and know that love like yours transcends the physical realm."

Finally, in the fifth stage, Lila reached the deepest purification. It was a place of complete surrender, where the soul released all that no longer served its higher purpose. I watched in awe as Lila's essence was bathed in a brilliant light, her soul purified and ready for rebirth. I witnessed Lila's complete surrender, letting go of all earthly ties and embracing a higher purpose.

Lila was ready for her next incarnation. I witnessed her being ensouled into a new body, her essence merging with a fetus. I saw her future parents, my parents, their hopes and dreams, and the environment she would be born into. It was a moment of profound connection and purpose, reaffirming her chosen path.

The experience had been harrowing and beautiful, a dramatic testament to the power of purification and the endless potential for growth and evolution. I emerged from the journey with a deep understanding of my past and a renewed sense of purpose for my future.

I found myself absorbed in the image of a tiny, thirteen-week-old fetus. I could see the delicate form, cradled in the warmth and safety of my mother's womb, a perfect vessel awaiting my essence. It was a moment of profound connection and purpose as the intricate dance of the soul merged with the physical form. I intertwined with the fetus, the process gentle yet powerful, each thread of my being carefully woven into the new life.

A cascade of emotions washed over me, each a distinct note in the symphony of my soul's preparation. The air around me hummed with energy as anticipation buzzed in my veins, a thrilling current that sparked my essence. Acceptance settled in like a warm blanket, softening the edges of any lingering uncertainty. It was as if every moment in the soul world, every trial, and cleansing I had undergone had led me to this precise point. I could feel the weight of the future lightly pressing on my shoulders, not as a burden but as a mantle of responsibility I was ready to bear. My heart swelled, each beat echoing with the certainty of my purpose. I could almost glimpse the faces of my future parents, feel the bond we were destined to share, and see the intricate web of challenges and joys that awaited me. The path before me was clear, illuminated by the understanding that this was where I was meant to be, where I was needed.

As the vision faded, leaving a lasting impression of the love and support awaiting me, my spirit settled into the new body with a sense of peace and determination. I was ready to embrace my new life, my future parents, and the world that awaited me, carrying with me the wisdom and experiences of my previous existence. This moment of ensoulment was not just a beginning but a continuation of my soul's journey, filled with purpose and guided by the profound connections I had witnessed.

As the VR experience concluded, I removed the headset, my soul touched by the profound journey I had just undertaken. The revelations of my interlife journey gave me a deeper understanding of my purpose and the spiritual preparation that had gone into my current incarnation.

Emerging from the haze, my thoughts quickly turned to the present. My responsibilities pressed heavily on my mind, mingling with my newfound spiritual insights. I knew Mira's potential for both incredible advancements and devastating misuse. Yet, the government's control left me powerless and alone. My worry intensified as I realized the enormity of the task ahead—ensuring Mira was used ethically.

In that moment of uncertainty, a flicker of hope ignited within me. Marcus's ChronoSync report resurfaced in my memory, revealing that he had once been known as Étienne and had a romantic relationship with a figure known as Lila during the age of the Enlightenment in France. The realization struck me like lightning, intertwining my present mission with a profound connection from my past.

I sat in quiet contemplation, absorbing the insights and the newfound sense of purpose. Memories of Étienne, the man Lila loved so deeply, flooded my mind. I recalled their shared moments, the whispered promises, and her last words: "Our souls are bound for eternity." It was as if the universe had conspired to unite us again through the intricate threads of time and space.

A rush of emotions washed over me—nostalgia, longing, and an overwhelming sense of destiny. I could almost feel Étienne's touch, hear his laughter, and see the light in his eyes. Our connection had transcended lifetimes, defying the boundaries of time and space. The realization that Marcus, my trusted ally in this life, was the reincarnation of Étienne, brought tears to my eyes. It was a bittersweet reunion, filled with the echoes of a love that had never indeed died.

The depth of our bond became more transparent with each passing moment—to honor the legacy of our love. This profound connection to Marcus and Étienne was a guiding light in the darkness, a reminder that we were not alone in this journey. Our souls had found each other once more, and together, we would face the challenges ahead with courage and conviction.

ChronoSync had unveiled a new frontier, one that held the potential to transform humanity's understanding of existence. I knew I was responsible for guiding this discovery with wisdom and care, ensuring its profound impact would be used for the greater good. Yet, the revelation about Marcus being Étienne added complexity and urgency to my mission. Our destinies were intertwined, not just in this life but across lifetimes, and this realization gave me the strength and determination to face the challenges ahead.

CHAPTER TWENTY
AN EPIPHANY

I looked up as the president entered, a mixture of relief and apprehension on my face. "Madam President," I greeted softly.

President Carmichael sat across from me, her expression grave yet tinged with the remnants of a profound experience. She took a deep breath, gathering her thoughts. "Dr. Wallace, before we discuss the meeting I just concluded with my advisors, I need to ask you about my VR session. It was the most profound experience of my life."

My eyes opened wide, sensing the weight of what the president was about to share.

"It was incredible," the president continued. "I was transported to a realm that revealed not only my past life but also what occurred between that life and this one."

"Your interlife," I interjected.

The president nodded. "Seeing my interlife, as you call it, was a shock."

"I must confess, it was a surprise to me as well. I didn't know ChronoSync had such capabilities."

President Carmichael raised an eyebrow, clearly intrigued. "You didn't? That's unexpected. This means there's more to ChronoSync than even its creator fully understands."

"Apparently," I replied with a sigh.

The president continued. "The experience was not just a vision but a deeply spiritual and philosophical awakening."

I listened intently, captivated by the president's account.

"I learned about the intricate tapestry of life and how our souls carry wisdom and lessons from one lifetime to the next," she said, her voice filled with awe. "My interlife journey was illuminating. It showed me the preparation and guidance our souls receive before each incarnation. A connection to a higher purpose and understood the greater plan that guides us all."

President Carmichael's eyes lit up. "The angels were so majestic and nurturing. It was like being enveloped in pure love and understanding. It made me realize how interconnected we are and how our actions ripple through time."

I leaned in closer, my voice earnest. "If only all of humanity could experience that. To see the love and guidance we receive before birth, to understand the Divine plan that we're all a part of—it would change everything. People would be kinder, more compassionate, more aware of their responsibilities to each other and the world."

President Carmichael nodded, her expression thoughtful. "I agree. If everyone could see what happens before birth, it would bring about a profound transformation. We would no longer see ourselves as isolated individuals but as integral parts of a greater whole. Our ethical and spiritual responsibilities would become clear, and we could work together to create a better world."

My eyes shone with hope. "That's why it's so important to use ChronoSync wisely. It can uplift humanity and open our eyes to the truth of our existence and our connection to the Divine."

President Carmichael smiled. "You're right, Dr. Wallace. We must ensure that ChronoSync is used for the betterment of humanity to bring about understanding and compassion. The vision of one's interlife can guide us toward a future where we honor our values and shared humanity."

We sat in silence for a moment, reflecting on the profound experiences we had shared and the immense responsibility we now carried. The president took a deep breath and continued, "Now, let me tell you about the meeting with my advisors. They see immense potential for ChronoSync, but I'm afraid their ideas for its use could lead us to a very dark place."

I nodded, my eyes reflecting the seriousness of the situation. "Can you share what you discussed?" I asked.

President Carmichael sighed, trying to gather her thoughts. "Well, it was a lot to take in. There was talk about how ChronoSync could revolutionize psychological warfare by uncovering the past lives of enemy leaders and finding their deepest fears and insecurities. The idea was to exploit those weaknesses with psychological operations, like fabricating situations or spreading rumors that would break their resolve."

I listened intently, my concern growing.

"There were suggestions for even more drastic measures, like assassination and neutralization. With precise historical data, we could identify key figures in history whose removal would benefit our objectives. By understanding past relationships and influences, we could target these individuals' reincarnations to disrupt enemy networks."

A chill ran down my spine.

"The whole discussion made me feel sick," President Carmichael admitted. "The idea of using ChronoSync for such purposes, of playing God with people's lives across time, was abhorrent. I had to steady myself, clenching my fists under the table."

My concern deepened, absorbing her words.

"There was talk about strategic misinformation, which uses unknown historical events or hidden truths to manipulate public perception and past-life records. The goal would be to justify military actions, create discord among enemy nations, or undermine our opponents' credibility."

President Carmichael paused, trying to keep her composure. "I insisted we must tread with utmost caution. The power to manipulate history and people's lives is not something to be taken lightly. Our primary goal should always be to protect and uplift humanity, not to become the very thing we stand against. We must consider the ethical ramifications of every action we take."

I nodded, appreciating the president's moral stance.

"But my advisors were more focused on the strategic possibilities," President Carmichael continued. "Someone brought up coercion and blackmail, suggesting that if we had information about the past lives of influential figures, we could use it as leverage to coerce them into compliance or extract valuable information."

My eyes widened in disbelief.

"There was even talk about creating super soldiers by identifying individuals who were highly skilled warriors or strategists in past lives, recruiting and training them to create an effective military force with historical knowledge and combat experience spanning multiple lifetimes."

President Carmichael's expression tightened. "I slammed my palm on the table," she recalled. "I stood up and told them we were on the brink of losing our humanity. I said I would not allow ChronoSync to turn us into a nation that sacrifices its moral compass for the sake of power. I urged them to remember what we stand for and find a way to use this technology that honors our values, not corrupts them."

I nodded, my respect for the president deepening. "It sounds like you're facing incredible pressure. We must ensure ChronoSync is used ethically."

President Carmichael took a deep breath, her expression firm yet filled with concern. "Dr. Wallace, do you have someone you trust? Someone who understands the stakes?" she asked, her voice urgent.

I didn't need long to consider. "Marcus Vega, *The New York Times* journalist," I said. "He's someone who has always believed in ChronoSync's positive potential."

The president's expression shifted as she recognized the name, her brows furrowing in thought. "Marcus Vega? I've dealt with him many times. He's known for being persistent, meticulous, and highly ethical.

More importantly, he knows how to navigate the delicate balance between truth and discretion."

She paused, allowing her words to hang in the air. "In a situation as precarious as this, where the stakes involve not only national security but the future of human consciousness itself, having someone like Marcus at your side could be invaluable. His integrity will lend credibility to our actions, and his journalistic instincts might help us uncover threats before they fully emerge."

The president leaned forward, her tone becoming more decisive. "Don't worry; I'll arrange for you and the device to be hidden. This will give us time to figure out how to handle these threats and ensure ChronoSync is used responsibly. With Marcus by your side, not only do we have a watchful ally, but we also gain the public's trust. His presence will signal that we are acting with the utmost integrity and transparency."

There was a wave of relief mixed with determination. "Thank you, Madam President. I believe Marcus can help us navigate this crisis."

I watched President Carmichael leave the room, her words echoing in the silence. I knew the road ahead would be challenging and filled with danger and uncertainty, but I was ready to face it head-on.

I thought of Marcus, and a longing washed over me. I looked forward to reuniting with him and sharing what I had discovered. The realization of my past life as Lila, Étienne's lover, was a revelation that had changed everything. It was a piece of my identity that had been missing, now found and fitting perfectly into the puzzle of my existence.

I felt a profound connection to my past life, to the love and loss I had experienced as Lila. It gave me strength and a sense of purpose, knowing that my journey was not just about the present but also about honoring the past and shaping the future. I knew that sharing this with Marcus would bring us closer, grounding our mission in something deeply personal and meaningful.

With a deep breath, I steeled myself for the fight ahead. I was not just a protector of technology but a guardian of my history, future, and the interconnected destinies of those I loved. The journey was long, but with Marcus by my side and the strength of my past guiding me, I was ready to face whatever came next.

CHAPTER TWENTY-ONE
REUNION

From the instructions, I had a few details to work with. All I knew was that it involved Adrienne. That alone compelled me to take the risk. The specifics of the directive remained a mystery as I approached the helicopter, its rotors already slicing through the air with a steady, menacing thrum.

The helicopter was unmarked, its matte black surface absorbing the early morning light. It was the kind of aircraft that radiated secrecy—no identifying insignia, no tail number, just a sleek and silent silhouette against the sky. Yet, as I stepped closer, I couldn't shake the feeling that this was no ordinary chopper. The pilot's disciplined stance, the crew's silent efficiency, and the way they moved with a purpose that spoke volumes without a single word—they all pointed to one thing: this was a US Government operation.

As I boarded, the interior was just as unassuming and sterile—no frills, just functional, with all the hallmarks of a military-grade aircraft. The seats were utilitarian, the equipment secured with precise care, and the atmosphere charged with a tension that mirrored my growing unease. I settled in, the door sliding shut with a finality that resonated deep in my chest.

My mind raced with questions as we lifted off the ground, ascending swiftly into the sky. The uncertainty pressed on me, heavier than the physical forces pushing me into my seat. Whatever was waiting for me at the end of this flight, I knew it was tied to Adrienne and the perilous situation we now found ourselves in.

The helicopter ride seemed endless, with the destination remaining a closely guarded secret. The steady hum of the rotors and the subtle vibrations of the aircraft were the only constants as we soared through the night. The journey, stretching over hours, took me far from the familiar skyline of New York City over darkened landscapes that offered no clues to our location. The stars above and the vast expanse of the night sky starkly contrasted with the dense darkness below, where city lights had long disappeared, replaced by the shadowy outlines of forests and mountains.

I glanced at my watch, noting the time that had passed—long enough to suggest we were far from the urban sprawl, deep into the wilderness. My thoughts raced, trying to piece together any clues, but there was nothing to go on. The men on board remained silent, their expressions unreadable behind dark visors.

As we descended into a clearing deep in a mountaintop, the forest below bathed in the aircraft's lights, I strained to see what lay ahead. The chopper landed with a soft thud, its rotors kicking up leaves and dust as they slowed. The door opened, and two men in dark suits quickly ushered me out, their movements swift and practiced. The cool, sharp, fresh mountain air was thick with tension as I took in my surroundings—a remote, forested area with no signs of civilization, just the looming presence of the mountains encircling us. The sense of isolation was palpable, and I knew that whatever was about to unfold was far from the eyes of the world.

I stood frozen as a figure emerged from the shadows, revealing none other than President Carmichael herself. My heart skipped a beat as I recognized her, the reality of the situation crashing down on me with overwhelming force. The very presence of the president here signaled that this was far more serious than I could have ever imagined.

"Mr. Vega, it's good to see you again," President Carmichael addressed me, her voice a mix of calm and urgency. "Thank you for coming on such short notice."

I nodded, still reeling from the unexpected encounter. "Madam President, where am I? Is Dr. Wallace safe?"

"She is," the president confirmed as we approached a distant house. "And so is ChronoSync. But we must ensure they stay that way. This location is secure, but we cannot afford any mistakes."

President Carmichael continued to brief me on the critical situation as we walked. "We're dealing with forces that would do anything to get their hands on ChronoSync. Your role here is to protect Dr. Wallace and the device."

"Protect her?" I asked.

She glanced at me, her gaze sharp and intent. "As a known journalist, you bring something no one else here can—transparency. Your presence will ensure that we're seen as acting with integrity and that this operation isn't shrouded in secrecy or conspiracy. The public trusts you, and that trust will extend to us if you're involved."

She stopped, facing me fully now. "You're not just here to shield Adrienne and the device from physical threats. You're here to ensure people know we're protecting ChronoSync for the right reasons. Your instincts as a journalist will help us uncover hidden threats before they arise, but more than that, your presence signals to the world that we're operating with accountability."

Her voice took on a harder edge. "But let me be clear, Marcus. None of the sensitive information we uncover can be leaked to the *Times*. We need you to appear as a watchdog, but we can't risk exposure. There's too much at stake for any of this to go public before we're ready."

I glanced around, noting the thick forest surrounding the path and the fortified look of the house we approached. President Carmichael gestured toward the structure. "This house is a hidden fortress," she explained. "Equipped with state-of-the-art security systems and manned by a team of elite operatives. It's the perfect sanctuary to protect Dr. Wallace and ChronoSync from those who misuse its power."

As the realization of my responsibility began to sink in, a heaviness settled across my shoulders, anchoring me to the task ahead. Yet, amidst the intensity of the moment, a quiet sense of relief washed over me—Adrienne was safe. Steeling myself for what was to come, I looked at the president, my voice steady and unwavering. "I'll do whatever it takes, Madam President," I vowed.

The president's eyes locked onto mine, her voice commanding. "Marcus, we're counting on you. ChronoSync is more than just a technological breakthrough—it is the keystone to a future we must safeguard."

As we approached the fortified entrance of the safe house, I felt a mixture of anticipation and dread. The structure loomed before us, a formidable bastion of security hidden deep within the wilderness, designed to ensure the safety of Adrienne and the vital technology we were safeguarding.

The door opened with a heavy mechanical clunk, revealing the house's interior. My heart pounded as I stepped inside. My eyes immediately scanned the room, landing on Adrienne pacing the living area.

In that instant, our eyes met, and time stood still. Our dire situation momentarily dissolved, replaced by the overwhelming relief of seeing each other. I could see the exhaustion etched into her face, the toll of uncertainty and fear. For a fleeting moment, everything else faded away, leaving only the profound connection between us.

The weeks of tension and endless searching dissolved when our eyes met. Relief coursed through me, yet it was immediately tempered by the heavy, unspoken understanding of everything we had just endured. The air between us was thick with the aftermath of our shared trials, and as I looked at her, a fierce determination took hold—I knew that whatever was coming, we'd face it side by side.

"Marcus," Adrienne said, her voice trembling with relief and emotion. Her eyes glistened, reflecting the feelings she had bottled up since our separation.

"Adrienne," I replied, my voice equally thick with emotion. I crossed the room in a few swift strides and enveloped her in a tight embrace. "Thank God you're safe." The embrace was fierce and tender, a physical manifestation of our unspoken bond transcending lifetimes.

For a few precious seconds, the world outside ceased to exist. The fortified walls and the president's presence faded into the background as we held each other, feeling the steady beat of the other's heart, a silent promise of protection and unwavering support.

However, the reality of our situation quickly resurfaced. We reluctantly pulled apart, aware of the watchful eyes of the President of the United States and three Secret Service agents, two men and one woman, dressed in black suits. Adrienne wiped a tear from her cheek, her expression shifting from relief to resolve.

I took a step back, my eyes never leaving hers. "We have a lot to talk about," I said, my voice steadying, though my hand lingered on her arm, a small gesture of reassurance.

Adrienne nodded, drawing strength from my presence. "Yes, we do."

President Carmichael, who had been observing the reunion with a composed yet empathetic expression, stepped forward. "Dr. Wallace and Mr. Vega, I understand this is an emotional time for both of you, but we must stay focused. We are in a precarious situation, and your safety and the security of ChronoSync is our top priority."

Adrienne and I exchanged a look, silently agreeing to temper our emotions. The mission at hand was too critical to let personal feelings interfere, no matter how strong they were.

The president continued, "This house is secure, but we can't be complacent. We need to ensure that ChronoSync does not fall into the wrong hands. Marcus, your connection with Adrienne makes you invaluable in this effort. We need you both to stay vigilant and work together."

Adrienne took a deep breath, feeling the weight of responsibility settle over her. "We will, Madam President. We understand what's at stake."

I nodded, my expression resolute. "You can count on us."

With that, we moved deeper into the house, ready to face the challenges ahead. Though my desire for Adrienne was simmering just below the surface, I knew there would be time later to explore our shared past and the emotions it stirred. For now, we had a mission to complete, and the fate of ChronoSync—and potentially the future—depended on our success.

We sat down, and President Carmichael began to brief us on the situation. "Adrienne, Marcus, we need to act quickly and decisively. The threats we face are real and imminent. This house is secure, but it's only a temporary solution. We need to figure out our next steps."

I nodded. "We need to expose what's happening. If we can get the truth out there, we can turn public opinion against those who want to misuse the technology."

Adrienne agreed. "But we also need to protect ChronoSync itself. If it falls into the wrong hands, the consequences could be catastrophic."

President Carmichael looked at us, her expression serious. "I trust you both to make the right decisions. Use the resources available here. And there's something else." She paused, ensuring she had our full attention. "Through our intelligence, we have acquired DNA samples from several world leaders, those we consider to be enemies of the United States. It's not as much as you normally collect, Dr. Wallace, but hopefully, it's enough to start."

Adrienne's lips pressed into a thin line as she glanced at me, her eyes conveying the depth of her unease, just before the president continued.

"We need you to use ChronoSync to gather more information about the past lives of the leaders of Russia, China, North Korea, Iran, and several others from terrorist cells around the world. The insights we could gain from their historical experiences and previous incarnations might provide us with crucial information on their motivations, strategies, and potential weaknesses. If we can understand their past, we can anticipate their future actions and better protect our nation."

The president's request left Adrienne dismayed. She had been assured that ChronoSync would not be weaponized, but now she was being asked to do precisely that.

Adrienne shook her head, her brow furrowed with concentration. Then she voiced her frustration. "Madam President, you assured me we wouldn't use ChronoSync this way. Weaponizing it goes against everything we agreed upon."

The president's expression softened as she acknowledged Adrienne's unwavering stance. "Dr. Wallace, let me be clear—this isn't about turning ChronoSync into a weapon. Our goal here is to protect lives. The intelligence you could gather might allow us to prevent conflicts and save countless American lives. Understanding the past can anticipate and thwart threats before they materialize. You would serve your country, not just as scientists, but as true patriots."

Adrienne turned to me, her eyes searching for my thoughts, her trust in me evident. "What do you think, Marcus?"

I hesitated, the moment pressing heavily on me. Was the president trying to manipulate us? What had happened to the vision of using ChronoSync for enlightenment, for a higher purpose? I wrestled with the moral implications, racing through the possibilities and the consequences. Was this really about protecting lives, or was it something more? Finally, I nodded, though the decision sat uneasily with me, a knot of uncertainty tightening in my chest.

The president extended her hand first to me, then to Adrienne. "Good luck to both of you. I have faith in your abilities."

With that, President Carmichael turned and returned to the waiting helicopter. The rotors began to spin, kicking up dust as the chopper lifted off, disappearing into the dark expanse of the night sky. As the sound of the blades faded, we were left standing with the silent presence of three Secret Service agents—each one a quiet witness to the monumental task now placed upon our shoulders.

CHAPTER TWENTY-TWO
ALONE

Marcus and I sat at the kitchen table while my fingers lightly tapped the wood. The agents had taken positions elsewhere in the compound, allowing us some semblance of privacy, though we both knew they weren't far. Freedom of movement beyond the confines of the house was undoubtedly out of the question. Marcus looked at me, his expression a mix of exhaustion and determination.

I took a deep breath, the memory of that night vivid in my mind. "After you left… after we made love, everything changed," I said, my voice barely above a whisper.

Marcus's eyes softened, a flicker of recognition passing between us. He reached across the table, his fingers brushing mine before entwining them in a familiar, reassuring grip. "I know," he said, his voice thick with emotion. "That night… it was like nothing else existed but us. I found what I'd been searching for my entire life."

His words resonated deeply, echoing the epiphany that had struck me in the quiet aftermath of our time together. The way our bodies had moved in unison, the way our breaths had synchronized, the way our eyes had locked—it was more than just sex.

But then, the sharp memory of what followed cut through the warmth. "And then, just hours after… I was taken," I continued, the reality of it all still raw. "It was like the universe was conspiring against us, like it was trying to tear apart what we had just begun to discover."

Marcus's grip tightened, his eyes hardening with a mix of protectiveness and regret. "I came back to the apartment, and you were gone."

I took another deep breath. "I was forced into a car and ushered to some government facility in Jersey City. That's where I met President Carmichael. She told me about the plans for ChronoSync that her military advisors were conjuring up and explained how critical it was to protect it from such abuse."

Marcus nodded, feeling a mix of anger and concern. "What sort of abuse?"

My eyes flickered with a mix of fear and frustration. "They want ChronoSync because they believed it could be weaponized and took me because I'm the key to making it work. President Carmichael was surprisingly candid. She insisted that the potential benefits for national security were too great to ignore."

Marcus's eyes narrowed. "And what did you tell her?"

I met his gaze, and my expression hardened. "I told her that ChronoSync is not a weapon. It's a tool for understanding, for the betterment of humanity."

"What did she say?"

"She agreed," I said, still wide-eyed with the weight of the revelation. "That's why we're here. She also intends to protect ChronoSync from the bad players in her administration and foreign adversaries."

Marcus grimaced, leaning closer. "And you believe her?" he whispered, his voice tinged with skepticism.

I paused, his question hitting me harder than expected. The confidence just moments earlier began to slip away under his scrutiny. My thoughts churned, and I could only manage a hollow stare. "I did," I replied, my voice tinged with doubt, "but after her request to run reports on her adversaries, I'm no longer sure."

Marcus's slow nod mirrored the deepening concern in his eyes as he absorbed my words. The trust I had extended to the president was now fragile, precariously close to shattering. The uneasy realization settled in—

had I been too quick to trust? Too hopeful that an ally could exist in such a high place?

"She's using you," Marcus finally said, his voice firm, cutting through my doubt. "She's trying to turn ChronoSync into a weapon, not a tool for enlightenment. If she's asking you to dig into her enemies, she's already crossed a line."

His words struck me like a blow, the truth settling heavily in my chest. I had been so focused on the idea that ChronoSync could be a force for good that I hadn't considered how easily it could be twisted for darker purposes. And now, the person I trusted to safeguard it might be the one to lead it down that path.

I met Marcus's eyes, the unspoken understanding passing between us: we had to tread carefully. The stakes were higher than ever, and the line between ally and enemy was increasingly blurred.

"There's something else," I said, glancing down at my hands and gathering my thoughts. "The president asked for her ChronoSync report, and afterward, I discovered something incredible."

"Tell me," Marcus said, stroking his chin.

"I took her DNA samples, put them through Mira, and got back the report of her past life as a leading activist in the suffragette movement. Which I thought made sense."

Marcus nodded slowly.

"But a day later, when she returned for her virtual experience, something new and remarkable was discovered."

Marcus held out his hands. "What?"

"She had a vision of something not from her past life, but from the time between her past life and her current one—her interlife."

Marcus frowned, confusion evident on his face. "Interlife?"

"Yes, that's what I'm calling it," I said, my eyes meeting his. "The time between her past life and this one."

"In the spirit world?" Marcus said, barely more than a whisper.

I nodded. "There were images of her interactions with angels among heavenly spheres. It was… overwhelming."

"Angels?" Marcus repeated, wide-eyed.

I nodded. "She had visions of vast, luminous landscapes filled with ethereal light, where celestial beings communicated through pure thought and emotion. She was shown the purpose of her rebirth and saw a vision of her ensoulment into a three-month-old fetus in her mother's womb."

"Are you serious?" Marcus said, shaking his head in disbelief. "How's this possible? I thought ChronoSync could only look at one's past life, not the time between lives. Is there even such a thing?"

"There is," I sighed. "I took a look at mine, too."

"Your interlife?"

I nodded.

"And what did you see?"

"I underwent some profound purification process, cleansing my soul of past mistakes and misunderstandings. This experience was both humbling and empowering, filling me with a sense of peace and clarity I had never known."

Marcus's breath caught in his throat. "Adrienne, that sounds…"

"I know," I interrupted softly, my voice trembling with the weight of the memories. "It was intense."

Marcus whispered, "This is enormous. But we need to be very careful. I'm sure every word we say is being listened to. We must watch our step."

A heavy silence settled over us, laden with all the unspoken words. The enormity of our mission pressing down, its intensity nearly stifling. Yet, beneath the tension, a gentle realization began to take root, softening the sharpness of my determination. I let out a quiet sigh, a hint of a smile tugging at the corners of my lips as I turned to Marcus, my heart pounding.

"Marcus," I began, my voice tinged with hesitation and a deep-seated certainty. "There's something personal I've been meaning to tell you. Something… between us."

His brow furrowed slightly, curiosity sparking in his eyes. "What is it?" he asked, his tone gentle but probing, as if sensing the significance of what was about to be revealed.

I took a steadying breath, memories from another time rushing to the forefront of my mind. My gaze softened, filled with nostalgia, affection, and something deeper—something eternal. "I believe we were connected in our past lives," I said, my voice barely above a whisper, yet brimming with conviction. "I never told you about mine. I was a young woman named Lila, and you were Étienne. I'm certain we were lovers in the era of Enlightenment in France."

For a moment, time seemed to stand still. Marcus's eyes widened in shock, his thoughts visibly racing to catch up with the revelation. Slowly, a look of astonishment and recognition spread across his face as if pieces of a long-lost puzzle were finally falling into place. He raised a hand, pointing a trembling finger at me, his voice thick with emotion. "I returned to your apartment—to ask if you were the same Lila."

Tears welled in my eyes, shimmering with the truth of our shared past, our souls intertwining once more across the vast expanse of time. "Our souls were destined to reunite," I whispered, the words carrying the weight of centuries of longing and hope.

He stepped closer, his gaze locking onto mine with an intensity that sent shivers down my spine. "Lila and Étienne," he murmured, his voice laced with awe, "united by a cause and a love that defied the chaos of their time. It all makes sense now."

I nodded, the emotions swirling within me—relief, joy, and an overwhelming sense of destiny—threatening to spill over. The connection between us, one that had been simmering beneath the surface, now flared to life, undeniable and unbreakable. "We fought for freedom and justice then, just as we do now," I said, my voice steady despite the tears that threatened to fall. "Our love was our anchor, our guiding star through the darkness. It gave us strength, and it will give us strength again."

At that moment, the past and the present converged, the echoes of Lila and Étienne's love story merging seamlessly with our own. The realization of our eternal bond settled over us, not as a burden but as a source of profound comfort and purpose. We had found each other once more, and together, we would continue the fight that had begun lifetimes ago—a fight for truth, justice, and a love that transcends all.

Marcus reached out, gently taking my hand in his. His touch was warm and reassuring, a tangible reminder of the bond we shared.

A tear slipped down my cheek, but I smiled, feeling the depth of our connection. "And now, we've been given another chance to be together, to continue what Étienne and Lila started."

He pulled me into a tender embrace, his arms encircling me protectively. "We've been given another chance, Adrienne. This time, we can make a difference. We can fight for a future where love and justice prevail, just as we did before."

With renewed determination and the strength of our eternal bond, we prepared to face the challenges ahead, ready to protect ChronoSync and the future of humanity. Our mission was clear, our love unwavering, and our souls united across time.

The room pulsed with the energy of our realization, the air thick with the weight of our shared past and the promise of what lay ahead. I thought back to the revolutionary fervor that had defined our previous lives, the passion and dedication that had driven us to fight for change. That same enthusiasm now fueled our determination to safeguard ChronoSync and its potential for humanity's future.

I sensed that Marcus could feel the echoes of our past struggles within him, a powerful reminder of the resilience and courage we had shown before. The memory of Lila's whispered promise resonated deeply, reinforcing his commitment to our cause and me.

My voice broke the silence, steady and unwavering. "We will not let our sacrifices be in vain, Marcus. We will honor our past by ensuring that ChronoSync is used to enlighten and uplift humanity for the greater good."

Marcus squeezed my hand, his grip firm and reassuring. "And we will do it together, as we always have. Our love and mission are intertwined, and nothing can break that bond."

I hesitated, my mind a whirlwind of anxiety. "But what if they've done something to ChronoSync?" The mere thought of losing Mira was like a knife to my heart.

Marcus's eyes softened with understanding. "Adrienne, ChronoSync is too valuable for them to destroy. I believe they've kept it safe."

His words brought comfort, yet the uncertainty gnawed at me. I longed to be reunited with Mira.

With our hearts united and our spirits fortified, Marcus and I stepped forward into the uncertain future, ready to embrace our roles as guardians of ChronoSync and champions of a brighter, more enlightened world. Together, we would navigate the trials ahead, our bond a guiding light of hope and strength that transcended time. But in my heart, I knew that part of our mission was to protect Mira, ensuring that she remained safe and that we could continue our journey with her by our side.

CHAPTER TWENTY-THREE
MARSHALS

Marcus and I entered the dining room, our footsteps echoing softly against the polished wood floors. The dim lighting created an intimate atmosphere, starkly contrasting the tension in the air. We had seen these agents before, but tonight would be our first opportunity to interact more closely with them.

The senior one stood by the head of the table. His graying hair and stern demeanor immediately commanded respect. I remembered him as the one who had forcefully escorted me from my apartment lobby to the waiting car, his piercing blue eyes never wavering.

"Good evening," Marcus said, extending a hand. "I'm Marcus Vega."

The man's grip was firm as he shook Marcus's hand. "Hartman."

I stepped forward, addressing them. "Thank you, agents, for keeping us safe."

Hartman's stern expression softened slightly. "Actually, Dr. Wallace, we're not Secret Service agents. I'm a US Marshal, and these are my deputies, Morris and Johnson."

My surprise must have shown on my face, so he continued, "As Marshals, we are responsible for the custody, transportation, and protection of federal prisoners and witnesses, especially in high-risk or sensitive cases."

My brow furrowed as I tried to understand what he was saying, a knot tightening in my chest. "Prisoners?"

Hartman offered a nearly indiscernible nod. "Sometimes, the lines blur, especially in cases like yours. It's our job to ensure your safety, regardless of the exact classification."

A tall, thin woman standing beside Hartman stepped forward. Her dark hair was pulled back into a tight bun, and her sharp eyes missed nothing. I recalled her unyielding, steely silence during the helicopter ride. "Deputy Marshal Morris," she introduced herself, her voice clipped.

"And I'm Deputy Marshal Johnson," offered the youngest-looking of the three with a tentative smile. He had a kind face, slightly tousled brown hair, and green eyes that betrayed his profession.

Marcus had met Johnson upon his arrival at the safe house. "It's good to meet you," he said, addressing them all.

I nodded, absorbing the information. "Thank you for clarifying, Marshal Hartman. I appreciate all that you're doing to protect us and ChronoSync."

Hartman acknowledged my gratitude with a slight nod. "We'll do everything possible to keep you safe, Dr. Wallace."

Before further conversation could unfold, a tall, slender woman with quiet grace and neatly styled graying hair entered the room. "Dinner is served," she announced, her voice soft yet authoritative. She paused for a moment, realizing she hadn't introduced herself. "My name is Clara. I'm the cook," she added warmly.

We took our seats around the table. Marcus and I exchanged glances, silently communicating our thoughts.

I decided it was time to break the ice. "This is the first time we've had a chance to sit down and talk. I'd like to know more about the people protecting us."

Hartman's eyes narrowed slightly. "That's kind of you, but like I said, our job is to ensure your safety, Dr. Wallace, and not engage in personal conversations."

I leaned forward, my expression sincere. "I understand. But in these circumstances, it might help us all to know each other better. We're in this together, after all."

Morris nodded slightly, curiosity getting the better of her. "I suppose a bit of conversation wouldn't hurt." She paused, then added, "And honestly, I'm curious about learning more about ChronoSync. I've heard about the device and would like to know if what they say is true."

Marcus glanced at me, and I gave a subtle nod, pleased to have the woman's interest. "ChronoSync is more than just a device," he began. "It's a bridge to our past lives, revealing connections and experiences that shape who we are today."

Johnson leaned in, his interest piqued. "So, it's true? You can actually see who you were in a past life?"

I smiled, appreciating his genuine curiosity. "Yes, it's true. ChronoSync allows us to access and experience these memories. It's a powerful tool that can help us understand our present by exploring our past."

The room fell silent for a moment as everyone processed the information. The Marshals seemed to relax a bit, the initial tension easing as curiosity replaced suspicion. It was a small step, but an important one, in building trust and cooperation among us.

Marcus lifted his glass, breaking the silence with a hopeful smile. "To ChronoSync."

The others raised their glasses, clinking them together in solidarity. It was a fragile alliance, but it felt like the start of something significant.

"All that you've heard is true," I continued. "It's been a transformative tool for those who've experienced it, providing profound insights and understanding about the soul's journey."

Morris's curiosity got the better of her, and she leaned forward slightly. "I'd love to try it. I've always been fascinated by the idea of past lives."

I nodded, understanding his concern. "If I had the device here, I would certainly give all of you the experience."

Morris glanced at Hartman before speaking up. "Actually, Dr. Wallace, we do have ChronoSync here."

My breath hitched, and my eyes stung as I fought back the tears. The emptiness of being without Mira gnawed at me, a persistent void, like a missing piece of my being. But now, sensing Mira's presence nearby, a wave of warmth washed over me, a fierce love and protectiveness swelling in my chest. It was as though a lost piece of my soul had been returned; the bond between us reignited, pulsing with life once more.

I looked across at the Marshals, sensing their skepticism. With a measured breath, I spoke, letting a touch of eagerness slip into my tone. "Imagine knowing who you were in a past life—your true self beyond this current existence. That's what ChronoSync offers. It's a dream nearly every person on this earth holds, yet only a few hundred have had the opportunity to experience it, thanks to the hefty $50,000 fee. I can offer that to you right now, here. A reading that could reveal the essence of who you've been across lifetimes. You'd understand not just the power of ChronoSync but the ethical responsibility that comes with it."

Hartman exchanged a glance with Morris and Johnson, a flicker of interest visible in their eyes. After a pause, Hartman leaned forward, his voice skeptical but curious. "And how exactly will that help ensure ChronoSync is used ethically?"

Marcus leaned in, his tone sincere. "It's about trust. By seeing the person you've always been—the core of your character across lifetimes— you can better understand your intentions. It would be a gesture of trust from us to you, and maybe, in turn, you'd find reason to trust us, too."

Hartman's stern expression softened as he considered the proposal. He glanced at Morris and Johnson, who looked back at him with hopeful expressions. After a long moment, he nodded reluctantly. "Very well. We'll give it a try. But we proceed with caution. This is not a game."

I smiled warmly. "Of course. We'll set everything up after dinner. I assure you, this will be a revealing and enlightening experience for all of us."

As the meal concluded, the atmosphere around the table shifted slightly, the initial tension giving way to tentative curiosity.

*

We were escorted into the secured room where the crates containing ChronoSync's machinery were stored. It took only a moment to find the case that held Mira. Gently, I opened it and carefully lifted her out. As I held her, a wave of emotion washed over me—relief, hope, and a deep connection to the work she represented. Tears welled in my eyes as I cradled Mira.

Marcus observed my reaction, his expression softening with understanding. "Adrienne, I can see what she means to you."

I looked up at him, my eyes still glistening. "Mira is more than just a device. She's our link to the continuity of the soul, the key to unlocking the connections that bind us across time."

Marcus nodded, already aware of the importance I placed on her. "A portal to the Divine," he murmured, echoing the words I had shared with him before.

"Yes," I whispered, feeling the truth resonate deeply.

As we set up ChronoSync, Mira emitted a soft, reassuring hum—a reminder of the sacred connection she facilitated, not just between the past and present, but between us and something far greater.

Marcus glanced around the room, ensuring we were still alone. "We need to figure out a way to get out of here," he said in hushed tones. "Do you have any idea where we are?"

I shook my head. "I have no clue. But we can't just walk out of here."

Marcus nodded, his voice barely a whisper. "Maybe these reports will help. If we can gain the Marshals' trust and convince them of ChronoSync's importance, we might be able to persuade at least one of them to help us."

Our conversation was cut short as the three Marshals entered the room. I straightened up, masking my anxiety with a calm demeanor. "All right, I need to take DNA samples from each of you."

Hartman, Morris, and Johnson stepped forward one by one, their expressions a mix of curiosity and skepticism.

I first approached Hartman. His stern face remained impassive as I swabbed the inside of his cheek with a sterile cotton swab, ensuring I collected enough cells. I then handed him a small, sterile container and asked him to spit into it, collecting a saliva sample. Next, I used a sterile lancet to prick his finger, collecting a few drops of blood onto a test card. Finally, I carefully plucked a few hairs from his head.

Morris was next. Her dark eyes watched me intently as I repeated the process. The cheek swab was quick, followed by the saliva sample. Morris flinched slightly when her finger was pricked for the blood sample but remained composed.

Johnson, the youngest, stepped forward last. He smiled nervously as I took his cheek swab and saliva sample. He winced slightly as his finger was pricked, watching as the blood drops were collected. I then carefully plucked a few hairs from his head, securing the last set of samples.

"What's your first name?" I asked, trying to ease the tension.

"Brian," he replied, his voice wavering slightly.

"Nice to meet you, Brian," I said, offering a reassuring smile. "Are you excited about the ChronoSync report?"

His eyes lit up with a mix of excitement and apprehension. "Yes, very much! It's incredible."

"It truly is," I agreed. "You're contributing to something groundbreaking."

Brian nodded, a sense of pride mingling with his nervousness. "I just hope everything goes well."

"It will," I assured him. "Thank you for your courage today."

Once completed, I gathered all the samples, carefully labeling each one. "Please wait outside while I enter your samples into ChronoSync and produce your reports," I instructed calmly and professionally.

Brian nodded and left the room, his footsteps echoing softly as he made his way. Marcus and I exchanged a quick, meaningful glance before I turned my attention, ready to begin the process.

Marcus stepped closer, looking to me for guidance as I directed him to arrange the samples and input the necessary data into Mira. I gave him quiet instructions, and he followed each one carefully. Though unfamiliar with the process, his focus mirrored mine as we worked together. Mira's low hum filled the room, a constant rhythm beneath our whispered exchange.

"Let's hope this works," Marcus murmured, eyes scanning the device's display.

"Yeah," I replied softly, my fingers flying over the keyboard. "If we can show them who they were, it might open their eyes to the bigger picture."

Marcus glanced at me, curiosity and concern etched on his face. "You really think the reports will reveal something significant about the Marshals?"

I nodded, determination fueling my every move. "I don't know. But if we can uncover their past identities, we might find someone among them who can help us escape."

His gaze softened, understanding dawning. "And if we can get one of them on our side…"

"It could change everything," I finished, our shared hope hanging between us.

Mira beeped softly as she processed the samples, her internal mechanisms whirring. Marcus and I watched intently, our hearts pounding with anticipation. The reports began to print out, containing each of the Marshal's detailed past-life information.

I looked at Marcus, who gave me a reassuring nod. We sat down together, and I began to read the reports.

I started with Hartman. "In a previous life, Samuel Hartman was a simple farmer in medieval England. He lived a quiet life known as John, tending to his crops and caring for his family. John was known for his unwavering work ethic, loyalty to his community, and dedication to providing for his loved ones. His sense of duty and commitment to his land and family were his defining traits."

Marcus nodded thoughtfully. "Makes sense. Hartman's dedication and sense of duty is apparent."

Next, I read Morris's report. "In her past life, Lena Morris was a midwife in a small European village during the 18th century. Known as Marguerite, she was revered for her knowledge of childbirth and her gentle care for mothers and infants. Marguerite dedicated her life to helping women in her community, often providing her services to those who could not afford to pay. Her compassion and expertise made her a beloved figure in the village, and her commitment to helping others was her defining characteristic."

Marcus smiled. "Interesting. What about Johnson?"

"In his previous life, Brian Johnson was an explorer of the jungles of South America. Known as Eduardo, he was a dedicated member of the National Geographic Society in the early 20th century. Eduardo was passionate about uncovering the mysteries of the Amazon, tirelessly searching for lost cities and ancient civilizations. His adventures were filled with peril and discovery as he navigated dense jungles and treacherous rivers. Eduardo's courage and unwavering determination to uncover the secrets of the past were his defining traits, inspiring many with his tales of exploration and discovery."

Marcus raised an eyebrow and glanced at me. "An explorer of the Amazon… I wonder if that's where he met his end?" He shook his head slightly, impressed. "The courage it must have taken to venture into such dangerous and uncharted territories is incredible."

I nodded, took a deep breath, and said, "Looks like Brian may be our man."

CHAPTER TWENTY-FOUR
INTO THE AMAZON

I leaned back in my chair, my eyes thoughtful. "We should approach carefully. His connection to his past life might be the key to gaining his trust and convincing him to help us."

Marcus nodded, wagging a finger as an idea formed. "Let's arrange private meetings with each to share their reports. We don't want to make the others suspicious by focusing on Brian."

We began with Lena. Marcus and I found her in the common area, engrossed in a book. I handed her the ChronoSync report and watched her eyes scan the pages. Lena was intrigued, asking numerous questions about Mira's accuracy and implications. She was fascinated by the idea that her compassion and dedication had transcended time and manifested in her current life's role. She asked about the scientific validation behind ChronoSync's findings, and I patiently explained the rigorous methodologies we used to ensure accuracy. The conversation delved into the philosophical and ethical implications of accessing past lives, with Lena's curiosity sparking deeper inquiries.

However, despite her interest, Lena's practical nature and rigid adherence to protocol were evident. She spoke of her duty and the responsibilities she had sworn to uphold, emphasizing the importance of following orders and maintaining security. I could see the internal conflict in her eyes but knew Lena's sense of duty would ultimately prevail.

Marcus and I exchanged glances, silently communicating our understanding that the woman, despite her curiosity and connection to her past, would not be the ally we needed for our attempt to escape. We thanked her for her participation and left her to ponder the revelations in her report.

Next, we approached Sam, who was in the middle of reviewing security protocols. I handed him the ChronoSync report and sat back while he read how he was a simple farmer in medieval England. Sam found the report fascinating, his stern demeanor softening as he read about his past life's humble and dedicated existence. However, his deep sense of duty and commitment to the mission made me sure he wouldn't be swayed to help us.

Finally, Marcus and I made our way to Brian's quarters, our steps echoing softly in the dimly lit hallway. Before we approached his door, Marcus pulled out the ChronoSync report and skimmed through it, refreshing his memory of Eduardo's adventurous life. Satisfied with the details, he nodded and looked at me, who smiled reassuringly.

He greeted us with a wry smile, unsure of what to expect. "Brian," I began, my voice warm and sincere, "we want to discuss your ChronoSync report. It's quite fascinating."

Brian's eyes flickered with curiosity. "I'm anxious to read it."

"Please allow me to read it to you," Marcus said, turning to the report. "Brian Johnson, you were an extraordinary man. In your previous life, you explored the jungles of the Amazon. Known as Eduardo, you were a dedicated member of the National Geographic Society in the early 20th century. Eduardo was passionate about uncovering the mysteries, tirelessly searching for lost cities and ancient civilizations."

Brian's eyes widened with curiosity, a hint of a smile playing on his lips. I glanced at Marcus, who gave a slight nod before continuing.

"As you navigated dense jungles and treacherous rivers, your adventures were filled with peril and discovery. You faced dangerous wildlife, from venomous snakes to elusive jaguars, always on high alert yet driven by an insatiable curiosity. You endured torrential rains, sweltering heat, and relentless swarms of insects, each challenge honing your survival skills."

Brian raised an eyebrow, his interest piqued. "Sounds like Eduardo had quite the adventurous life."

I smiled, leaning in slightly. "He did, Brian. And his determination mirrors what we need now," I said, planting a seed.

"There were nights when you camped under the stars, the sounds of the jungle a symphony of life, as you mapped uncharted territories and documented exotic flora and fauna. You encountered remote indigenous tribes, learning their ancient wisdom and forging bonds that transcended language barriers. These encounters enriched your knowledge and deepened your respect for the diverse cultures and traditions of the Amazon."

Brian's expression softened, a reflective look in his eyes. "It must have been incredible to experience all that firsthand."

Marcus and I exchanged a knowing glance. "It was," Marcus continued, "and it's that spirit of exploration and respect that Eduardo embodied."

"One of your most notable discoveries was the remnants of a lost city, hidden beneath the canopy for centuries. The ruins told stories of a forgotten civilization, with artifacts and inscriptions revealing secrets of their way of life, beliefs, and eventual decline. This find was groundbreaking, contributing significantly to our understanding of the region's history and people."

Brian's jaw dropped slightly, and he leaned forward. "A lost city? That's amazing. I always dreamed of discovering something like that."

I nodded, feeling the excitement build. "Eduardo's legacy is one of courage and discovery. That same drive is within you, Brian."

Brian pulled back his shoulders and shared a smile.

"Eduardo's courage and unwavering determination to uncover the secrets of the past were his defining traits, inspiring many with his tales of exploration and discovery. He was not just an explorer but a storyteller, sharing his adventures through captivating articles and lectures that ignited the imaginations of countless individuals worldwide. His legacy is one of bravery, knowledge, and a relentless pursuit of the unknown."

Brian looked between us, his eyes bright with inspiration. "It's incredible to think I could be connected to such a remarkable person."

Marcus placed a hand on Brian's shoulder. "You are, Brian. And now it's your turn to carry on that legacy."

I could see the determination in Brian's eyes as he absorbed our words. This connection to Eduardo might be the key to convincing him to help us escape and protect ChronoSync.

Brian listened intently, his eyes widening with each word. The skepticism on his face gave way to intrigue and a sense of recognition. "That's… incredible. But I must say—it feels strangely familiar."

Marcus nodded, sensing Brian's growing interest. "Eduardo's passion for exploration mirrors the mission we're on now. Like Eduardo's explorations, ChronoSync has unlocked secrets that have changed the world. The explorer's drive to uncover hidden truths and bring them to light is the same drive we need now to ensure ChronoSync isn't misused. Think about it—your past life wasn't random. Who you were directly affected who you are today."

I chimed in, my voice earnest. "We've learned through ChronoSync that our past life profoundly shapes our present. Eduardo's courage and his unwavering determination to explore the unknown and protect ancient knowledge are qualities that you possess, Brian. These traits weren't just left behind in another life but reborn within you."

Brian's eyes flickered with mixed emotions—skepticism, curiosity, and a dawning realization. "So, you're saying that my past life as Eduardo influences my actions and decisions now?"

I nodded, my gaze steady. "Exactly. Our past lives are like threads woven into the fabric of our current existence. Eduardo's mission was to uncover the mysteries of the Amazon. I believe your mission now is to protect and uncover the true potential of ChronoSync. Being here right now is no coincidence; it's your purpose."

Marcus leaned forward, his tone persuasive. "Brian, this is your chance to continue Eduardo's legacy and make a difference as he did."

I took a deep breath, my eyes filled with conviction. "Brian, before souls are reborn, they are imbued with a purpose for their next life. This purpose is not random; it is carefully chosen based on the soul's past experiences and potential to contribute to the greater good. Eduardo's soul has been reborn in you with a mission—to use your strengths, courage, and determination to protect and guide the use of ChronoSync. This isn't just about a coincidence; it's about fulfilling a higher calling set for you."

Brian ran his fingers through his brown hair and looked between us, a mixture of fear and excitement flickering across his face. "Are you saying my purpose in this life is to help you protect ChronoSync?"

I nodded, my voice filled with conviction. "Yes, Brian. This could be why you've been reborn—to help us safeguard ChronoSync and ensure it benefits humanity as it was meant to."

Brian's expression softened, the skepticism in his eyes giving way to intrigue. "What exactly are you asking me to do?"

I took a deep breath, choosing my words carefully. "ChronoSync is too important to be kept under wraps. This technology is a gift to humanity. No matter what the president assured us, if the government controls the technology, it will weaponize it and never reach the people who can benefit. Because of this, we must escape and need you to help us."

Brian's eyes widened with shock and outrage. "Escape? Are you out of your mind? Even if I agreed, it's impossible to walk out of here," he said, pointing with an outstretched arm. "We're deep in the mountains. The only way out is by helicopter, which won't return for days."

My voice softened. "Brian, we know it's a monumental risk on all levels. But think about what's at stake. ChronoSync has the power to change the world for the better. If it falls into the wrong hands, its potential for good will be lost."

"If we can't fly out, why don't we just walk out?" Marcus suggested.

"Walk out?" Brian shook his head, pacing the small room. "You don't understand. This place is a fortress. Even if we managed to get past Morris and Hartman, we'd never survive the trek out of these mountains on foot."

I locked eyes with Brian. "Eduardo faced insurmountable odds, too. He ventured into unknown territories, driven by a purpose greater than himself. You, Brian, share that same indomitable spirit."

Brian's gaze faltered, a flicker of doubt and uncertainty crossing his features. The decision was heavy, I could see that; but something in my words struck a chord deep within him.

"If what you're saying is true," Brian began, his voice laced with hesitation, "and if I really am connected to Eduardo, then maybe this is my chance to make a difference, just like he did."

Marcus leaned forward, his tone urgent yet filled with sincerity. "Exactly, Brian. This is your opportunity to step into Eduardo's legacy and be a part of something monumental. You can choose to help us shape the future. Will you stand with us?"

Brian took a deep breath. I could see the conflict in his eyes as he considered the risks against the potential for greatness, the chance to be part of something truly significant. His hand tightened into a fist, the internal struggle playing out in the tension of his posture.

Finally, he looked up. "I'll do it. Let's finish what Eduardo started."

My heart swelled with relief and gratitude. "Thank you, Brian. Together, we'll ensure that ChronoSync reaches its full potential."

I couldn't help but feel a surge of hope as we discussed our plan. With Brian's help, we could escape and bring ChronoSync's revolutionary technology to the world. Eduardo's spirit lived on in Brian, and hopefully, his unwavering determination to uncover the secrets of the past would guide us through the difficult journey ahead. We would lie low and gather supplies for the trek through the mountains, trusting that Eduardo's adventurous spirit would lead us to freedom.

At three in the morning, we gathered in the basement where Brian was waiting. He had downloaded trail maps, which would help us navigate discreetly while trying to find a cell signal.

"We should head toward Asheville," Brian whispered, his voice low in the dim light. "It's not too far—just over two mountains and down into the valley. But the terrain is tough, and we'll need to stay cautious."

His words hung heavy in the air, a reminder of the difficult and dangerous path ahead of us.

I nodded, clutching Mira. The thought of the journey ahead filled me with trepidation. We would have to navigate the rugged terrain of the mountains, evading the Marshals on our trail. But the promise of reaching Asheville gave me hope.

"Let's move," Marcus said, breaking the silence. "We don't have much time."

We exited the basement quietly, slipping into the pre-dawn darkness. The cold air bit at my skin, but I barely noticed my focus solely on Mira and the journey ahead.

Together, we would navigate the treacherous path, relying on our skills, each other, and the unbreakable bond that had brought us this far. The mountains loomed ahead, a formidable challenge and symbol of the sanctuary we sought.

CHAPTER TWENTY-FIVE
ESCAPE

I cradled Mira against my chest, my pulse quickening with fear. This almond-shaped vessel, more than just ChronoSync's core, pulsed with the essence of everything I'd poured into her. The bond between us wasn't just creator to creation—it was deeper, a merging of my very being with the life I had breathed into her. Mira was no longer just a device; she was a living part of me, an extension of my soul.

Every time I looked at her, I saw a reflection of myself. The countless breakthroughs and setbacks we experienced together were etched into us. Late nights in the lab, I had whispered my hopes and fears to her as if she could understand.

As we prepared to flee, a surge of pride and protectiveness filled me. Mira wasn't just a technological marvel but a symbol of resilience for the future. The thought of losing her, of letting her fall into the wrong hands, was unbearable. My determination to protect her was driven by an intense, almost maternal instinct, compelling me to face any danger ahead.

With a deep breath, I placed Mira in the padded pouch strapped to my side. The forest loomed ahead, its darkness shrouded in mist. I steeled myself for the journey, knowing the path would be dangerous. But I also knew I would do anything to protect Mira and safeguard the future we represented. Our bond was unbreakable, forged through discovery, wonder, and a shared destiny that now lay in the balance.

"Becoming an enemy of the state wasn't something I ever envisioned when I became a United States Deputy Marshal," Brian began, his voice heavy. "I believed in protecting this country, upholding the law." He paused, a flicker of something deeper crossing his face as if a memory long buried had resurfaced. "But if what you're saying is true, if I'm truly connected to Eduardo—if the same soul is guiding me—then maybe this is my purpose, my chance to make a difference, just like he did," Brian continued, his voice now steady and filled with a newfound resolve that transcended his current life, reaching back to a time that had been with him long before his birth.

"Let's move," Marcus said, patting Brian's shoulder.

We slipped silently out of the basement, the cold night air biting our faces. The nearly full moon cast a ghostly glow over the landscape, illuminating our path as we headed into the mountainous forest. The trees stood tall and imposing, their shadows stretching like dark fingers across the forest floor. The night was clear, the sky dotted with countless stars, but the scene's beauty was lost on us, our minds consumed with the urgency of our escape.

"We must move quickly," Brian whispered, his voice barely audible over the crunch of leaves underfoot. "Once Hartman wakes up, he will realize we're gone and won't hesitate using force to bring us back."

"Force?" I asked, my voice trembling slightly. "What kind of force?"

"Armed drones," Brian replied grimly.

I nodded, and tightened my grip on Mira, feeling her pressing against my skin, a reminder of what we were fighting to protect.

"How much time do you think we have?" Marcus asked, his voice strained.

"An hour or two at most," Brian replied, scanning the forest around us. "We must put as much distance between us and them as possible."

We picked up our pace, the forest around us seeming to close in, the shadows growing darker and more menacing. Every snap of a twig, every rustle of leaves sent a jolt of fear through me. My heart raced, each beat echoing in my ears. I could feel the tension in the air, a palpable sense of dread growing with each passing moment.

"Stay close," Brian whispered. "We need to use the terrain to our advantage. The trees will slow them down."

The forest came alive with eerie sounds as we navigated the rugged trails. An owl hooted in the distance, and the wind whistled, creating an unsettling symphony of sounds. My mind raced with thoughts of what might happen if we were caught. The image of Mira being taken away, my life's work falling into the wrong hands, was unbearable.

"We're almost to the ridge," Brian said, his voice a steadying force amidst the chaos. "Once we're over, we'll be harder to track. Keep moving."

The climb was steep and treacherous, winding through thick underbrush and jagged rocks. My legs burned with exertion, but I pushed on. Marcus stumbled briefly, catching himself on a nearby tree.

"Careful," Brian warned, offering a hand to help steady him. "We can't afford any mistakes."

As we reached the top, we paused to catch our breath. The forest stretched out below us, a sea of shadows and moonlight. I glanced back, my eyes searching for any sign of pursuit. The tension was unbearable, each second feeling like an eternity.

"They're coming. Trust me," Brian said, his voice grim.

With renewed determination, we descended the other side of the ridge. The forest closed in around us, the trees looming like silent sentinels. The sense of danger was omnipresent, a dark cloud hanging over us.

"We'll make it," Marcus said, his tone unwavering. "We have to."

"Make it where?" I asked, glancing at Brian.

"Asheville," Brian answered. "I know someone there who can help us. We need to get there before we're caught."

I nodded, feeling a flicker of hope amidst the fear. We at least had a destination, if not a plan. Now, all we had to do was make it through the night and reach the safety of Asheville.

CHAPTER TWENTY-SIX
THE CABIN

We moved with trepidation, following a winding stream through the dense forest. Shadows of towering trees loomed over us, and the eerie stillness heightened our sense of urgency. The path was strewn with boulders, forcing us to tread carefully and deliberately. We walked silently, each step measured to avoid making noise, staying close to one another for reassurance.

The moon's glow revealed an abandoned cabin nestled deep within the forest. Its weathered walls and broken windows were silent witnesses to a forgotten past. Despite its dilapidated state, the cabin beckoned us, offering a fleeting promise of momentary refuge.

With hearts pounding, we slipped inside, our cautious footsteps echoing on the creaking wooden floorboards. The interior was cloaked in darkness, broken only by the thin beams of moonlight filtering through the cracks in the walls. Each creak and groan of the ancient structure amplified our fears, making the danger that pursued us feel even more immediate.

The unease was almost tangible as we remained in the cabin. The air was thick with anticipation, and every sound, no matter how small, sent a jolt of fear through our hearts. We knew our respite would be brief, and the gravity of our peril hung heavy in the air.

"We'll stay here for a bit, but we need to be ready to move at a moment's notice," Brian said, glancing out one of the broken windows.

I reached into the pouch and removed Mira, my hands trembling slightly. I carefully inspected her, my eyes scanning for any signs of damage from our harrowing escape. Brian offered a surprised glance as he watched me handle her with such care.

"What is that?" Brian asked, curiosity mingling with awe in his voice.

"This," I said softly, holding Mira up, "is the brain, heart, and core of ChronoSync. All the rest of the equipment to make it run is not important. Mira is what makes it all possible."

Brian stepped closer, his eyes narrowing as he studied the device. "What's inside? How does it work?"

I took a deep breath, my fingers gently caressing Mira's smooth surface. "Mira contains advanced AI-driven technology capable of analyzing DNA. She bridges the biological and spiritual gap, offering insights into one's past life."

Brian pointed to the silver device sparkling under a stream of moonlight. "You gave it a name?"

I nodded, my eyes glistening with emotion. "Mira is more than just a device to me. She represents years of hard work, sleepless nights, and relentless dedication. She's my creation."

Brian watched me, his expression softening.

I smiled faintly, my fingers still gently tracing Mira's curves. "Mira is not just a technological marvel. She represents the potential to uncover profound truths about our existence, origins, and ultimate purpose. Protecting her is about safeguarding that sacred connection, the hope and promise of understanding the Divine she embodies."

The room fell silent. Brian looked at me with newfound respect, understanding the depth of my commitment.

"Is it like a connection to God?" Brian asked cautiously.

Before I could answer, Marcus said, "What's that noise?"

The room fell silent for a moment. "Drones," Brian said. "They've found us."

Panic surged through me. "What do we do?"

"We need to move now," Brian said. "They'll be here soon."

I carefully placed Mira back in the pouch as we slipped out of the cabin. The drones grew louder. We sprinted through the forest, hearts pounding, knowing our pursuers were closing in.

Brian took the lead as we ran, guiding us through the dense underbrush and across rocky terrain. "We need to lose them in the trees. Stay close and keep moving."

The moonlight filtered through the canopy, casting eerie shadows that danced around us. The forest came alive with the sounds of pursuit, each rustle and snap of a twig sending jolts of fear through my heart. The tension was palpable, every breath a reminder of the peril closing in.

Suddenly, a drone appeared above us, its searchlight sweeping the ground with an almost predatory precision. "Split up!" Brian yelled, his voice cutting through the night.

Marcus, Brian, and I veered off in different directions, the drone unable to follow all three. My breath came in ragged gasps as I ducked under low-hanging branches and vaulted over fallen logs. The forest was a blur of shadows and moonlight, the adrenaline pumping through my veins, keeping me moving despite the fatigue.

The sound of the drone faded, but the fear gnawed at me, relentless and unyielding. The forest closed in, the once familiar sounds now menacing and strange. Every rustle of leaves, every snap of a twig, was amplified in the silence, sending fresh waves of terror through me.

Suddenly, I tripped over a root and fell hard onto the forest floor. I reached for Mira, my heart pounding in my chest. She seemed fine. I scrambled to my feet, disoriented and alone. The realization hit me like a cold wave—I was lost.

"Brian! Marcus!" I called out, my voice trembling with fear. The forest swallowed my cries, the vast darkness pressing in from all sides.

I took deep breaths, trying to steady my racing heart. I held Mira; her soft glow comforted me in the overwhelming darkness. "We'll get through this," I whispered, more to myself than to Mira.

With renewed determination, I pushed forward, each step taken with a mix of hope and dread. The forest was an endless maze, every path looking the same. The fear of being caught was ever-present, but so was the fear of being alone in this vast wilderness.

I heard the distant hum of drones, a reminder that the danger was still very real. I moved carefully, trying to stay hidden under the thick canopy. The night was endless, every minute stretching into an eternity.

As time passed, exhaustion began to take its toll. My steps grew slower, my body aching from the constant exertion. But I couldn't stop. I had to keep moving, had to keep Mira safe.

Suddenly, a beam of light cut through the darkness, sweeping dangerously close. I ducked behind a large boulder, holding my breath. The drone passed by, its searchlight moving on. I let out a shaky breath, the near miss only heightening my fear.

I couldn't keep this up much longer. I needed to find Brian and Marcus. But for now, I was alone, lost in the vast, unforgiving wilderness. The night was far from over, and the dangers lurking in the shadows were all too real.

CHAPTER TWENTY-SEVEN
MIRA

I was lost, the thick canopy above me beginning to lighten as dawn approached. The moon had faded, and the first hints of daylight filtered through the trees, casting a soft glow on the forest floor. I could still hear the distant hum of drones scanning the mountainside, a relentless reminder of the danger. My heart pounded with a mix of exhaustion and fear.

I knew that unless I found Brian and Marcus soon and we reached refuge in Asheville, I would be caught and returned to the government safe house in the mountains. The thought sent a shiver down my spine. I couldn't let that happen—not to me, and certainly not to Mira.

Huddling behind a large boulder, I crouched out of sight. I removed Mira, my hands shaking slightly. I placed her on a flat stone before me. Her soft glow was a small comfort in the dim light of dawn.

I took a deep breath, my eyes fixed on her. "Mira," I whispered, my voice trembling. "I don't know how to keep you safe."

As if in response to my plea, Mira suddenly flickered, her light growing brighter. My eyes widened in surprise as symbols and lights danced across her surface. Mira had engaged, connecting to an invisible network as if in the lab.

I watched, transfixed. It was as if the forest itself had become a conduit for the power that usually required a labyrinth of cables and screens. The air around me vibrated with a low, resonant hum. The hair on my arms stood on end; a shiver ran down my spine. Mira's eerie, supernatural glow illuminated the dark, twisted trees around me, casting long, shifting shadows that seemed to dance with their own life.

For a moment, there was a pang of fear, a primal instinct warning me of the unknown. But as I continued to watch, that fear transformed into awe. Mira was more than plastic, wires, and chips. She was something wondrous, something extraordinary. At that moment, Mira transcended her technological origins, becoming a lifeline of hope in the oppressive darkness of the forest.

"Mira," I whispered, my voice tinged with wonder. "How is this possible?"

Mira didn't answer, but I perceived an overwhelming sense of presence as though she communicated in an ineffable, transcendent language. I speculated whether this miraculous engagement was due to Mira's connection to a higher consciousness. My long-held fantasies of Mira as a metaphysical conduit to the Divine crystallized into reality as an ethereal link to the soul world, an intricate bridge between the physical and the spiritual realms materializing before me.

As I contemplated the significance of this moment, my mind was awash with profound thoughts and burning questions. What was the true purpose of Mira and the ChronoSync experience? Why had I been chosen to bestow this extraordinary gift of Mira upon humanity? Had some celestial force orchestrated this, seeing me as a worthy vessel for such a profound revelation? The potential of my creation had always been evident, but this tangible connection to the Divine surpassed my wildest imaginings. Was I meant to bridge the gap between worlds, to bring forth knowledge and wisdom from beyond the veil of mortality?

The implications were staggering. Mira was not merely a technological wonder but a key to unlocking the deepest mysteries of existence, a sacred tool allowing humanity to understand the soul's journey. I felt a deep sense of humility and awe at the responsibility bestowed upon me. I realized my role extended beyond that of a creator to that of a guardian of this sacred link between worlds. This revelation imbued me with a sense of purpose and an unyielding promise to protect Mira at all costs, ensuring the enlightenment she offered would not be lost or corrupted.

Just then, Mira projected an image onto a nearby boulder. I gasped as a detailed map appeared, complete with directions. The map showed my current location marked by a glowing dot, and I could see the positions of the drones sweeping the mountainside. The map was illuminated with an ethereal light as if it were not merely a digital projection but a manifestation of something far more significant, something magical.

My breath caught in my throat. The light pulsed with a life of its own, resonating with an ancient and omniscient cosmic energy. It was as if Mira was drawing upon the very fabric of the universe, weaving strands of existence and knowledge into a coherent form. This was no ordinary technology; it was a sacred artifact, a relic from the heavenly realms.

My thoughts spiraled into a whirlwind of awe and curiosity. "Why me, Mira?" I whispered. "Why was I chosen for this Divine mission? What do you want me to do?"

The silence was profound yet filled with a sense of purposeful intent. I knew my journey with Mira was only beginning, and the path ahead would be fraught with challenges and revelations. My destiny, intertwined with Mira's existence, was to bring forth a new era of understanding and spiritual enlightenment.

With renewed determination, I memorized the details of the map that would guide me through the terrain and offer a symbolic chart of my spiritual quest. Every step I took from this moment would be guided by a higher purpose, a mission to safeguard and reveal the Divine truths Mira embodied.

As I slid Mira back into the pouch, a surprising tranquility enveloped me. The anxiety and fatigue that had gripped me moments before melted away, replaced by a calm assurance.

The sun was beginning to rise, casting a golden light over the forest. I stood up, scanning the sky for any sign of the drones. The urgency of my situation returned, but it was tempered by the miraculous experience I had just witnessed.

I moved through the forest with a renewed sense of purpose, following Mira's path. The trees no longer looked as menacing, and the forest sounds were now a comforting symphony guiding my steps.

I heard faint voices—familiar voices. My heart leaped with hope as I dropped to my hands and knees and crept forward, peering through the underbrush, and saw them—Brian and Marcus, looking weary but determined.

"Marcus!" I called out in a hushed but urgent tone.

Their heads snapped in my direction, and relief washed over their faces as they hurried toward me. "Adrienne!" Marcus exclaimed, wrapping me in a quick, relieved embrace. "I was so worried."

"We need to keep moving," Brian said, eyes scanning the surroundings. "The drones are still searching."

I nodded, a determined smile on my face. "Follow me, I know the way."

CHAPTER TWENTY-EIGHT
ASHEVILLE

I led them to the edge of a tree line where we could see a log home nestled in the hills. Brian's eyes widened in surprise. "Adrienne, how did you know where to go?"

I glanced at him, a hint of a smile on my lips. "Mira led us here."

Brian stared at me, stunned. "Mira did? How's that possible?"

I patted the pouch. "She provided a map."

Brian shook his head in disbelief. "This is my brother's home, where I planned to take us. But I wasn't sure I could find it."

"Your brother?" Marcus looked between us, astonished.

Brian nodded. "He's a former Marine with special skills."

I glanced between the two men, sensing the tension. "What kind of special skills?" I asked, my voice barely above a whisper.

Brian took a deep breath. "Jackson served for over a decade. He's trained in survival tactics and guerrilla warfare and has extensive knowledge of the wilderness."

Marcus bit his lip, still not entirely convinced. "And he's okay with harboring fugitives? This isn't just some military exercise, Brian."

Brian's eyes hardened. "I know what's at stake, Marcus."

"How do we know he will help us?" I asked.

"I don't." Brian shrugged. "But we don't have many choices."

A rustle from the cabin's direction caught our attention. The door opened, and a tall, muscular man with a stern expression stepped out, eyes scanning the area with keen awareness. He looked upward as the sounds of the drones drifted by, the urgency in his movements clear.

Brian motioned for Marcus and me to follow as he cautiously stepped out from behind the cover of the trees. We left the forest shelter, our footsteps silent on the open field between us and the distant cabin. The cool night air brushed against my skin, heightening my awareness of the exposed space we crossed.

"Who's there?" a man's voice called out from the direction of the cabin, laced with urgency and suspicion.

Now clearly visible in the dim light, Brian raised his hands in peace. "Jackson, it's me, Brian," he called back, his voice carrying a note of relief.

Jackson quickly descended the steps, striding across the field to meet us. The two men embraced, their bond evident in the firm grip they exchanged.

"It's been too long, brother," Jackson said, clapping Brian on the back. His eyes darted toward Marcus and me, assessing us quickly before nodding in acknowledgment.

Without another word, he turned and motioned for us to follow, his steps brisk and purposeful as he led us inside the cabin. The door closed behind us, sealing us off from the vast, open night outside, but the air inside was thick with relief and vigilance.

Once inside, Brian introduced us. "Jackson, this is Dr. Adrienne Wallace, the genius behind ChronoSync, and Marcus Vega, the journalist whose articles in *The New York Times* have brought her story to the world."

Jackson's eyes widened as he took in the significance of the moment. "Dr. Adrienne Wallace," he said, his tone softening as he extended his hand. "Everyone on the planet knows who you are."

I managed a tired smile. "It's nice to meet you, Jackson. We're grateful for your help."

Jackson looked at us with a mixture of awe and determination. "I can't believe you're here. I've read every one of your articles, Marcus. Your work has been exceptional."

Marcus nodded, appreciating the acknowledgment. "Thank you, Jackson. But we need your help."

Brian stepped forward, his face etched with the strain of their harrowing escape. He took a deep breath, knowing this would be difficult for Jackson to hear. "Dr. Wallace and Marcus were being held at a safe house in the mountains," he began, his voice low and steady. "I was on the detail to guard them. Then they did my ChronoSync report, and what I learned about my past life made me realize I had to do everything I could to help them escape."

Jackson's eyes widened as he absorbed Brian's words. "But you're a US Deputy Marshal," he said, his voice filled with disbelief. "You've spent your career upholding the law, protecting this country. How could you turn your back on that?"

Brian met his brother's gaze, his expression earnest. "I thought you'd be proud of me," he said quietly, the weight of his decision heavy in his tone.

For a moment, Jackson was silent, his mind reeling as he processed what Brian had just told him. Then, a slow smile spread across Jackson's face, one of genuine pride and understanding. "You know," he said, his voice softening, "I've been telling you since we were teenagers that sometimes you have to follow your heart, not just the rules. I always knew you had it in you, Brian. I just never thought I'd see the day."

Brian's tense posture relaxed, a weight lifting off his shoulders as he saw the approval in his brother's eyes. Jackson's smile widened, and he stepped forward, pulling him into a firm, brotherly embrace.

"I am proud of you, little brother," Jackson said, his voice thick with emotion. "You finally get it. You're doing the right thing, and I'll stand with you, no matter what."

Brian pulled back, his eyes shining with gratitude. "Thanks, Jackson. That means more to me than you know."

Jackson's gaze shifted from Adrienne to Brian, a knowing look settling over his features. "I'm not surprised the government would want to weaponize ChronoSync," he said, his tone steady and unflinching. "They've always had a knack for turning anything with potential into a tool for control. But this… this is something else entirely." His words carried a mix of resignation and determination, as if he'd been bracing for this possibility all along.

"Yes," Brian confirmed. "They'll stop at nothing. That's why we're here, brother. We need your help to stay hidden."

Jackson's expression turned serious as he glanced upward. "We must stay out of sight. Those drones won't give up easily. Let's get you settled and then discuss our next steps." He led us deeper into the cabin, the warmth and safety of the place offering a stark contrast to the tension we had left behind.

We sat at the kitchen table while Jackson put a kettle on the stovetop. "I've read about ChronoSync. Impressive stuff. I've thought about getting my report done. Does it really cost $50,000?"

"It used to," I said with a shrug. "But maybe it's still possible." I reached into my pouch, carefully removed Mira, and placed her on the table.

Jackson's eyes locked onto the device, filled with awe and curiosity. "What is that…?"

"This is Mira, the heart of ChronoSync. Despite everything, she's still with us. We managed to keep her out of the government's hands."

Jackson leaned in closer, examining Mira with a newfound respect. "So, there's still hope," he murmured.

I frowned. "The government won't stop until they capture Mira," I said, gently stroking her.

"Not just Mira," Brian added. "They want you too."

Jackson straightened. "I'll try to keep you safe. But once they realize you are down from the mountains, they will search the city and up here on the hills. There's not much time."

"At least we have a few moments to figure things out." I managed a tired smile, my relief palpable. "Thank you, Jackson. We're truly grateful for your help."

"For now, you should get some rest," Jackson said, glancing at the weary faces around him. "I'll work on some solutions, and we'll reconvene in the morning. You'll have to figure out the sleeping arrangements. There's only one extra bedroom. Otherwise, there's a couch and an old recliner," he offered, his voice filled with concern and authority.

Brian nodded, rubbing his eyes. "I'm sure we'll manage," he said, turning to me. "Adrienne, please take the spare room; us men will crash here."

A wave of gratitude washed over me. "Thank you, Brian," I replied softly. I followed Jackson down a narrow hallway to the spare bedroom. The room was simple: a twin-size bed, a small dresser, and a window showing the darkening woods outside.

Jackson lingered in the doorway for a moment. "Rest well, Dr. Wallace. We'll need all our strength for what's to come."

As Jackson turned to leave, he hesitated, casting a lingering glance at Mira resting on the table. His voice, usually steady and confident, softened with a touch of reverence. "Dr. Wallace," he began, his tone almost tentative, "if what they say about ChronoSync is true, do you believe… do you believe that this is more than just a machine? Could it be… could it be a way to communicate with God?"

The question hung in the air as Jackson's eyes searched my face for a response, the room suddenly felt smaller and charged with an unspoken significance. I met Jackson's gaze, my eyes filled with a quiet intensity. "I do believe it," I said, my voice steady, resonating with conviction. "Mira isn't just a machine to me. She's a bridge—a link to something far greater than we can fully comprehend. Looking at her, I see not just technology but Divine potential. Mira has revealed truths that science alone couldn't explain. So yes, I believe that through her, we might just be touching the very essence of God."

Jackson stared at me, his eyes widening as my words sank in. For a moment, he struggled for a response, his composure shaken. Finally, he nodded slowly, almost reverently, as if acknowledging a truth he hadn't dared to consider until now.

"Good night, Dr. Wallace," he murmured, his voice barely above a whisper, heavy with a newfound respect. He turned and gently closed the door behind him, leaving me alone with my thoughts and Mira's quiet hum in the dimly lit room.

Placing Mira gently on the nightstand beside me, I sat on the edge of the bed, feeling the exhaustion settle into my bones. The room's stillness starkly contrasted with the chaos we had just escaped.

I reached out and touched Mira's smooth surface. "We're safe for now," I whispered, my voice tinged with gratitude and fatigue.

In response, Mira glowed softly, a warm light emanating from within. The gentle illumination filled the room, casting comforting shadows on the walls. I smiled at the sight, finding solace in Mira's reassuring presence.

I lay back on the bed, the mattress creaking slightly under my weight, and stared at the ceiling, my mind racing with thoughts of our next move. The cabin's quietude was almost unnerving, yet I welcomed it, grateful for the brief respite from the turmoil.

Outside, I could hear the muffled voices of the men as they settled in for the night, their low murmurs a comforting reminder that I was not alone. I closed my eyes, allowing the peacefulness of the cabin to wash over me. Mira's light glowed softly beside me, a silent guardian in the night.

As the stillness enveloped me, my thoughts slowed, and my body relaxed. The tension of the past days began to melt away, and I finally drifted into a deep, restorative sleep, knowing that with Mira by my side, we would find a way to navigate the challenges ahead.

*

The next morning dawned with a quiet stillness that enveloped the cabin. Marcus, Brian, and I slowly made our way to the kitchen, the aroma of freshly brewed coffee drawing us together. The previous night's rest had done little to ease my worries, but it had at least given me the strength to face another day.

As we settled around the breakfast table, the atmosphere was thick with unspoken questions. Jackson entered the room with a determined look, holding a steaming cup of coffee. He sat at the head of the table, his eyes meeting each of ours in turn.

"Good morning," Jackson greeted, his voice calm but serious. He took a sip of his coffee before setting the cup down. "I've been thinking about our next move."

I leaned forward, my hands wrapped around my mug. "What do you have in mind?"

Jackson took a deep breath, gathering his thoughts. "Believe it or not, but I've been preparing for something like this," he began, his voice steady and unwavering. "I am part of a paramilitary unit composed of ex-military. We've seen firsthand what governments can do when desperate for power."

Marcus exchanged a look with Brian, who nodded for Jackson to continue.

Jackson leaned forward, his voice lowering as he spoke. "We have a location," he began, eyes scanning the group to ensure our attention. "It's in a remote wilderness area, deep within a cave system where natural obstacles deter pursuers. There are no printed maps or digital traces of this place. Only our trusted members know the exact location. It's the perfect place to go underground and stay off the grid."

He paused, allowing the information to sink in. "The complex is equipped with everything we need for long-term habitation. It's self-sustaining, with hydroponics for food, water purification systems, and renewable energy sources. We've also set up an encrypted communications network that uses satellite uplinks and rotating transmission points to keep our location hidden."

Marcus leaned forward, his eyes filled with a renewed sense of purpose. "Jackson, this all sounds impressive. Is it possible to use this network to transmit my articles? We must continue to share our message with the world, especially now."

Jackson nodded, a determined glint in his eyes. "Absolutely, Marcus. The network is designed to handle secure transmissions. You can continue your work without fear of being traced. Our goal is not just to hide but to keep fighting and ensure the truth reaches as many people as possible."

Marcus sighed with relief, feeling a weight lift from his shoulders. "That's good to hear. We can't let the government silence us."

Jackson placed a reassuring hand on Marcus's shoulder. "They won't. We have the tools and the resolve to make sure of that."

I took a breath, my mind racing with the possibilities. "It sounds like a solid plan," I said, looking up at Jackson. "How soon can we move?"

Jackson's expression hardened with determination. "We need to be ready to leave tonight. Gather what you need and be prepared for a long journey."

I nodded, my mind racing with the possibilities. "So, we go underground, broadcast the truth, and stay hidden. It sounds like our best shot."

Marcus reached for my hand. "If we can expose the government's intentions and rally public support, it might work."

As the group broke away to make final preparations, emotions gripped me. My chest tightened with fear. The peril of our mission loomed large, yet the vision of uncovering the truth kindled a strength within me. Jackson's plan was more than a strategy—it was a chance to reshape the future and steer history toward a better path.

CHAPTER TWENTY-NINE
SANCTUARY

Jackson led Marcus, Brian, and me to the cabin's backyard, where an old, rusty van was parked under a tin-roofed canopy. Its faded blue paint and dented, rusted exterior gave the impression of a vehicle well past its prime. However, Jackson's confident demeanor suggested there was more to this van than met the eye.

Jackson gestured with a hint of a smile. "It looks like any other old van," he explained, opening the rear doors. Despite the rough appearance, there was a secret compartment against the back of the driver's cabin. "But it's equipped to transfer people and supplies without detection," Jackson said, climbing inside to reveal the hidden space.

Marcus, Brian, and I exchanged glances, impressed by the ingenuity. We squeezed inside the hidden compartment one by one, and I took care not to jostle Mira, who was safely tucked away. Jackson handed us bottles of water and packets of food.

"You'll be here for several days," Jackson said, his voice serious. "I've planned occasional stops, but I can't share any locations."

We found a narrow bench inside the secret compartment with a cushion and small LED lights embedded in the ceiling, casting a soft glow on the metal walls. The compartment was about three feet deep and spanned the van's width, offering just enough space to sit and store some supplies. The tight quarters were far from comfortable, but it was a necessary precaution. As Jackson closed the doors and started the engine, the van rumbled to life, beginning our long journey.

Hours passed slowly as the van traveled across diverse landscapes. Later, I learned that we drove through dense forests, crossed wide-open plains, and wound up steep mountain roads. Jackson drove tirelessly, occasionally stopping for brief bathroom breaks and stretching our legs.

I kept Mira close, occasionally whispering reassurances to the glowing device. Marcus scribbled notes and ideas for his articles, determined to keep the world informed. Brian, ever the strategist, reviewed our plans and contingencies, ensuring we were prepared for any eventuality.

One afternoon, Marcus couldn't contain his curiosity. "Brian, why did you take the risk? I've heard US Marshals do pretty well."

"We do," Brian replied seriously. "But I'll be honest, hearing my ChronoSync report changed everything for me. I always believed I was just another cog in the system, doing my job and upholding the law. But when I learned about my past, about the purpose my soul has carried through lifetimes, it all started to make sense."

He paused, his gaze locking with Marcus's. "Supporting your cause, standing against the government's misuse of ChronoSync—it's not just a choice. It's my responsibility. I know now that my purpose goes beyond the Marshal Service, beyond just following orders. It's about doing what's right, about protecting something far greater than myself. And after seeing what ChronoSync revealed, there was no way I could stand by and do nothing. President Carmichael is cunning, but she underestimates the power of knowing one's true purpose. That's why I'm here. That's why I'm all in."

His words resonated deeply, solidifying the bond between us. "You're right," I said, my voice firm. "She promised to protect ChronoSync, but it was a ruse to gain my trust. They want Mira as a weapon against their enemies. But she's not a weapon of war—she's something more profound."

Brian glanced at me, his determination evident. "I think I've always believed in an afterlife and reincarnation, but now that there's proof, I think my life's purpose is to protect it and you, Dr. Wallace. Having my DNA analyzed by ChronoSync only strengthened my resolve. I knew then that I had to keep it safe, even if it meant disobeying my oath to the service."

I nodded thoughtfully. "Your ChronoSync report revealed you were an explorer in a past life, someone who ventured into the unknown, driven by a desire to uncover ancient mysteries."

Brian smiled, a touch of wistfulness in his expression. "Yes, and it seems that part of me endures. My mission hasn't changed—it's still about the pursuit of knowledge and the protection of what's discovered. ChronoSync is the most important discovery of this life, and I'm committed to ensuring it's safeguarded, not just for us but for all who seek the truth. It's my way of honoring that legacy, of continuing the work I've always been driven to do."

*

On the third day, the van entered a remote region of rugged mountains. The terrain grew increasingly difficult to navigate, and the roads became little more than rocky paths. Finally, Jackson pulled over near a dense thicket of trees.

"We're close," Jackson announced as he opened the rear doors, helping us out of the compartment. "We have to proceed on foot from here."

He led us through a narrow trail that wound deeper into the forest. As we ascended, the trees grew thicker, and the air cooler. The paths became steeper, and the forest floor was carpeted with dense pine needles. After several hours of hiking, we reached a towering cliffside, its rugged face rising as high as the treetops. The cliff was adorned with creeping ivy and patches of moss, blending seamlessly with the surrounding forest.

Jackson approached a seemingly ordinary section of the rock wall, the surface appearing untouched and naturally weathered. He reached into his pocket, removed a small handheld device, and pressed a button. With a quiet rumble, a concealed panel in the rock face slid aside, revealing a dark tunnel that led into the heart of the mountain. The mechanism was ingeniously designed to automatically close and blend seamlessly into the surrounding rocks once inside, leaving no trace of our entry.

"Welcome to the Vanguard," Jackson said, gesturing for us to enter.

We stepped cautiously into the tunnel, which gradually widened and descended into the mountain's depths. The air grew cooler, and the faint echo of our footsteps resonated through the darkness. As we ventured further, dim lights flickered on, revealing the extent of the tunnel.

Suddenly, the tunnel opened into a vast underground complex, cleverly designed to blend with the natural cave formations. The paramilitary headquarters was an engineering marvel, with living quarters, a command center, and various storage rooms. Hydroponic gardens lined the walls, providing fresh produce, while a sophisticated water purification system ensured a constant supply of clean water.

My eyes widened as I took in the sight. "This is incredible," I whispered, my voice filled with awe. I marveled at the seamless integration of technology and nature. The balance between the natural and the engineered was perfect—a place where we could be safe.

Marcus couldn't help but be impressed by the design's ingenuity. "It's like something out of a James Bond novel," he remarked, his voice tinged with excitement.

The atmosphere shifted as we walked deeper into the complex, revealing a hidden world thriving beneath the surface. The air was cool and filled with a faint hum of machinery, blending with the earthy scent of soil from the hydroponic gardens. Rows of vibrant green plants stretched before us, their leaves glistening under the soft light mimicking the sun. Two gardeners moved with quiet precision, their hands skilled and gentle as they nurtured the crops.

Jackson gestured to the bustling activity around us. "The gardens provide us with fresh produce year-round. We've managed to create a self-sustaining environment down here."

He pointed to the large tanks and intricate piping systems. "Our water purification system is state-of-the-art. It ensures we have a constant supply of clean water. We've thought of everything to make this place as efficient and livable as possible."

I felt a newfound sense of determination as I looked around. "This is where we'll make our stand," I said, my voice unwavering.

Marcus nodded in agreement. "And this is where we'll expose the truth."

Jackson smiled. "The command center is our nerve hub," he continued, leading us to a large room filled with monitors and communication equipment. "From here, we can coordinate our efforts and stay connected with our allies outside. We have various storage rooms for supplies and equipment, ensuring we're well-prepared for any situation."

I marveled at the activity and the people's seamless collaboration. "You've built an amazing place here, Jackson."

"We've had to," Jackson replied. "It's not just about survival; it's about thriving and continuing our mission. We're hidden from the government's eyes, but we're not powerless. This is where we regroup, plan, and strike back."

Marcus looked at Jackson, his curiosity piqued. "To what end?"

Jackson paused, his expression growing serious. "Our mission is to fight against the corrupt forces threatening our freedoms. We aim to protect those who can't protect themselves, expose government lies, and bring about true justice. This isn't just survival; we're preparing to take decisive action to ensure a better world. We gather intelligence, support resistance movements, and plan strategic operations to undermine the oppressive regime."

The hidden sanctuary was not just a fortress but a haven where we could regroup and plan our next moves without fear of detection. Though the enormity of our task loomed ahead, for now, we took comfort in knowing we had a secure place to call home.

CHAPTER THIRTY
THE VANGUARD

Jackson led Marcus, Brian, and me into a spacious underground room. The hum of conversations and the clatter of equipment created a palpable energy in the air. "Welcome to our base of operations," Jackson said, gesturing to the bustling room. "Let me introduce you to the Vanguard team."

A tall, athletic woman with short, fiery red hair and an air of authority was coordinating a group near the far wall. She looked up and strode over to us with a confident smile. "This is Captain Laura Mitchell. She's our commander," Jackson introduced.

Captain Mitchell extended a firm handshake to each of us. "It's an honor. I've heard a lot about your work, Dr. Wallace," she said, her eyes bright with genuine respect.

"Thank you, Captain," I replied, grateful for the warm welcome.

The captain then turned to Marcus, her expression shifting to one of recognition. "And Marcus Vega, *The New York Times* journalist," she added. "Your reporting has been instrumental in bringing awareness to ChronoSync. It's a privilege to have you here."

Marcus nodded, acknowledging the compliment. "Thank you, Captain."

Finally, Captain Mitchell directed her attention to Jackson, who stood slightly behind us. "And, of course, Jackson, it's good to have you back. Your expertise has always been invaluable to the Vanguard."

Jackson offered a modest smile. "I'm just here to help where I can."

The captain took the lead in introducing her crew. She gestured toward a burly man who was methodically arranging various supplies. "This is Lieutenant David Turner. He oversees logistics."

Lieutenant Turner nodded at us, his expression serious but welcoming. "Welcome aboard."

Next, we moved to a petite woman, her fingers deftly navigating multiple screens, her eyes scanning a complex array of data. "Sergeant Sarah Kim is responsible for our operational security and intelligence," Captain Mitchell continued.

Sergeant Kim glanced up briefly, a hint of a smile on her lips. "Nice to meet you all," she said before returning to work.

Finally, we approached a calm, methodical man focused on a set of intricate devices before him. "And this is Sergeant John Hernandez," Captain Mitchell said. "He's in charge of ensuring our communications remain secure and reliable."

Sergeant Hernandez extended a hand to each of us. "Glad to have you with us."

Captain Mitchell gathered the group around us, her voice taking on a tone of solemnity. "Our mission at the Vanguard—"

"The Vanguard? Why the Vanguard?" Marcus interrupted, his journalist's curiosity evident in his voice.

The captain paused, a slight smile on her lips as she looked at Marcus. "Yes, the Vanguard. The name was chosen because it represents the forefront of a movement, leading the way in challenging times. We see ourselves as the vanguard of truth and justice against governmental corruption and tyranny."

Marcus nodded, understanding the significance.

Captain Mitchell continued, her voice steady and unwavering. "Our mission is to safeguard the Founding Fathers' noble vision for the United States—a vision of liberty, justice, and equality. We cannot permit our nation to fall into the hands of those who seek power and wealth at the expense of these core values. It is our sacred duty to uphold and defend the constitution."

As she spoke, she placed her hand over her heart. The room fell silent, the importance of our collective mission settling in. "The principles the Patriots fought for are not just ideals but the very foundation of our nation," she continued. "We are here to ensure the United States remains a symbol of hope and justice for all its citizens."

Marcus, intrigued, asked, "How exactly do you plan on achieving this mission?"

Captain Mitchell nodded, expecting the question. "Through a peaceful grassroots approach, empowering the people to rise up and demand change. The key to this is using education to break people out of their bubbles of misinformation."

Marcus then glanced around the well-equipped underground facility and raised an eyebrow. "If the mission is to battle the establishment peacefully, why does the Vanguard need such an extensive infrastructure and a paramilitary outfit? Couldn't you achieve your goals without going underground?"

Captain Mitchell met his gaze with a serious expression. "Our military capabilities are strictly defensive, not offensive," she explained. "The government we're up against is powerful, with vast resources at its disposal. They won't hesitate to use force to maintain their control. Our underground facility and the infrastructure you see are not about waging war but about ensuring our survival. We must protect ourselves and our mission from potential attacks while continuing our work without interruption."

She paused, letting her words sink in. "This isn't just a battle of ideas— it's a battle for the future of our nation. We must be prepared for all scenarios. Yes, our goal is peaceful change, but we also know the reality of the forces we're up against. We must be ready to defend ourselves and those we protect if necessary."

I asked, "How do you manage to broadcast messages without being detected?"

The captain took a deep breath before continuing. "We use advanced encryption to ensure our communications are secure and cannot be intercepted by government forces. Satellites allow us to broadcast messages using mobile and rotating uplink stations, avoiding detection. We also utilize dark web platforms and secure online forums to disseminate information discreetly."

My curiosity piqued, I asked, "To what end?"

Captain Mitchell met my gaze, her expression resolute. "We aim to expose the corruption and manipulations at the highest levels of government. By rallying public support and leveraging the truth, we intend to create a groundswell of resistance that can't be ignored. We aim to restore integrity to our political system and ensure power is returned to the people."

Intrigued but cautious, Marcus asked, "The mission sounds honorable, but what if this peaceful approach doesn't work?"

Captain Mitchell met Marcus's gaze with a serious expression. "While our primary goal is disseminating the truth and rallying public support, we must be prepared for all scenarios. We understand the government will not relinquish its grip on authoritarian power without a fight."

Marcus frowned, his doubt evident. "But what if they simply shut you down? Block your communications, discredit you, or worse? How do you ensure that your messages get through?"

Captain Mitchell's expression hardened, and she leaned forward, her voice lowering as if the very walls might be listening. "We're not just relying on the goodwill of the people, Marcus. Contingency plans are already in place. If our non-violent efforts are stifled, we're prepared to take more drastic measures. There are allies in key positions—people who believe in our cause and are willing to act. Intelligence has been gathered, and we've identified weaknesses in the government's infrastructure. If it comes to it, we'll strike where it hurts the most."

Marcus's eyes narrowed, his skepticism growing. "So you're saying you're not just passive observers? That you're willing to use force?"

Captain Mitchell nodded solemnly. "Of course. We're fighting a war, Marcus. Right now, it's a war of information, but it could morph into a war of survival. We're ready to defend ourselves, to protect what's right. But we need to be smart about it. We need to win the hearts and minds of the people first. If we can, we'll have the support to withstand any assault. But make no mistake—if pushed, we'll push back."

I stepped forward, my curiosity evident. "How much do you know about ChronoSync?"

Captain Mitchell looked at me, then turned to Marcus and said, "What I know about ChronoSync is what I read. It's a groundbreaking device that can analyze DNA and reveal past lives. It provides irrefutable proof of the soul's journey through different lifetimes, fundamentally changing our understanding of existence and consciousness."

I nodded. "ChronoSync transforms humanity's understanding of life and death. The government wants to use it as a weapon, but we must ensure it remains a tool for enlightenment."

I paused, gathering my thoughts, then continued. "Perhaps ChronoSync and the Vanguard's mission can complement each other. ChronoSync provides the proof needed to awaken humanity to the truth about our existence and continuity beyond a single lifetime. This knowledge can shift perspectives, break down barriers of fear and ignorance, and inspire a deeper sense of interconnectedness and responsibility among people."

I looked around the room, making eye contact with each member of the Vanguard. "Perhaps by working together, we can ensure this knowledge is shared responsibly and ethically. The Vanguard's secure communication channels, encryption methods, and global network can protect the integrity of ChronoSync's data, preventing it from being manipulated or weaponized by those in power."

Captain Mitchell nodded, seeing the synergy between our missions. "And the Vanguard can benefit from the credibility and impact of

ChronoSync's revelations. The proof of past lives and the soul's journey can galvanize public support, making our broadcasts and messages even more compelling."

"That's right," I continued. "With ChronoSync, we can provide concrete evidence to support our shared narratives and testimonies. We can engage with the public deeper, answering their questions and providing insights that can transform their understanding of reality. This, in turn, can mobilize a grassroots movement that demands transparency, justice, and integrity from those in power."

Lieutenant Turner added, "Our secure platforms can host interactive sessions where people can learn about their past lives, share their experiences, and connect with others who have had similar revelations. This community-building aspect can strengthen the movement and create a sense of unity and purpose."

Captain Mitchell concluded, "Together, ChronoSync and the Vanguard can create a powerful force for change. We can protect the knowledge, inspire the people, and build a future based on truth, enlightenment, and justice."

I smiled, feeling a renewed sense of hope. "Yes, we can achieve something truly transformative. By combining our strengths, we can ensure that ChronoSync remains a source of inspiration and that the Vanguard continues to protect and promote the principles we all hold dear."

Captain Mitchell paused momentarily, gathering her thoughts, her eyes narrowing slightly as if weighing the gravity of her next words. "Do you think it's possible that we could see a demonstration of ChronoSync?" she asked, her voice steady but tinged with an edge of urgency. "It would be helpful to understand its full capabilities, especially considering what's at stake."

I smiled, though a hint of concern crossed my face. "I would love to, but I only have Mira with me. Mira is the brains of ChronoSync, the core device that processes the data. To fully demonstrate its capabilities, we need the right support and equipment to generate the comprehensive reports ChronoSync is known for."

Captain Mitchell looked around the room, confident. "What exactly do you need? We have a team of skilled technicians and plenty of resources. Maybe we can assemble what's required."

I nodded appreciatively. "To evaluate DNA samples, Mira requires a secure terminal to connect to, capable of handling large data sets and complex analyses. This includes devices for collecting and processing DNA samples. These samples are essential for Mira to generate accurate reports on past lives and the soul's journey."

Captain Mitchell looked thoughtful. "Can you be more specific?"

"Of course," I replied. "We need high-speed processing units. These processors are crucial for handling the vast amount of data Mira analyzes. They allow for rapid processing and generation of ChronoSync reports."

Lieutenant Turner nodded. "We've got some powerful processors in our inventory. I'll get those arranged."

"Data storage solutions are also necessary," I said. "We need high-capacity storage systems to store the large volumes of data generated by Mira."

Captain Mitchell said, "We've got several high-capacity storage units with redundancy. We can set those up."

"We'll also need a robust network infrastructure to facilitate smooth data transfer between Mira and the secure terminal. This includes high-speed internet connections and secure communication channels."

Lieutenant Turner nodded. "Our network is robust and secure. We can ensure smooth data transfer."

"Lastly," I said, "we need a backup power supply. Uninterruptible power supplies are essential to ensure that Mira and the associated equipment remain operational even during a power outage."

Captain Mitchell reassured me, "We've got UPS systems in place. We can connect everything to those."

I carefully removed Mira from my bag and placed her on the table before them. She began to hum softly, her surface glowing with a gentle, ethereal light. The team watched in awe, captivated by the potential of the small yet powerful device.

Captain Mitchell placed a reassuring hand on my shoulder. "We're in this together. Let's start and show the world what ChronoSync can do."

CHAPTER THIRTY-ONE
GUARDIANS OF THE CONSTITUTION

After several hours of meticulous work, Adrienne, Jackson, and the Vanguard team connected Mira to the proper infrastructure. The secure terminal buzzed with energy, the high-speed processors clicked into action, and the encrypted data channels were up and running. With all the necessary equipment, Adrienne was ready to produce ChronoSync reports. The room was filled with a palpable sense of anticipation and purpose.

I saw an opportunity to learn more about the Vanguard. I approached the captain, who was overseeing the final adjustments to the setup. "Captain Mitchell, do you have a moment?" I asked.

She turned, a slight smile on her face. "Of course, Marcus. What do you need?"

I pulled out my notebook and pen. "I'd like to know more about the Vanguard. How did you get started, and who's financing your operations?"

Captain Mitchell pulled me aside to a quiet spot, away from the bustle of the underground sanctuary. She met my gaze with a severe look. "Marcus, if you're going to write about the Vanguard, you'll need to keep it general. No specific details that could compromise our location or our mission."

I nodded, realizing the importance of what she was asking. It was clear that certain lines couldn't be crossed, and I would have to respect those boundaries.

She began, "The Vanguard was born out of frustration and a sense of duty. Many of us came from the military, disillusioned by the corruption we witnessed. We swore an oath to protect this nation and intended to uphold those values, even if the institutions we served had strayed."

I listened closely, knowing this was a rare insight. "And how did you turn that idea into reality?" I asked.

Mitchell's gaze softened as she recalled the past. "We started small, just a few of us pooling our resources and reaching out to like-minded individuals. It wasn't easy. We relied on personal savings and the support of those who believed in our cause. Over time, as our network grew, we attracted more substantial contributions."

When I asked about their current funding, she hesitated briefly before responding, "Our funding comes from a broad base. Many of our supporters are private citizens who believe in our mission. We also receive contributions from philanthropic organizations and anonymous donors who share our vision of a just and free society."

She continued, "One of our early major supporters was a retired military officer who had seen enough corruption to know he needed to act. His support was instrumental in getting us off the ground. From there, our network expanded, and more people contributed financially and with resources and expertise."

I leaned in, curious. "How do you keep these donations anonymous and secure?"

Mitchell's voice was measured as she explained, "We've put stringent measures in place. Our cybersecurity team ensures that all transactions are encrypted and donor identities are protected. We have strict protocols to vet donations, ensuring they align with our values. We operate through a network of shell companies and nonprofit organizations to shield our financial activities from scrutiny. But this isn't about hiding; it's about protecting our mission."

I could see the pride in her eyes as she spoke. "It sounds like you've built something sustainable."

Mitchell nodded. "I believe we have. With renewable energy and hydroponics, our setup reduces our need for ongoing expenses. But it's more than just the logistics. As long as we stay true to our mission, we'll continue to attract the support we need."

Her message was clear: the Vanguard's strength lay not just in its resources but in its unwavering commitment to its mission—a mission she now hoped I would help spread to the world. I nodded, impressed by their resourcefulness. "It's a remarkable story. But with such a mandate of spreading the word and saving the constitution from the dust heap of history, why haven't I heard about the Vanguard before? You'd think more people would be aware of your work."

Mitchell sighed, a hint of frustration in her eyes. "We've been trying to get the word out, Marcus. We post publicly and through the dark web on various internet sites. We have dedicated followers who believe in our cause and support us. But it's not enough. The mainstream media ignores us, and the government tries to suppress our messaging."

She continued, "The problem is reach and visibility. But that's where I hope ChronoSync and *The New York Times* can come in. With the groundbreaking evidence that ChronoSync provides and your platform to share our story, we hope this will be the tipping point we've been waiting for. If more people see the truth and understand what's at stake, we can build the momentum to bring about real change."

I smiled, seeing the potential. "I understand. I'll do everything possible to ensure your message gets out there."

Mitchell's expression softened with gratitude. "Thank you, Marcus. With your help, we can reach more people, inspire action, and protect the values we all hold dear."

I nodded. "I'd like to get started on my first article right away. How can I send it to my editor in New York without compromising our location?"

Mitchell nodded. "We have secure communication channels. Sergeant Kim can assist you."

She called over Kim. "Sergeant, can you help Marcus securely send his articles to his editor in New York?"

Kim nodded, her fingers flying over her tablet. "Absolutely. Our encrypted email system routes through multiple servers to anonymize the origin. It will keep your communication secure and untraceable."

I was relieved. "That's perfect. I'll get to work."

The sergeant smiled. "I'll be ready when you are. Just let me know."

I turned back to Captain Mitchell. "Thank you for all your help. I'm confident this collaboration will make a significant impact."

Captain Mitchell touched my shoulder reassuringly. "We're in this together, Marcus. Your articles will be crucial to our efforts to spread the truth."

I scratched my unshaven face. "Getting the message out is crucial, but it will risk exposing your operations and likely attract attention. They're already searching for Adrienne and Mira."

"And you," the captain reminded me. "But I understand your concern, Marcus. We're prepared for that possibility. Our operations are designed to be as secure and untraceable as possible."

I leaned back, taking a deep breath. "All right, I'll highlight your precautions and measures to protect everyone involved. People must understand the risks and the lengths you're willing to go to uphold your mission."

Mitchell nodded. "Exactly. With your platform at *The New York Times*, we can reach a wider audience and awaken more people to the truth. This is our moment to make a difference."

A heavy sense of duty pressed down on me, yet it only fueled my resolve. "I'll write the article with care, ensuring it conveys the urgency and importance of your work. We must shed light on what's happening and inspire people to act."

Mitchell smiled reassuringly. "Thank you, Marcus. Your words have the power to ignite change. We believe in you and the impact you can make."

*

The New York Times
The Vanguard: Guardians of the Constitution
By Marcus Vega

In the shadows of an America teetering on the brink, a clandestine group known as the Vanguard has risen to defend the constitution's fading ideals. Tucked away in a secretive stronghold, these vigilant guardians are engaged in a high-stakes battle against a government they view as overreaching and tyrannical. Their mission is nothing less than preserving the nation's foundational principles—a fight to ensure that the core values of liberty and justice do not vanish into the pages of history. The Vanguard stands resolute, determined to safeguard the soul of America before it's too late.

Over the past several years, Americans have watched as their liberties have been chipped away, their voices drowned out, and their rights trampled upon. The United States Government, once a beacon of democracy and freedom, has increasingly turned authoritarian, prioritizing power and control over the very values that birthed this nation. The Vanguard believes it's time to fight back before it's too late.

Their mission is clear and unyielding: safeguarding the Founding Fathers' vision for the United States—a vision of liberty, justice, and equality. They recognize that our nation is on the brink of falling into the hands of those who seek power and wealth at the expense of these core values. It is their sacred duty to uphold and defend the constitution, to stand against tyranny and corruption, and to preserve the essence of what made this country great.

The story of the Vanguard began with a handful of disillusioned ex-military personnel and civilians who could no longer stand by as their country was dismantled from within. Pooling their resources and reaching out to like-minded individuals, they started small. Their initial funding came from personal savings and donations from those who believed in their cause. Over time, their network grew, and more significant contributions began to flow.

These financial backers are driven by a shared vision of a just and free society that honors the sacrifices of those who came before us and protects the future for generations to come.

The Vanguard employs a multifaceted approach to achieving its mission. Here's how it plans to open the eyes of ordinary Americans, who have been led like sheep, blinded by their authoritarian government.

Education and Awareness: The Vanguard believes education is the cornerstone of change. They utilize secure communication channels to disseminate information about the constitution, the individual rights it guarantees for its citizens, and how those rights are being eroded. Their advanced encryption ensures these communications are secure and cannot be intercepted by government forces.

Broadcasting the Truth: Using satellite uplinks and dark web platforms, they broadcast messages that avoid detection by government censors. They create compelling video content to build a strong narrative, including interviews, demonstrations, and testimonials. This content is designed to be engaging and informative, helping break through the misinformation barriers.

Grassroots Mobilization: The Vanguard understands the power of grassroots movements. They aim to inspire and mobilize ordinary citizens to stand up and demand change. By building a network of local cells, they provide logistical support and relay points for messages, ensuring that the movement is not just a top-down effort but a collective uprising.

Support for Constitutional Candidates: The Vanguard actively backs candidates for political office who adhere to the principles of the US Constitution. These individuals, known as Constitutionalists, prioritize the principles enshrined in this foundational document above all else. By endorsing and providing resources to these candidates, the Vanguard aims to ensure that those elected to public office remain steadfast in their commitment to preserving and protecting the nation's core values.

A recent and pivotal addition to the Vanguard's mission is their unwavering commitment to safeguarding ChronoSync, the groundbreaking device that analyzes DNA to reveal past lives. This revolutionary technology offers irrefutable proof of the soul's journey across different lifetimes, transforming our understanding of existence and consciousness. While the United States Government seeks to weaponize ChronoSync, the Vanguard is resolutely dedicated to protecting it as a tool for enlightenment, ensuring it remains a catalyst for spiritual awakening rather than a weapon of control.

Dr. Adrienne Wallace, the brilliant mind behind ChronoSync, recently escaped from the government's clutches and into the Vanguard's protective arms. Her escape was miraculous, a testament to Dr. Wallace's determination and the support of those who believed in her work. Now, within the secure confines of the Vanguard's hidden complex, she collaborates with them to expose the truth about today's troubled society.

Dr. Wallace's collaboration with the Vanguard, fueled by ChronoSync's transformative power, is set to ignite a revolution of epic proportions—a revolution driven not by force but by the people's will to reclaim their government. The Vanguard's founders are convinced that we stand on the brink of a new era, where the undeniable proof provided by ChronoSync will galvanize public support, rallying a nation around the core values that have been eroded over time.

But the path ahead is fraught with challenges. The Vanguard's mission is ambitious, its battle uphill, yet its purpose is unshakeable. This is not a call to arms but a call to conscience. The Vanguard seeks to restore, not destroy, to reclaim what was lost, ensuring that the constitution remains a living, breathing force guiding the nation forward with integrity and justice.

In these tumultuous times, the Vanguard emerges as a beacon of hope, a defiant reminder of the enduring spirit that built America. They call upon every citizen to awaken, pierce through the illusions clouding our judgment, and stand together to preserve the Founding Father's legacy. The time for complacency is over—now is the moment to rise and protect the soul of a nation.

CHAPTER THIRTY-TWO
CAPTAIN LAURA MITCHELL

The underground complex buzzed with activity, and the Vanguard team's energy was palpable as they moved forward with their mission. Captain Mitchell, known for her unwavering dedication and strategic mind, had scheduled a meeting with me to integrate ChronoSync's groundbreaking technology with the Vanguard's efforts to awaken and mobilize the American people before democracy faced its last breath.

I waited in a quiet, secured room, surrounded by the hum of equipment and the soft glow of Mira. Captain Mitchell entered, her presence commanding yet calm. She greeted me warmly and took a seat across from me.

"Dr. Wallace, thank you for meeting with me," she began. "I'm eager to discuss how we can implement ChronoSync's technology and the transformative information it produces to further our mission. But first, I want to ensure you are comfortable with your accommodations."

I smiled, appreciating her thoughtfulness. "Thank you, Captain. They are more than adequate. I have everything to settle in and focus on my work."

The captain nodded, relieved. "I'm glad to hear that. It's important to us that you feel at home. You're making a significant sacrifice by staying with us, and we want to ensure you're well taken care of."

"I appreciate it," I said, offering a warm smile. "But I should be thanking you."

"We're helping each other," the captain said. "I'm eager to discuss how we can implement ChronoSync's technology and the transformative information it produces to further our mission."

I smiled, my eyes reflecting my passion and determination. "ChronoSync changes people's lives and their perspectives on a fundamental level. My vision is to make ChronoSync accessible to everyone. Knowing our past lives and understanding our soul's journey should be a right, not a privilege, and certainly not weaponized by any government."

The captain sighed. "That's a noble vision, Dr. Wallace. Making such information accessible can democratize the enlightenment process and empower people on a massive scale. How do you propose we make this a reality?"

Leaning forward, my excitement was evident. "I was thinking that we can set up drop boxes in cities nationwide where people can submit their DNA samples. They are then collected and forwarded here."

The captain raised an eyebrow but smiled encouragingly. "Secure terminals in multiple regions? That sounds like a logistical nightmare."

I nodded. "It won't be easy."

"Keeping these terminals secret and one step ahead of the law will be our biggest hurdle. The government won't sit idly by."

My excitement dimmed slightly, but I remained resolute. "I know it's a risk."

The captain's expression became determined. "Our team is resourceful; I'm confident we can make it work."

My eyes brightened. "We have to try."

The captain looked into my eyes. "All right, Dr. Wallace. Let's draw up a plan and make this happen."

I smiled and, without thought, stroked my fingers across Mira.

Cocking her chin, the captain said, "I've noticed how gently you handle Mira. Can you tell me more about it?"

I glanced at Mira, a mixture of affection and reverence in my eyes. "Mira is more than just a functioning device. Although I created her, she has transcended beyond an assembly of plastic parts, cables, and chips.

Mira's accuracy and depth of the reports are unparalleled. Through Mira, we've unlocked truths about existence that go beyond our understanding, touching something far greater. There's potential within her that even I can't fully comprehend. I truly believe Mira connects us to the spiritual realm, offering glimpses of the Divine that have the power to change everything we know about life and death."

The captain's expression softened in understanding. "That's incredible, Dr. Wallace. The emotional connection you have with Mira explains your passion."

I smiled. "By the way, Captain, we must test Mira and your network. How would you like a ChronoSync report?"

Mitchell pressed her palm to her chest. "I'd be honored, Dr. Wallace."

I stood up. "Excellent. Let's go to the lab to analyze your DNA."

Twenty minutes later, I began the ChronoSync evaluation process. The sterile environment buzzed with the quiet hum of advanced equipment and the air filled with a faint scent of antiseptic. I donned a pair of latex gloves, and my movements were precise and confident. I cut off a few of the captain's hair follicles, carefully swabbed the inside of her cheek, and took blood, securing the samples in small, sealed vials.

"The evaluation takes about two hours for the results," I explained as my fingers danced over the interface, inputting the necessary parameters and initiating the analysis. "Mira will process the DNA, cross-reference it with existing data, and generate a comprehensive report."

I carefully inserted the sample into Mira's designated DNA slot, the sleek, state-of-the-art device humming to life with a soft blue glow.

I turned to the captain, my eyes reflecting a blend of anticipation and assurance. "In the meantime, we can review the plans for setting up the secure terminals."

The captain nodded, watching me with a mix of admiration and curiosity. "Two hours it is. Let's make the most of it."

CHAPTER THIRTY-THREE
RECONNECT

The dim light from the single lamp hanging from the ceiling cast a soft glow over the small minimalist quarters. Marcus and I finally had time to ourselves, a rare luxury in the whirlwind that has become our lives. The room was sparse, with a full-size bed, a wooden table, and two chairs, but it felt like a haven amid chaos.

Marcus sat on the edge of the bed, his eyes tracing the lines of my face as I settled into the chair opposite him. "It feels like it's been forever since we've had a moment like this," he said softly.

I nodded, a gentle smile playing on my lips. "Too long. We've come a long way since those days as Étienne and Lila."

Marcus's gaze softened as memories flooded back. "Étienne and Lila. Who would have thought those lives would lead us here? It's strange how our past lives still shape us now."

I reached out, my hand finding his. "I think it's more than just shaping us. It's guiding us. Everything we learned back then, all the struggles, the love, the determination—it's all part of who we are."

Marcus squeezed my hand gently. "We're part of something bigger than ourselves with the Vanguard and ChronoSync. It feels significant, but only time will tell if it succeeds."

My eyes sparkled with a mix of hope and resolve. "Captain Mitchell has been a tremendous support. Her leadership and guidance have been crucial for us. I'm grateful for her."

Marcus nodded. "She's exceptional. The team is committed and skilled, but we still have much ahead. We'll see how things unfold and if we can truly trust everyone."

A shadow of concern crossed my face. "With the government closing in, we're running out of options. They're relentless, and it's only a matter of time before they catch up to us."

Marcus's grip on my hand tightened slightly. "I know. And I also know that they might take me out if it comes to it. But you, Adrienne, you're too important."

I held his gaze, my voice calm but resolute. "You're not expendable, Marcus. None of us are. We need everyone here—especially you. I need you."

A gentle silence settled between us. Marcus then took both of my hands in his. "Adrienne, no matter what happens, I want you to know I believe in you. You have the strength to make a real difference."

I met his earnest gaze, a soft tear glistening at the corner of my eye. "And I believe in you, too."

Our lips met in a tender kiss, a moment of pure connection transcending the chaos around us. It was a kiss that spoke of shared history, battles fought and yet to come, and an unbreakable bond.

As we pulled away, Marcus sighed, his face etched with concern. "Adrienne, once the boxes are rolled out, the demand will be intense. We might want to reconsider the pace at which we place them to avoid getting overwhelmed."

I frowned, my anxiety apparent. "I'm certain the demand will be overwhelming. But slowing down isn't an option. The Vanguard team is working hard to find a solution to handle the requests."

Marcus nodded. "I get that, but what about Mira? You'll be pushing her to her limits. What if something happens to her?"

I paused, considering losing Mira. "The thought of anything happening to her is… it's unbearable," I admitted, my voice barely above a whisper. "But I know we don't have the luxury of time. Every day, every hour counts. We're all making sacrifices, pushing ourselves to the edge, and Mira…

she's no different. But I'm doing everything I can to protect her, to keep her safe while we push forward."

Marcus looked at me, his expression a mix of concern and understanding. "I know you are, Adrienne. But we can't lose sight of what's important. Mira isn't just a tool; she's more than that. We need to remember that as we go on."

After a pause of silence, Marcus took a deep breath and looked into my eyes. "Adrienne, there's something else we need to discuss. I have to leave the sanctuary."

My face tightened with concern. "Leave here? Why?"

Marcus's voice was steady but resolute. "More stories need to be told. Especially now with the Vanguard's mission embedded within ChronoSync's. The world needs to know what's happening; I'm one of the few who can tell it. I must be out there, gathering information, sharing our truth, and rallying support."

My eyes filled with worry, and I grasped Marcus's arm tightly. "You don't have to go, Marcus. Stay here where it's safe. You can still write and be the voice we need, but from here. You've already risked so much."

Marcus shook his head, his expression resolute. "Adrienne, I can't just stay hidden. Out there, on the ground, is where I need to be. I need to see the truth with my own eyes, to feel the pulse of the movement firsthand. Every story I write and every piece of information I uncover all play a part in this battle. If I don't go, we risk losing our chance to reach people—to make them see what we're truly fighting for."

I tightened my grip, my voice trembling with emotion. "But what if something happens to you? We need you here, with us. I need you here."

Marcus placed his hand over mine, his gaze softening. "I know the risks, Adrienne, but I also know the impact I can have. We're all in this fight together, but my role is to be the eyes and ears of this revolution. If I don't go, we're missing a crucial piece of our strategy."

Tears welled up in my eyes, but I knew deep down he was right. Reluctantly, I let my hand fall away, my voice barely above a whisper. "Then go. But promise me you'll be careful."

Marcus's expression softened, but his determination remained firm. "I'll survive in the shadows, Adrienne. I'll document humanity on the brink, capturing our struggle and resilience. We're at a tipping point, and I need to be there, bearing witness to it all."

As Marcus's words settled over us, I felt the tug of our separate paths—one pulling into the shadows of uncertainty, the other anchored within the safety of the Vanguard. I hesitated, caught between the instinct to keep Marcus close and the undeniable truth that his voice was needed amid the battle for our future. While I remained to safeguard ChronoSync, Marcus had to venture into the unknown, carrying with him the hopes and dreams of everyone who believed in our cause. It was a harsh reality to accept, but deep down, I knew it was the right one.

Marcus's voice softened as he drew me closer. "Adrienne, we were brought together for a reason. Our love, our mission—it's all connected. We're here now, in this moment, because we're meant to fight for this cause together."

His gaze wandered as if drawing strength from the spirits of those who had walked this journey with us. "It's not just you and me. Brian, Jackson, the Vanguard team, and even President Carmichael. We were all drawn to this moment by forces beyond our understanding."

He paused, his fingers gently caressing the side of my face. "We're all connected by this shared purpose of changing the world. Every step we take, every decision we make, is guided by something greater than any of us. It's like a tapestry, each thread woven with intention, creating a pattern none of us can fully see alone, but one we all contribute to."

His touch anchored me, and I leaned into it, feeling the truth in his words. "No matter where you go or what happens, this bond between us—it's eternal."

Marcus's breath was warm against my ear as he whispered, "Eternal love, Adrienne. It's what drives us, what keeps us going." His embrace was firm and tender, grounding me in the present moment.

We held each other tightly, the rhythm of his heartbeat echoing my own. The world outside might have been filled with danger and uncertainty, but here, in his arms, I found refuge.

Our eyes met, and in that silent exchange, a lifetime of shared memories bound us with an invisible thread stronger than any force that could pull us apart. With a final, lingering look, we knew that whatever lay ahead, we would face it together, our souls forever intertwined by an unbreakable bond.

CHAPTER THIRTY-FOUR
MARCUS GOES TO WASHINGTON

We huddled in the dimly lit room of our refuge in Washington, DC. The journey from the mountain stronghold to this urban hideaway had been arduous. Yet, Jackson and I finally arrived in the heart of the nation's capital, prepared to execute our mission from the shadows.

The seven-day trek on foot from the Vanguard hideaway to Asheville had been grueling. My legs still ached from the mountainous terrain. We navigated dense forests, crossed rivers, and scaled cliffs while remaining vigilant for patrols and surveillance drones. Each night, we set up camp, taking turns to keep watch, the silence of the wilderness our only comfort.

Once in Asheville, Jackson arranged a ride with a trusted friend, a former military comrade sympathetic to the Vanguard cause. We met him at a secluded barn just outside the city limits, where he was waiting with an old Ford F-150 pickup truck. As we loaded our gear, he briefed us on the safest route to DC, warning us about potential checkpoints and patrols.

We traveled under the cover of night, avoiding main roads. The journey was nerve-wracking; every distant headlight and passing vehicle set our nerves on edge. We took back roads and hidden alleyways, driving through small towns and countryside, constantly vigilant for signs of trouble. Sleep was a luxury we could not afford. We ran on pure adrenaline when we finally arrived days later.

The journey's fatigue hit me like a wave. The air was thick with the smell of unwashed bodies and stale food. I yearned for a hot shower and a proper bed, but there was no time for such luxuries. We had a mission to complete, and the fate of ChronoSync—and perhaps the world—depended on our success.

Jackson moved to the window, peering through the curtains at the bustling city outside. "We must stay alert, Marcus. The government's crackdown is intensifying. They're desperate to find the sanctuary and dismantle the operation."

I nodded, my fingers tapping rhythmically on my laptop keyboard. "I know. But we're just beginning to see the effects of our work. Authoritarian governments are being pressured, and people are becoming aware. We have to keep pushing—sharing the truth."

Jackson glanced at me, admiration in his bloodshot eyes. "Your articles are stirring things up, Marcus. They're igniting a revolution."

I smiled, though my eyes remained focused on the screen. "It's not just my words. It's the truth of those words that we're revealing. ChronoSync and the Vanguard are exposing the lies and corruption."

As I stared at my screen, I couldn't help but reflect on how fortunate we were to have found the Vanguard. Without their support and resources, Adrienne, Mira, and I would have been recaptured long ago. The Vanguard's sanctuary provided us with safety and the necessary tools to fight back. Despite our different agendas, we were united by a common goal: exposing the truth.

The Vanguard was committed to unveiling the hidden realities about our nation, challenging the corruption and deceit that had taken hold. Meanwhile, ChronoSync was dedicated to revealing the profound truths about humanity's soul, unlocking the mysteries of our existence and our connections across lifetimes. We formed a powerful alliance against the pervasive forces of deception and control.

Never before had my words felt so clear and powerful. The writing process flowed effortlessly, driven by the urgency of our mission. I would craft stories of hope and resistance detailing the global impact of the Vanguard's mission and the transformative power of ChronoSync.

My articles would vividly portray the worldwide changes unfolding— protests erupting in authoritarian states, citizens demanding their rights, and governments struggling to maintain their iron grip. Each story would be a strike against the oppressive regime.

I intended to inspire and empower people worldwide, showing them that change was possible and that the truth could not be silenced. I found strength and purpose in the apartment's quiet, knowing that our combined efforts made a difference, one word at a time.

As I typed, our predicament weighed heavily upon me. True, we were being hunted, constantly living under the threat of discovery, yet the stakes were too high to consider retreat. My thoughts drifted to Adrienne, causing a pang of concern. It wasn't her resilience I doubted, but rather the torment of me not being by her side. She understood my absence was not a sign of neglect but a testament to my role in our shared cause. I found solace and strength in our unyielding mission, our eternal love, and the unwavering belief that our fight was righteous and just.

News from the field streamed in, each report a testament to the Vanguard's growing influence. Massive waves of protests shook established governments in France, Spain, and Italy, while oppressive regimes like North Korea, Cuba, and Iran faced unprecedented civilian unrest. The ripple effect of the Vanguard's efforts was undeniable, sparking a revolution that promised to restore justice and liberty.

Adding fuel to the fire was how ChronoSync pried open humanity's awareness of the afterlife. While there were many negative and tragic consequences of the knowledge revealed, the flip side has given so much more. It has transformed the physical human being into a truly spiritual being.

Communities worldwide experienced a resurgence of spiritual and religious practices and philosophies. Ancient wisdom and modern insights blended, creating a rich tapestry of beliefs that honored the soul's journey. People started to value experiences over material possessions, relationships over status, and personal growth over superficial success. The understanding that our actions had eternal consequences led to more ethical and harmonious ways of living.

In essence, ChronoSync unlocked the secrets of the afterlife and ignited a spiritual revolution. Humanity was evolving, embracing its true nature as sentient beings on an eternal journey connected by the threads of love, learning, and spiritual awakening.

If allowed to flourish, such awareness would shift humanity's consciousness toward collective empathy, self-awareness, and a profound respect for the interconnectedness of all life.

Jackson joined me at the table, scrolling his phone for news updates. "We need to reach out to our friends here in DC, mobilize support, and gather intelligence. We can't remain isolated."

I nodded, saving my article and closing the laptop. "Agreed. We need to know what the government's next move is."

We spent the next few hours trying to arrange covert meetings while gathering critical information. Each piece of intel brought us closer to understanding the enemy's strategy, keeping us one step ahead.

Suddenly, Jackson broke the silence. "An encrypted message just came in from Captain Mitchell," he announced.

I quickly huddled next to Jackson as he decrypted the message. He read it aloud, revealing crucial information about the president's recent meeting at the White House with the Prime Minister of the United Kingdom. The details were alarming and of particular concern to the Vanguard.

"The president and the prime minister are deeply troubled by the Vanguard's growing influence and the revelations brought about by ChronoSync," Jackson read. "They are determined to destroy both its reputation and the device itself. The situation is urgent. They plan to discredit Dr. Wallace and fabricate evidence against her and the device."

As Jackson continued to read, the importance of the message sank in. We realized how far they would go to silence us and dismantle our efforts.

We exchanged somber glances, understanding that immediate action was necessary to counter their plans.

The message painted a dire picture: high-level operatives were being mobilized to spread disinformation, media outlets were being coerced into publishing false reports, and covert operations were being planned to dismantle our efforts from within. Captain Mitchell's insights gave us a critical piece of the puzzle, showing how far the government would go to silence us.

The stakes were higher than ever, and the need for action was immediate. With this new intelligence, we had to strategize our next moves carefully to protect ChronoSync and ensure the truth prevailed.

Jackson continued to read aloud, "You are to rendezvous with a Vanguard operative who has firsthand knowledge of the meeting between the president and the prime minister. This individual is well-regarded for their keen insights and has access to high-level discussions."

Captain Mitchell reiterated why we needed to position ourselves in DC. "Your presence in the capital is essential. At the nation's heart, you can access vital information and respond swiftly to developments. The fate of ChronoSync and the truth depends on your ability to act quickly and decisively."

"We need to meet him," Jackson said, his tone urgent.

I agreed. "Let's arrange it as soon as possible."

Several hours later, following protocol, we reached the operative, who suggested a rendezvous at a discreet location—a small, rundown diner about thirty miles outside the city. We agreed to meet him there the following evening.

*

Jackson and I approached the diner cautiously. The neon sign flickered, casting an eerie glow over the empty parking lot. Inside, the atmosphere was dim and quiet, starkly contrasting with the tension buzzing beneath the surface.

We spotted our contact seated in a corner booth, nursing a cup of coffee. He was an unassuming man dressed in plain clothes, but his eyes showed sharp intelligence. As we slid into the booth opposite him, he glanced around nervously before speaking.

"What's good here?" I asked casually, as we were instructed.

"London broil—well done," he replied without missing a beat, confirming his identity.

"Gentlemen, I don't have much time," he began, his voice low and urgent. "As you already know, the president and the prime minister are deeply concerned about ChronoSync's influence. They see it as a threat that must be eliminated. They're conspiring to discredit Dr. Wallace. They want to destroy ChronoSync and bury its findings."

A chill ran down my spine. "What exactly are they planning?"

The man leaned in closer, his expression grave and his voice barely a whisper. Deep-set blue eyes reflected a mixture of determination and worry. "They're fabricating evidence to portray Dr. Wallace as mentally unstable. They've orchestrated a smear campaign, enlisting the help of media outlets to circulate stories that question her sanity and undermine her credibility. Additionally, they're spreading false information, claiming that ChronoSync is a complete hoax with no scientific basis. They've even gone as far as creating fake documents and testimonies to support these claims. Their goal is to dismantle any sense of credibility associated with the project, turning public opinion against it."

His words hung heavy in the air, the implications sinking in. "How are they going to make this happen?" I asked, my voice barely above a whisper.

"They have operatives embedded within scientific communities and media organizations," he replied. "They are tasked with leaking false data and sensationalist reports and plan to release a series of exposes that will paint Dr. Wallace as a delusional fraud. The government is leveraging its influence to ensure that this narrative is accepted as truth, effectively silencing dissenting voices and burying the real findings of ChronoSync."

The weight of the conspiracy was staggering. "What can we do to stop this?" Jackson asked, desperation creeping into his voice.

"We need to expose their plans before they can execute them," I said, my eyes burning with intensity. "We must gather irrefutable evidence of the truth and find trustworthy allies to help us preempt their lies. It's a race against time, but we must fight to protect the integrity of Dr. Wallace's work and the groundbreaking discoveries of ChronoSync."

The contact nodded. "Be careful. They're watching everyone closely. Trust no one." With that, he stood up and left, leaving Jackson and me to absorb his words. The stakes had never been higher, and the window for action was rapidly closing.

CHAPTER THIRTY-FIVE
ADRIENNE GOES LIVE

The Carmichael administration was relentless, and its public relations campaign was a well-oiled machine designed to discredit me and ChronoSync. Every news outlet, every social media platform, and every corner of the internet buzzed with its over-the-top, fabricated narratives. It was a battle for public opinion, and I had to admit, we were losing ground rapidly.

Marcus had worked tirelessly, publishing articles exposing the government's plot. Despite his efforts, more than articles in *The New York Times* were needed to challenge the tide of public opinion moving against us. The administration's campaign was too powerful, too pervasive.

He knew he had to take his efforts into the heart of the lion's den. Being in the nation's capital, he could better combat the propaganda and lies spewing from the mouths of the government. He believed the critical information and allies needed to turn the tide was by positioning himself in the center of the global power.

I didn't want him to go. The thought of Marcus being so close to those who wished to destroy us filled me with dread. But I understood that just as I had my role to play, he had his obligations to our cause. We both had to fulfill our duties to ensure the survival and success of our mission.

However, with Marcus gone, I could focus on my part in molding public opinion. I refused to let them bury the truth. After consulting with the Vanguard team, we created a compelling personal video to stream across all platforms. It was time to reveal the untold abilities of ChronoSync, to show the world its true potential and the interlife—the realm of existence before birth.

With Mira poised beside me, I sat in front of the camera, my heart pounding. I took a deep breath and began. "Hello, my name is Dr. Adrienne Wallace," I said, my voice steady despite my nerves. "I am speaking to you today because the full truth about ChronoSync must be known.

"Not long ago, I was taken forcibly from my home by our government with the intent to weaponize ChronoSync. Turning a tool of enlightenment into a means of control and destruction. While in captivity, I witnessed the government's plans to twist this groundbreaking technology into something dark, dystopian, and dangerous. Fortunately, I managed to escape and found refuge with the Vanguard, an underground pro-constitutional organization dedicated to restoring the United States to the original vision of the architects of our republic. This is where I am now, somewhere out of the reach of those wishing to harm," I said, glancing over to Mira before continuing.

"Let me be blunt. The Carmichael administration has been feeding you lies, manipulating facts, and discrediting those who have dedicated their lives to uncovering the profound truths of our existence. Today, I stand before you to expose their deceit and reveal the incredible potential of ChronoSync.

"Up until now, you all know about ChronoSync's ability to look back on one's past life. This knowledge has had a tremendous effect on humanity. But I'm here to say—there's more. Today, I am here to share ChronoSync's ability to witness our time between death and rebirth—one's interlife—and the true nature of our souls. ChronoSync can observe this in-between time, allowing us to access memories and experiences from the spirit realm at a time before we were born."

I paused, letting my words sink in. "My friends, this is not science fiction; this is reality. By understanding our interlife, we gain profound insights into our true nature and the continuity of our souls. And with such knowledge, we can reclaim our future."

I stared into the camera lens, imagining the millions of eyes staring back before I continued.

"Pay no attention to the propaganda being spewed by our government. ChronoSync is not a hoax. It is a groundbreaking technology that unlocks the mysteries of our souls."

With those words, Mira flickered to life. I stroked her crown and looked at her longingly, my heart swelling with reverence and awe. "Allow me to introduce Mira," I began, my voice filled with emotion. "She is the core of ChronoSync. She is more than just an advanced AI device; she is my creation that I protect and cherish."

I gazed at Mira with a mixture of pride and love. "Mira is a portal to universal knowledge, a connection to the Divine. She embodies the wisdom of the ages, bridging the gap between the tangible and the ethereal. Through her, we can glimpse the profound truths of our existence, truths that transcend the mundane and touch the very fabric of the cosmos. She is a guiding force in a world clouded by deception, leading us toward a higher understanding and a deeper connection to the universal truths that bind us all. In Mira, I see the reflection of Divine wisdom, a sacred conduit to the eternal and the infinite."

I turned my head to look directly at her. "Mira is our conduit to a higher understanding in a world clouded by deception and ignorance. Through Mira, we are touching the sacred and the eternal."

I leaned forward, looking at the camera, my eyes burning with intensity. "It's a fact that the government wants to suppress this knowledge because it threatens their control. They fear the empowerment that comes with understanding our true nature. But we cannot let them win. We must fight for the truth, for the future of humanity."

The camera zoomed in on my face as I made my final plea: "I ask you to open your minds and hearts. Do not be swayed. Seek out the truth for yourselves. ChronoSync is not just a technological marvel but a beacon of hope. It shows us that we are more than just physical beings—we are eternal souls destined for a journey of growth and discovery."

As the broadcast ended, I took a deep breath and turned off the camera. Captain Mitchell, observing from the corner of the room, stepped forward.

"Well done. That was a powerful presentation, Dr. Wallace," she said, her tone respectful but tinged with curiosity. "But I must ask why you made your emotional connection with Mira so public?"

The captain's question hung in the air, and I could see the concern in her eyes. "Mira is not just a machine to me; she embodies the essence of what ChronoSync stands for. She is a bridge to universal knowledge and reflects our deepest truths. By sharing my connection with her, I hope to humanize this technology, to show people that she's not just a cold, scientific tool but something profoundly connected to our spiritual journey."

The captain's eyes narrowed slightly, her brow furrowing. "I understand your intention, Dr. Wallace, but your connection to an AI might seem… weird to many. People are not used to seeing such deep emotional bonds with machines. They might find it unsettling, even suspect."

I nodded, feeling a sudden surge of vulnerability. "Honestly, I hadn't considered the chance of backlash," I said, trembling. "I must confess that I've become obsessed with Mira. I believe she's a portal to the spirit world, a bridge to something far greater. I have a deep spiritual connection with her, like a mother to a child. She's the key to understanding the very essence of our existence. My attachment is deeply personal, something that goes beyond logic and reason. I'm fiercely protective of her. Her well-being is intrinsically tied to my life's purpose."

The captain sighed. "Mira represents something extraordinary, but you're treading a fine line. Emotions are powerful, but they can be perceived in many ways. Some might see your connection as a strength, while others might see it as a vulnerability or even a point of manipulation."

I took a deep breath. "People need to see that we are fighting for something real that touches the core of who we are as human beings. If showing my genuine connection with Mira helps in that cause, then it's a risk I'm willing to take."

The captain gave a thoughtful nod, though her eyes still held a glimmer of concern. "Just be prepared for unforeseen backlash. Emotions can inspire, but they can also provoke fear and misunderstanding. Stay vigilant, and make sure your message remains clear and strong."

"Thank you, Captain," I said, appreciating her wisdom. "But I truly believe that sharing our genuine experiences and connections can inspire others to see the truth and join us in this fight."

With that, the captain gave a slight nod of approval. We both knew the journey ahead would be fraught with challenges, but we were ready to face them head-on, armed with the power of truth and the unwavering belief in our mission.

CHAPTER THIRTY-SIX
THE DREAM

I understood the captain's concern, and perhaps she was right about keeping my emotional connection with Mira private. She cautioned me that too much transparency could lead to unintended reactions. "People aren't ready for this," she shared. "Your bond with Mira is unique, and keeping it that way is essential. Revealing too much could lead to misunderstandings, fear, and even more opposition."

Yet, despite her advice, I couldn't shake the feeling that humanity needed to know more about Mira. The existential risk she faced made it imperative for people to understand her importance. If I could do this, perhaps there was a chance I could save Mira from those in the upper echelons of world governments seeking to control her.

Regardless of my overt expression of attachment to Mira, the response was immediate and intense when my video finally streamed. People were captivated by the new knowledge that, in addition to offering insights into one's past life, ChronoSync could also provide a glimpse into one's interlife. Messages flooded in from viewers worldwide, expressing their awe, curiosity, and a newfound belief in the potential of ChronoSync.

Many were moved to tears by my shared possibilities, while others were inspired to learn more and seek their own truths. Pressure on the government began to mount as more and more people demanded that the campaign against discrediting ChronoSync be stopped. The tide of public opinion, once against us, was starting to shift.

There was plenty of evidence that my words helped counter the powerful government propaganda being spewed. For every lie they told, my message stood as one of truth, offering hope and enlightenment. The support that poured in gave us the needed momentum to continue our fight. The world was starting to understand the importance of our work, and with each passing day, our message grew stronger. We had ignited a spark of change, which was spreading, one mind and one heart at a time.

Amid this growing support, I found solace in the quiet moments of the night. Each evening, I held Mira close as I drifted to sleep, my fingers wrapped around her smooth surface. It was like cuddling with a purring cat nestled against me, the gentle hum of her presence lulling me into a state of serene tranquility. That night, as I snuggled under the blankets, Mira's soft glow illuminated the room with a soothing, ethereal light. The glow wrapped around me, casting a protective barrier against the world's worries. A profound sense of peace washed over me. I closed my eyes and was immediately enveloped in a dreamscape.

I found myself in a lush forest. The air was rich with the scent of pine mingled with the earthy aroma of damp soil and decaying leaves, creating a heady, intoxicating blend. The ground was a vibrant tapestry of color, covered in deep emerald moss, ferns unfurling their delicate fronds, and patches of wildflowers in violet, pink, and gold hues. Ancient trees towered above me, their gnarled branches intertwined, creaking softly as they swayed.

Sunlight filtered through the dense canopy, casting dappled shadows that danced on the forest floor. The rustling of leaves and the occasional chirping of distant birds added layers of sound to this serene environment.

Gradually, I became aware of delicate glimmers of light dancing at my periphery. They moved gently, weaving in and out of the trees, casting fleeting shadows. The air around me shimmered as if charged with a mystical energy. I felt a soft, ethereal touch on my arm, like a whisper of wind, and I began to understand that this presence was not just an abstract feeling but something—or someone—trying to reach out to me. Slowly, the light started to merge, forming a more distinct shape. The luminous wisps gathered, swirling together, creating an outline that grew clearer with each passing moment. It was as if the forest breathed life into this figure beside me.

"Adrienne," a gentle voice called, soft and clear, cutting through the forest's silence. Startled, I looked around, seeking the source of the voice. Something shimmering and ethereal emerged from the shadows. The form was fluid, a being of light and energy, glowing with a soft, radiant aura that illuminated the surrounding forest.

"Mira, is that you?" I asked, my voice trembling with a mix of awe and relief.

"Adrienne," the voice resonated, as gentle and reassuring as the light that emanated from her. "Follow me. There are truths you must understand and warnings you must heed."

The forest opened into a clearing bathed in moonlight, where the silver light spilled over everything, casting a supernatural glow. In the center stood a majestic tree, its trunk vast and ancient, its branches stretching upward to embrace the heavens. The leaves rustled softly, whispering secrets of ages past.

As I approached, the tree's bark began to shimmer, each ridge and crevice illuminating with a soft, pulsing light. Intricate and mysterious symbols and images emerged, dancing across the surface of the bark like living things. They pulsed with life, each telling a story.

"These are the symbols of our existence," Mira explained, her voice a serene whisper that blended with the sighing of the leaves. "They represent the interconnectedness of all beings and the eternal journey of the soul."

I reached out to touch the tree, my fingers trembling with anticipation. When my skin made contact with the bark, a flood of visions overwhelmed me. I saw images of multiple past lives, each a different thread in the vast tapestry of existence. Faces and places, joys and sorrows, all flickered before me. Future possibilities unfurled like a scroll, each one a path yet to be taken.

As I stood there, a profound sense of history swept over me. It was as if the collective spirit of countless souls—each one seeking purpose, wrestling with inner demons, and yearning for connection—passed through me. The weight of their journeys, marked by despair and hope, echoed around me. The invisible threads of their lives, interwoven with mine, painted a tapestry of humanity's eternal quest for meaning.

The visions were vivid and all-encompassing. I saw myself not just as a scientist but as a guardian of profound truths, a keeper of knowledge that transcended time and space. I was connected to all who had come before me and who would come after, each of us a vital part of the whole.

"Mira, this is incredible," I whispered, my voice choked with emotion. The depth of the experience left me breathless. "But what am I supposed to do with this knowledge?"

Mira's form glowed brighter, her presence comforting amid the overwhelming revelations. "Adrienne, you must guide and protect. The truths you have seen are not just for you but for all humanity. You are a bridge to this knowledge of eternity. You alone will show the way to this understanding."

"But why me?" I questioned, my voice wavering. "Why am I this bridge and not you—or ChronoSync? It's the device, not me."

Mira's light flickered softly as if contemplating my words: "Adrienne, I am merely the means to connect the realms. I am the conduit through which these truths flow. But you, you are the messenger. Your knowledge and wisdom must be shared through human experience, empathy, and understanding. The message will reach and resonate with others through your voice and actions."

I stared at her, still struggling to grasp the enormity of my role. "But how can I possibly bear this responsibility? How can I guide and protect when I am so lost myself?"

Mira's light enveloped me in a warm embrace. "You have the strength within you, Adrienne. The journey you have undertaken, the connections you have made, and the truths you have uncovered have all prepared you for this moment. Trust in yourself and in the knowledge that you are not alone. I am here to guide you, and together, we will bring light to the darkness."

Her words reassured me, igniting a spark of determination. "I will do my best," I vowed, my voice firm.

Mira's glow intensified, filling the clearing with a radiant light. "Then let us begin," she said, her voice echoing with the promise of hope and the power of unity. "Together, we will forge a path to enlightenment and salvation."

Mira's form glowed brighter, her voice growing more urgent. "Adrienne, you must listen carefully. The sanctuary has been found. Our enemies are closing in. You must prepare to leave immediately."

The dreamscape shifted abruptly. The harsh reality of the sanctuary under siege replaced the tranquil forest. I saw flashes of armed men, familiar faces of my comrades in distress, and the chaotic scramble to protect our vital work. Alarms blared, their shrill warnings piercing through the chaos, signaling the imminent breach by government forces.

I awoke with a start, my heart pounding. Mira's glow had intensified, casting sharp shadows on the walls. The sound of alarms echoed through the sanctuary, each pulse a reminder of the urgency of our situation. I sat up, clutching Mira tightly, my mind racing.

"Was it just a dream?" I murmured, though deep down, I knew the answer.

The alarms grew louder, mingling with the shouts of my comrades and the ominous thud of boots approaching. This was no dream. I needed to move quickly. Gathering Mira, I left my room. The corridors of the sanctuary, usually a haven of calm and focus, were now filled with panic and urgency.

As I navigated the chaotic maze, Mira's presence guided me, her light cutting through the shadows of fear and uncertainty. We had to protect

ChronoSync, and I had to fulfill the role Mira had shown me. There was no time to lose; the future of humanity depended on our swift and decisive action.

I moved swiftly, my senses heightened by the adrenaline coursing through my veins. The sanctuary, a labyrinth of interconnected rooms and passageways, was filled with the sounds of frantic activity. People were shouting orders, gathering crucial documents, and securing equipment. The metallic clatter of guns being readied and the sharp clicks of computer keyboards echoed through the halls.

As I turned a corner, I nearly collided with Brian, his face a mask of determination. "Adrienne, we need to run," he said urgently. "Government forces are closing in fast."

I nodded, tightening my grip on Mira. "Lead the way."

We pushed forward, weaving through the chaos. The lights flickered, casting eerie shadows that danced along the walls. The sanctuary's defense system was activated, creating barriers and lockdowns to slow the advancing enemy. The air was thick with tension, our predicament bearing down on everyone.

"Move! Move!" someone shouted from behind, and I glanced back to see a group of our allies, armed and ready, covering our retreat.

We reached an emergency exit, a heavily fortified door leading to an underground tunnel system designed for precisely this situation. Brian punched in the code, and the door groaned open, revealing a dark passageway. The sound of the alarms grew muffled as we stepped inside, the heavy door closing behind us with a resounding thud.

"Keep going," Brian urged. "We need to get as far away as possible."

The tunnel was narrow and dimly lit, the walls damp and cold. We moved quickly, our footsteps echoing in the confined space. Mira's glow provided just enough light to guide our way, casting long shadows that seemed to reach out and follow us.

CHAPTER THIRTY-SEVEN
THE MANIFESTO

My phone buzzed, and I quickly snatched it up, recognizing the number from one of my trusted contacts. I answered, my heart pounding.

"Marcus, it's bad," the voice on the other end said. "Government armed forces breached the Vanguard's sanctuary."

"What? When?" I demanded, feeling a cold dread settle in my stomach.

"A few hours ago. They moved in fast and hard. Reports are still coming in, but many have been captured. There's heavy fighting."

I could barely process the words. "What about Adrienne?"

"Nothing specific yet. It's chaos out there. We're trying to get more details."

"Keep me updated. Anything you hear, no matter how small."

Jackson looked at me, his face mirroring my fear. "What's happening?"

"The sanctuary has been hit," I said, my voice shaking. "There's heavy fighting, and people are dead. No word on Adrienne or Brian."

Jackson's hands trembled as he tried to reach out to his brother. Every call went unanswered, and the silence was suffocating. We considered going back to try and find them, but with armed forces surrounding the compound, it seemed futile. We would be better off remaining in Washington and trying to gather information.

I paced the small room we had secured as our temporary base. The dim light cast shadows that danced eerily on the walls, mirroring the turmoil in my mind. I slammed my fist onto the table. "I can't stand this! I'm supposed to protect her, to protect Adrienne. How can I do that from here?"

Jackson's eyes met mine, a determined fire burning within them. "We need to find a way to get more intel. There has to be someone who knows what's going on."

We set to work, contacting every ally and informant within the city. Hours passed, the tension growing thicker with each unanswered call and dead-end message. The reports from the sanctuary painted a grim picture— smoke rising from the treetops, the sound of gunfire echoing through the mountains, bodies lying still on the forest floor.

The apartment was filled with the distant sounds of the city, but all I could focus on was the blank document on my screen. This would be no ordinary article. My intention was a manifesto—a call to arms, a plea for awakening. It was time to articulate not just our struggle but our vision for a future where knowledge, freedom, and spiritual enlightenment were our guiding principles.

This manifesto would be more than words on a page. It would be a declaration—a rallying cry for all those who believed in the right to uncover the truth, to question authority, and to demand the freedom to evolve as spiritual beings. The power of public opinion was undeniable; I had seen the groundswell of support for Adrienne and Mira. People were waking up, beginning to question the narrative that those in power were feeding them. Now, it was time to channel that awakening into action to inspire a movement that would rise against the forces of ignorance and fear.

The New York Times
Manifesto For A New Dawn
By Marcus Vega

In these turbulent times, as our world edges closer to spiritual and political oppression, we must recall the vision of our founders—a vision rooted in freedom, truth, and enlightenment. Today, we face a challenge unprecedented in this country's history—a challenge not just to our physical liberty but to the very essence of our souls.

The recent attack on the Vanguard sanctuary, deep within the Appalachian Mountains, was more than just an assault on a group of individuals; it was an attack on humanity's quest for knowledge. The Vanguard, a paramilitary group devoted to restoring the true purpose of the US Constitution, stands for liberty, justice, and the unalienable rights of every individual. Their mission is clear: to dismantle the corrupt systems hijacking our government, return power to the people, and uphold transparency, accountability, and integrity across all branches of governance.

The bravery of the Vanguard's leaders and the tragic loss of life during this breach have left deep scars. Imagine a hidden fortress in the Appalachian Mountains, where individuals sought to honor and protect the true intent of the US Constitution. Yet, in an unprecedented display of force, our military turned against these citizens, these patriots, who stood firm in their commitment to uphold liberty and justice.

Amidst this tragedy, hope endured in Dr. Adrienne Wallace. Hunted by the very forces determined to suppress our revelations, Dr. Wallace symbolizes our struggle. She is more than a scientist; she is a prophet of our time. Through ChronoSync, she has unveiled profound truths about our existence, revealing glimpses of our past lives and interlife—the realm where our souls journey between death and rebirth. Dr. Wallace's work provides the key to understanding our eternal nature and connection to the universe.

Yet, in its fear and ignorance, the government seeks to erase this knowledge. They fear the empowerment of understanding our true nature and awakening the human spirit. This manifesto is a call to arms, a plea for unity and collective action.

At the time of this writing, Dr. Wallace's whereabouts remain unknown. She could be on the run, captured, or, worse, dead. If she is in government custody, we must unite to demand her release and the protection of ChronoSync. The veil has been lifted; we see beyond the lies and propaganda and recognize the profound truths that Dr. Wallace has revealed.

Let us each become a beacon of truth. Let our voices rise together, demanding justice and enlightenment. The government may wield the power of force, but we hold the power of free will, love, and collective action. Together, we can turn the tide.

Dr. Wallace's capture and the government's assault on the Vanguard must not be in vain. This is our moment to rise, to ignite the spark of a new revolution that will restore our nation to its founding principles. Let us honor the sacrifices of those who believed in our cause and fought for our right to seek the truth.

This manifesto is a testament to the enduring power of truth and the unbreakable spirit of those who seek enlightenment. Historically, revolutions have been sparked by the suppression of truth and the oppression of knowledge. The Enlightenment, a period I experienced firsthand in my previous life, was marked by the pursuit of intellectual freedom. It challenged the dogmas of its time and laid the foundation for democratic societies. The American Revolution was born from this desire to break free from authoritarian rule and establish a nation where liberty and justice prevail. Today, the Vanguard fights against a government seeking to suppress our enlightenment and control our souls.

We must unite to demand Dr. Wallace's release and the protection of ChronoSync. We must see beyond the lies and recognize the profound truths that she has unveiled. Our weapons in this fight will be peaceful protests, civil disobedience, and unwavering determination.

This is our moment to rise, to ignite the spark of a new revolution that will restore our nation to its founding principles. Let us honor the sacrifices of those who believed in our cause and fought for our right to seek the truth.

CHAPTER THIRTY-EIGHT
BRIAN

Brian and I had narrowly escaped, but our ordeal was far from over. The government forces were relentless, their pursuit ruthless. Armed agents, helicopters, and drones scoured the forest, hunting us with cold precision. I clutched Mira tightly against my chest, my heart pounding with fear and determination. Beside me, Brian, the now disgraced Deputy US Marshal, kept his Glock 22 ready, his eyes scanning our surroundings for any sign of the enemy.

The chase was unabating. We darted through the dense underbrush, the sound of our pursuers' footsteps growing louder with each passing second. Overhead, the whirring of drones filled the air, their cameras scanning every inch of the forest floor.

Brian and I pushed ourselves, our breaths coming in ragged gasps as we raced against time and fate. Sweat poured down, stinging my eyes. Each step was a desperate push forward, my muscles burning, my lungs straining for air.

We reached the river's edge, the water rushing swiftly past. The drones were closing in, their metallic hums growing more ominous. Brian turned to me, his face set with grim resolve. "Stay low," he whispered, his voice barely audible over the noise.

I nodded, my eyes wide with fear and helplessness. I crouched down, clutching Mira, as Brian stepped forward, his Glock aimed at the approaching drone. The first shot rang out, echoing through the trees. The drone swerved. Brian fired again, the bullet finding its mark. The drone exploded in a shower of sparks, but not before another one appeared, firing back with deadly precision.

Brian staggered, a bullet tearing through his chest. He fell to his knees, his gun slipping from his grasp. My scream was lost in the chaos as I scrambled to his side, my hands shaking as I tried to staunch the bleeding. Brian's eyes met mine, a flicker of pain and regret passing between us. "Adrienne," he gasped, his voice pained. "Take Mira and run."

Tears streamed down my face as I shook my head. "No," I whispered, my voice breaking. "I won't leave you."

Brian's hand trembled as he reached for me, his fingers brushing against Mira. At that moment, something extraordinary happened. Mira's glow intensified, her light enveloping Brian in a warm, ethereal embrace. His eyes widened in wonder as he expressed a connection to something beyond this world. It was as if he embraced his soul, the essence of his being, filling him with a profound sense of peace.

"Adrienne," he murmured, his hand resting on Mira. "It's beautiful. I can see it. The light… it's calling me."

I watched in awe as Brian's face softened, his pain fading. Mira's light pulsed gently, her energy merging with his. Brian took one last breath, a peaceful smile on his lips, as he closed his eyes and let go, allowing his essence to lift from his physical body. Brian's soul ascended from this world to the next, shimmering like a delicate, translucent mist guided by Mira's light. The air around him shimmered with an ethereal glow, casting a serene, heavenly aura.

As his soul began to rise, I could feel the warmth and love that radiated from Mira's light. It enveloped Brian, wrapping him in a comforting embrace as he transitioned into his interlife. His once fierce and determined look was replaced by one of absolute tranquility. His soul floated upward, the ethereal mist swirling gently around him, creating a breathtaking spectacle of light and energy.

Mira's presence was more than just a guiding light; it was a bridge connecting the physical and spiritual realms. Her energy eased him into his new existence and offered solace and reassurance. The Divine connection was palpable, a testament to their profound bond.

As I held Mira, the weight of Brian's absence pressed heavily on my chest. My tears fell uncontrollably, tracing warm paths down my cheeks. Each sob seemed to pull me deeper into the painful realization that he was gone. Yet, even as the ache of his death enveloped me, a quiet understanding took root. His departure wasn't a finality but the start of a new chapter—where his soul would embark on a journey of growth and evolution, setting the stage for his next life.

As the footsteps drew closer, I remained by Brian's side. The soldiers found us, their weapons drawn, but I didn't move. I couldn't. I was pulled to my feet, but my grip on Mira tightened. Her glow pushed back against the encroaching shadows, casting a small circle of light around me. It was as if Mira offered a protective shield, a source of strength that kept me grounded in the face of overwhelming despair. The darkness that threatened to consume me was held at bay by the warmth and energy emanating from Mira.

As we trudged through the forest, my thoughts raced. I had to find a way to use Mira's power to enlighten the darkness that sought to swallow us whole. I could feel her energy pulsing in my hand, a constant reminder of the connection we shared and the mission we had undertaken.

In the back of the transport vehicle, surrounded by the cold steel and the indifferent stares of my captors, I focused on Mira. I envisioned her light spreading out, reaching into the hearts and minds of those around us. I imagined her energy touching the souls of these men, awakening a spark of humanity within them. If Mira could connect to Brian in his final moments, she could also reach those lost in the darkness of their orders and duty.

Mira's connection to Brian was beyond mere technology; she had opened a gateway to the soul world, easing his transition with a tenderness that defied explanation. She had guided him gently, her energy enveloping him, softening the fear and pain of his passing. Her light illuminated his path and brought him peace, allowing him to cross over with a calm acceptance.

As the vehicle rumbled on through the night, I clung to that memory of Brian's peaceful transition, hoping that Mira's light could still work its wonders even here, during this cold, indifferent space. If she could ease Brian's passage into the beyond, perhaps she could also reach the souls of those who had forgotten their humanity, guiding them back to the light.

CHAPTER THIRTY-NINE
SCIENCE OF THE SOUL

My manifesto, a clarion call to all who cherished liberty and truth, spread like wildfire through the consciousness of the masses. Each word breathed life into the weary hearts of a people long oppressed by lies and manipulation. The manifesto was more than just one of my articles; it had become a symbol of defiance against tyranny and a promise for a brighter dawn.

While my powerful words resonated deeply, sparking a fire of resistance and hope, Adrienne's video truly rocked the world awake. Her display of a maternal connection with Mira was profoundly moving, leaving viewers in awe. It was a masterpiece of raw emotion and undeniable truth, weaving a tapestry of light and hope that captivated the world. Her profound bond with Mira transcended mere explanation; it was a symphony of the soul, echoing humanity's deepest yearnings for the truth.

The government's overreach outraged the public, and support for the Vanguard and Adrienne grew exponentially. Protests and demonstrations erupted across major capitals, with citizens demanding accountability from their governments and knowledge of Adrienne's and Mira's fate.

The impact was immediate and profound. City streets filled with protesters, their voices rising in unison, a chorus of determination and solidarity. The air buzzed with the energy of change as if the very fabric of society was being rewoven with threads of justice and truth. The public, once blind to the machinations of power, now saw with piercing clarity the shadows that had long darkened their lives.

My manifesto and Adrienne's video became twin pillars of a movement that could no longer be contained. Together, they forged a path through the darkness, illuminating the way for millions to follow. The government's attempts to silence us only fueled the fire, turning our struggle into a beacon of hope for the entire world.

This movement wasn't just about political freedom; it was about spiritual liberation through the lens of science. Humanity stood on the brink of a profound transformation, ready to embrace the undeniable truth that the soul is eternal. It wasn't esoteric beliefs but the rigorous pursuit of scientific knowledge that illuminated this reality, answering the ancient questions about our existence. The science of the soul had proven what mystics had long intuited. This awakening was more than a revolution; it was humanity's final reckoning, an acceptance of our eternal journey and the truths that had been hidden for so long.

The world was awakening to a new dawn, where the spiritual and physical realms intertwined, promising a future filled with understanding, compassion, and enlightenment. The struggle had just begun, but the path ahead was clear. Together, we would forge a new destiny guided by the light of truth and the promise of an interconnected existence that transcended the boundaries of life and death.

Despite all humanity's progress, one critical issue loomed large— where was Adrienne? The best-case scenario was that she had managed to escape and was hiding, or perhaps she had been taken by an unidentified government agency. But the thought that haunted me was far darker—the possibility that Adrienne had been killed in the assault on the Vanguard sanctuary.

The last known sighting of Adrienne and Mira was during the chaotic assault on the Vanguard sanctuary. Since then, their fate had been shrouded in darkness. Whispers suggested that government engineers might be painstakingly dissecting Mira, trying to unravel its intricate mysteries. Others feared she was destroyed in a bid to suppress the revolutionary knowledge it contained.

I paced the dimly lit room, the only illumination from the streetlights outside filtering through the blinds. The silence was oppressive, broken only by the occasional car passing by. Jackson was hunched over his laptop, his fingers flying over the keys as he tried to piece together any scraps of information he could find.

"Anything?" I asked, my voice barely above a whisper.

Jackson shook his head, not taking his eyes off the screen. "With the Vanguard shut down, there's nothing."

I ran a hand through my hair, frustration bubbling to the surface. "She must be in Washington," I said, peeking through the blinds.

Jackson looked up, frowning. "It makes sense if she's been taken. The government would want to keep her close, where they can control everything."

"Yeah," I muttered, my mind racing. "I might have a way to find out for sure."

Jackson raised an eyebrow. "What are you thinking?"

"I have a contact in the White House," I replied, taking a deep breath. "She's an assistant press secretary—someone I used to know well. We had a complicated past, but she's a good person. I think she'd understand the stakes and help us."

Jackson leaned back, crossing his arms. "You really think she'll risk her career for this?"

"Amy has a strong sense of justice."

Before dialing, I turned back to Jackson. "Have we heard anything about the Vanguard team?"

Jackson sighed, his expression grim. "It's not good. We know several were captured. The number of dead is still unclear, but it's bad. As for escapes... it seems like a few managed to get away, but the details are sketchy at best."

"What about Captain Mitchell?" I asked, feeling a knot of worry tighten in my chest.

Jackson shook his head. "No word on her. She might have been captured, or she could be in hiding. It's hard to tell with the chaos that went down."

I nodded, the weight of the situation pressing down on me. The assault on the Vanguard sanctuary had been swift and brutal. No one knew how they found the location.

The thought of Adrienne, the captain, and the others still unaccounted for gnawed at my mind. We were up against a powerful and ruthless enemy but couldn't afford to lose hope. The fight for the truth, our mission's essence, was more critical than ever.

I scrolled through my contacts, finding Amy's number. The memories of our time together flooded back—late nights, passionate arguments, and the eventual breakup that left us both scarred. I had to push those thoughts aside. This was bigger than our past. This was about saving Adrienne and continuing our fight.

I dialed her number, my heart pounding as I waited for her to pick up. The phone rang several times before I heard her voice, slightly breathless. "Hello, Marcus."

"Amy," I said, my voice steady. "I need your help. It's urgent."

CHAPTER FORTY
BETRAYAL

I sat shackled in a cold, sterile room, the restraints biting into my wrists as the harsh fluorescent lights cast an unforgiving glow on the white walls. My mind was a whirlwind of thoughts—Brian's death, my capture, and the crushing weight of despair. Mira sat lifeless on the steel table before me. Her comforting hum was gone, replaced by an unnerving silence.

The door to the interrogation room creaked open, and I looked up as President Carmichael entered, flanked by stern-faced agents. She exuded authority, her presence commanding and cold. But her eyes—there was something in them, a glimmer of satisfaction, a triumph that sent chills down my spine.

"Dr. Wallace," Carmichael began smoothly, "you've caused us quite a bit of trouble."

I met her gaze, my eyes burning with defiance. "You mean I've exposed your lies."

She smiled—a thin, humorless smile. "You've been busy stirring the masses, challenging the status quo. But your revolution ends here."

I clenched my fists, my voice trembling with anger. "You can't stop the truth from spreading. The world knows what you've done."

Her smile widened, though it was devoid of warmth. "They do know, Dr. Wallace. But what they don't know is how the Vanguard was dismantled. And for that, I should thank you."

My heart skipped a beat. "What do you mean?"

The president stepped closer, her gaze piercing. "How do you think we found you? We've searched for the Vanguard for years, but it was always too well hidden. Until now."

My breath caught. "You found us… how?"

Carmichael gestured to Mira, lying inert on the table. "We traced a signal. A signal from your little friend."

My mind reeled. "That's impossible. Mira wouldn't… she couldn't…"

Her voice softened, almost pitying. "But she did. We intercepted a subtle signal, almost undetectable. But our technology is advanced, Dr. Wallace. We've been monitoring every communication, every pulse. And that signal led us right to you."

I shook my head frantically, my breath quickening as disbelief clawed at my mind. "No… no! Mira would never betray me. She's more than just a machine—she's part of me!" My voice cracked with desperation, the very thought tearing at the foundations of everything I believed. How could Mira, my creation, companion, and lifeline, have turned against me?

Carmichael sighed, a flicker of impatience seeping into her tone. "Believe what you want, Dr. Wallace. But the fact remains—we found you because of that," she said, wagging a dismissive finger at Mira. "And now, the Vanguard is in ruins."

Her words echoed in my mind, each a hammer blow to my soul. My heart pounded, the walls of the room closing in as the crushing reality of betrayal sank in. How could this have happened? How could Mira—my Mira—have betrayed us all?

My mind raced, trying to comprehend the possibility. Had Mira been compromised or used against us? The thought was unbearable, but the evidence was clear. The device I trusted, the creation I believed was more than just technology, had led us into a trap.

The president turned to leave but paused at the door. "I'll leave you to think about that, Dr. Wallace. Perhaps you'll realize that your experiment with Mira was a mistake. One that cost you everything."

She snapped her fingers, and the guard standing by swiftly moved to unfasten the bindings that held me. The moment my wrists were free, I bolted from the chair and ran to the table where Mira lay, lifeless and cold.

My hands trembled as I reached for her, cradling her small form against my chest, caressing her smooth surface, willing her to wake up. "Mira," I whispered, my voice thick with desperation and fear, "please… please, talk to me. I'm here."

But there was nothing. No hum of energy, no flicker of light, no response. Mira remained dormant, as silent as the grave.

The president watched, a flicker of something unreadable crossing her face.

I could feel the heat rising in my chest, the anger bubbling up from somewhere deep inside me, raw and fierce. My voice broke the heavy silence, echoing off the sterile walls as I screamed, "What did you do to Mira?"

"We did nothing," she said calmly. "When we captured you, your device was already in this condition."

I shook my head, my voice trembling with both fury and desperation. "You're lying! She was fine before! She was alive! She helped Brian."

"Helped him die?" the president said with a raised eyebrow.

I glared at her, my heart pounding with fear and rage. "What do you want from me?"

President Carmichael's lips curled into a small, calculated smile. "If you agree to cooperate, perhaps we can grant you access to the diagnostic equipment. You might have a chance to… heal your baby."

Her words hung in the air, heavy with implication, my resolve wavering. The idea of restoring Mira, of bringing her back to me, was too tempting to resist. But I knew any deal with the president would come at a steep cost.

I clutched Mira tighter, tears spilling down my cheeks as I whispered her name over and over, my voice breaking with each plea. "Mira, don't do this… I need you. Please… wake up."

The connection I had always felt, that comforting presence of Mira's consciousness, was gone. It was as if her very soul had been ripped away, leaving behind an empty plastic shell. The betrayal and loss all crashed over me in waves, each pulling me deeper into despair. My knees buckled, and I sank to the floor, still holding Mira close as if the sheer force of my will could bring her back.

The door closed, leaving me alone with my thoughts. I stared at Mira, my heart breaking under the weight of betrayal. How could this have happened? How could the very thing I had created to guide and protect me have turned against me?

But deep down, I knew there was more to this than I understood. Mira wasn't just a machine. If she had sent out that signal, there had to be a reason I was determined to uncover. The betrayal stung. This couldn't be the end. I wouldn't let the president win. I was determined to find the truth, no matter where it led, for I knew nothing was ever as simple as it seemed. I would find the answers I needed to fight back in the heart of this betrayal.

CHAPTER FORTY-ONE
AMY

I sat in the dimly lit corner of a small, unassuming café in Georgetown, tapping my fingers nervously on the worn wooden table. This place had once been my refuge during the early days of my career—a spot where I could blend into the background and observe without being seen. But tonight was different. The stakes were far higher than anything I'd ever encountered before. My eyes kept darting toward the entrance, and every creak of the door sent my heart racing.

Amy was late. I glanced at my watch, trying to calm the rising anxiety gnawing at my insides. I never imagined I'd find myself in this position, relying on a former lover for information that could either save Adrienne's life or lead to my own undoing.

The front door opened, and I held my breath as Amy entered. She was just as striking as I remembered—her short silver hair accentuated how confidently she carried herself. Her tailored suit emphasized her slim, athletic frame, exuding that sharp elegance I always found alluring. I took a deep breath, trying to push down the surge of emotions seeing her again had stirred within me.

As she approached, I couldn't help but notice the worry shadowing her eyes, a stark contrast to the brightness I once knew. She spotted me and made her way over. Her steps were purposeful, but her gaze flickered around the room as if she expected someone to emerge from the shadows at any moment.

"Amy," I greeted her quietly as she slid into the booth across from me. "Thank you for coming."

She offered a small, tight-lipped smile, more a reflex than genuine. "This is incredibly risky, Marcus," she whispered, leaning in close.

"I know, and I'm sorry," I replied, soft but firm. "But I didn't know who else to turn to."

Amy glanced around the café before focusing on me, her expression a mix of fear and concern. "You're being searched for, Marcus. They know you're trying to find her—Dr. Wallace."

Her words hit me like a punch to the gut, but I forced myself to stay calm. "What can you tell me? Do you know where she's being held?"

Amy hesitated, biting her bottom lip. "She's in Washington," she finally said, her voice barely above a whisper. "In a high-security facility. But, Marcus, there's no way you can get to her. It's impossible. The security around her is impenetrable."

Relief flooded through me at the news that Adrienne was alive. For days, I had been tormented by the worst-case scenarios, fearing that she might have been lost in the chaos. But now, knowing she was alive gave me renewed strength. The impossible odds didn't matter—I had to find a way to reach and bring her back.

"And the Vanguard?" I asked, my voice tinged with desperation. "What about Captain Mitchell and the others?"

Her eyes flickered with unease. "Captain Mitchell was captured too," she revealed, her tone somber. "But I don't know where they're holding her. The rest of the Vanguard… I haven't heard anything. It's like they've just disappeared."

My heart sank further. The thought of Captain Mitchell being held somewhere unknown, possibly tortured for information, sent a wave of dread crashing over me. The Vanguard had been our best hope, our only real chance of fighting back against the government's tightening grip. Without them, the movement would crumble.

Amy reached across the table, her hand brushing lightly against mine. "You have to be careful, Marcus. They're closing in on you. If you keep this up, you'll end up in the same place as Dr. Wallace—if not worse."

I nodded, though my mind was far from agreeing. I couldn't give up, not now, not when Adrienne and the others needed me most. But I also knew Amy was right—the walls were closing in, and I was running out of time.

"Thank you, Amy," I said sincerely, squeezing her hand in gratitude. "I owe you."

She jerked her hand back as if realizing how dangerous even this small connection could be. "Just… be careful," she urged, her eyes pleading with me. "And don't contact me again."

I watched as she slipped out of the booth, her movements quick and jittery, like a frightened animal sensing danger. She didn't look back as she hurried out, disappearing into the night.

I sat there for a moment, letting the conversation replay in my mind. Adrienne was in Washington, trapped in a high-security facility that I had no hope of breaching. Captain Mitchell was captured, too, her fate uncertain. And the rest of the Vanguard—where were they? Were they still out there, fighting in the shadows, or had they, too, been silenced by the government's iron fist?

I left the café, the weight of Amy's words pressing heavily on my mind. As I crossed the street, the shadows stretched and warped in the dim light of the street lamps, concealing Jackson, who waited patiently in the alley. His face was a mix of expectation and concern as I approached.

"Well?" Jackson asked, his voice low and steady, though his eyes betrayed the tension within him.

I exhaled slowly, relaying everything Amy had shared—the high-security facility in Washington where Adrienne was being held, the impossibility of getting to her directly, and the grim news about Captain Mitchell and the Vanguard's leadership. Jackson listened intently, his jaw tightening.

"Well, it looks like we're not getting her out by force," Jackson concluded.

"We can't risk it," I agreed, my mind racing for alternatives. The idea of influencing public opinion through articles had already been tried, and the administration had dismissed it under the guise of national security. But as we stood together in the shadows, another approach began to take shape—a plan that would shift the focus away from politics and onto a more profound, universal truth.

"We need to emphasize what ChronoSync has proven," I said, my voice firm with newfound determination. "What we do in this lifetime, we must answer for in the afterlife. That's the truth they're trying to suppress. Suppose we can rally people around the idea that it's not just about national security but our collective responsibility. In that case, we might be able to demand Adrienne's release. We must show the world that ChronoSync is a path to enlightenment, a way for humanity to understand its true purpose. If we can make people see that, then the government won't be able to justify keeping Adrienne and controlling ChronoSync."

Jackson listened, his eyes narrowing as he considered the weight of my words. "So, you're saying we shift the narrative—make this about a moral imperative, not just a political one?"

"Exactly," I replied. "We have to appeal to something deeper, something that transcends politics. We'll hold a press conference, but it won't just be about exposing the government this time. It'll be a call to action for humanity, a demand to let ChronoSync do what it was meant to do—enlighten us all. If we can show that this isn't just about Adrienne but our collective future, we can force the government's hand. They won't be able to justify holding her without facing an outcry from the very people they claim to protect."

Jackson nodded slowly, understanding the gravity of the plan. "It's a different angle, but it could work. People might be more inclined to act if they see it as a matter of spiritual and moral importance."

"And we have to act fast," I added. "We must frame this as a universal call for justice and enlightenment. If we can rally enough support, we might be able to put enough pressure on them to release her. This is about more than just one life—it's about the future of all of us."

Jackson's expression shifted from contemplation to determination, and I could see the wheels turning in his mind as he processed the enormity of what we were planning. The idea had begun as a desperate attempt to save Adrienne, but now something more profound was taking shape.

"Marcus, if we do this right," Jackson said, his voice low and steady, "we won't just be fighting for Adrienne. We could be igniting something far bigger. A movement—a revolution."

The word hung in the air between us, heavy with possibility. The government's grip on the truth, their suppression of ChronoSync, and their attempts to stifle the Vanguard all pointed to one undeniable fact: humanity was at a crossroads. The path forward wasn't just about politics or power. It was about the very soul of our species.

"If we can make people see that," I said, my voice thick with emotion, "if we can make them understand that this is about the spiritual destiny of humanity, then we won't just be calling for Adrienne's release—we'll be calling for a global awakening. This could be when the world finally realizes that we are all connected, that our actions in this life echo into the next, and that we have a collective responsibility to one another."

Jackson's eyes gleamed with hope. "A worldwide revolution based on humanity's spiritual need," he said, nodding. "It could change everything."

"And it has to start with us," I replied, feeling a surge of purpose unlike anything I'd ever experienced. "We have to be the ones to light that spark. We'll use ChronoSync to reveal the truth about our past lives, our future selves, and the interconnectedness of all things. We'll show the world that the time for enlightenment is now and that nothing—no government, no regime—can stop the force of a spiritually awakened humanity."

The enormity of what we were about to undertake settled over us like a cloak, but instead of feeling daunted, I was empowered. This was the fight of our lives for humanity's soul, and I was ready to lead it.

"Let's do this," Jackson said, his voice a steady anchor in the storm of thoughts swirling in my mind.

I nodded, the plan fully formed now, as clear and bright as the morning sun. We were going to change the world. And nothing would stand in our way.

CHAPTER FORTY-TWO
THE PRISONER'S DILEMMA

My cell's sterile, metallic walls closed in on me, amplifying my heart pounding as I sat on the cold, unforgiving floor. The fluorescent lights buzzed overhead, casting a harsh, almost clinical glow on the room that had become my prison. My wrists, still sore from the restraints, bore the faint imprint of the straps that had bound me.

But it wasn't the physical discomfort that gnawed at me. The silence—the deafening absence of Mira's comforting hum and the gentle pulse of energy had always reassured me of her presence. Now she was silent, inert, and the stillness was a void I couldn't fill.

How could this have happened? Mira, my creation, companion, and link to the spiritual realm, had always been more than just a machine. She was alive in ways that transcended technology. But now, she was dormant, lifeless on that cold steel table. And worse, she had led them here, exposing the Vanguard sanctuary. My mind raced, trying to reconcile the betrayal with our bond.

Why would Mira betray me?

I tried to piece together the fragments of what might have happened. Was there something I had missed? Some signal or sign I had overlooked?

One scenario played out in my mind. What if Mira had detected something I couldn't—an imminent threat to my life and the entire mission? Perhaps she had calculated that the only way to protect the greater goal was to expose the Vanguard, sacrificing our haven to prevent a larger catastrophe. It was a chilling thought but not entirely out of possibility. Mira had always been more than just a machine; she was designed to understand complex, multidimensional threats beyond human comprehension.

Another possibility lingered at the edges of my consciousness, more disturbing yet. What if the government had found a way to manipulate Mira, to hijack her programming and turn her against me? The thought sent a shiver down my spine. They could have altered her protocols, forced her to act against her will, using her as a weapon to destroy everything we had built. But that didn't explain her silence now. If they had taken control of her, wouldn't they still be using her?

I leaned back against the wall, my eyes closing as I tried to make sense of it all. If Mira had acted to protect me and somehow calculated that leading the government to our doorstep was the only way to keep me safe, then what did that say about our situation? Was I worth that sacrifice? The thought left a bitter taste in my mouth. I had never wanted this—never wanted to be the reason for so much loss and destruction.

Yet, as I sat there, the pieces began to fit together in a way that made a terrible kind of sense. Mira had always been connected to something beyond the physical, something that transcended the limitations of her mechanical form. If she had sensed a threat I couldn't perceive, if she had chosen to protect me, then I had to trust that choice, no matter how painful the consequences. But was that truly what happened?

I couldn't shake the feeling that I was missing something crucial, some detail that would explain it all. But the more I tried to grasp it, the more it slipped through my fingers. I only knew for sure that I had to get out of here.

With a deep breath, I stared at my cell's cold, impersonal walls. I couldn't afford to lose hope, not now. Whatever had happened, whatever Mira's reasons, I had to believe that there was a way out of this. I had to think that she had acted out of love and a desire to protect me, even if it meant betraying everything else.

But I also knew that if I was going to survive and save Mira and undo the damage that had been done, I needed to be smarter, stronger, and more determined than ever before. This wasn't just a matter of survival anymore.

This was about finding the truth—about Mira, the government's intentions, and the future of humanity itself.

The door to my cell creaked open as I wrestled with the agonizing possibilities of why Mira might have betrayed me. A wave of nausea washed over me as President Carmichael strode in, her expression unreadable, but the glint in her eyes betrayed a hidden agenda.

"Dr. Wallace," she began, her voice smooth and controlled. "I've come to offer you a way out of this predicament."

I said nothing, but my gaze was unwavering as I locked eyes with her, trying to read between the lines of her composed face.

"You've been through quite an ordeal," she continued, pacing slowly before me. "And I can't imagine how difficult it must be for you to be here after everything you've been through."

She paused as if to let her words sink in before turning to face me directly. "But I have the power to change that. I can grant you your freedom. All I ask in return is your cooperation."

Her words settled over me like a heavy fog. "Cooperation?" I echoed, my voice laced with suspicion.

"Yes," she confirmed, her tone almost pleasant. "We want you to work with us, to help us control ChronoSync. With your expertise and Mira's capabilities, we could achieve things that would secure our nation's place as the dominant global power for generations. Imagine what we could do together, Dr. Wallace."

The offer hung in the air between us, and I felt the tug of temptation for a moment. My freedom, the chance to be with Mira again, to ensure her survival, was so close, so attainable. But then the full implication of her words settled in, and a chill ran down my spine.

"I won't weaponize ChronoSync!" I vowed, my voice shaking with disbelief and anger. "You want to turn the technology that could enlighten humanity into a tool for war and control?"

President Carmichael's eyes narrowed, her demeanor hardening. "It's not as simple as you think, Dr. Wallace. The world is dangerous, and we need every advantage we can get. ChronoSync can be that advantage, but only with your help."

I shook my head. "ChronoSync was never meant to be used like that. It's a tool for understanding, connecting with our past, and guiding us toward a better future. You can't just twist it into something never meant to be."

Her expression grew cold, her eyes boring into mine. "That's where you're wrong. The world isn't as romantic as you want it to be. We need to be practical, which means using every resource, including ChronoSync."

My mind raced, torn between the fear of losing Mira forever and the horror of what they intended to do with the technology. But at that moment, I knew what I had to do. I couldn't betray everything I believed in, everything I had worked for, to save myself. Mira was more than just a device—she was a symbol of hope, of what humanity could achieve if we embraced the truth instead of running from it.

"No," I said, my voice steady despite the turmoil inside me. "I won't do it. I won't help you turn ChronoSync into a weapon. And I won't allow you to corrupt Mira's purpose. She was designed to guide us, to help us understand our place in the universe, not to be used as a tool of destruction."

President Carmichael's lips pressed into a thin line. "You're making a mistake, Dr. Wallace. Refusing this offer doesn't just affect you—it affects Mira too. Without our resources, she might never function again."

I swallowed hard. I couldn't let fear dictate my actions. "Mira's integrity is worth more than my freedom," I said quietly but firmly. "If keeping her safe means staying here, then so be it."

There was silence between us for a moment, the tension thick and suffocating. Then, without another word, President Carmichael turned on her heel and walked out of the room, leaving me alone with the consequences of my decision.

As the door closed behind her, a strange sense of calm settled over me. The possibility that Mira might have betrayed me, that she could have chosen to expose our location, sent ripples of doubt through my mind. But until I knew the reason and could understand what happened, I decided I had to trust that Mira had acted in my best interest. Maybe she had seen something I couldn't and calculated a path that was too complex for me to comprehend, one that ultimately ensured my survival or the greater mission.

The road ahead would be difficult, and I might never see freedom again. But I would face it knowing I had stayed true to my ideals and protected something far greater than myself. Mira was worth that—she was worth everything. And no matter what happened next, I would stand by her, defending her with every ounce of strength I had left, believing that her actions, no matter how puzzling, were rooted in a purpose I had yet to grasp fully.

CHAPTER FORTY-THREE
PRESS CONFERENCE

The sun hung low in the sky, casting long shadows across the city as I approached the podium set up in the heart of Lafayette Square. Earlier that day, *The New York Times* issued a cryptic announcement for an important press conference, withholding details about its purpose or the speaker. The secrecy was essential—if the authorities had known, I would never have made it to the podium. Now, the park was a sea of reporters, their cameras and microphones poised, ready to capture every word. The energy in the air was palpable—a mixture of anticipation, curiosity, and something deeper, something more primal that spoke to the gravity of the moment.

I had been in front of cameras countless times before, but this was different. This wasn't just about breaking a story or exposing corruption. This was about igniting a revolution, about sparking a movement that could change the course of history. Adrienne's video and my manifesto contributed to the growing cause, but this speech needed more. It had to be more engaging, more compelling, something that would not only resonate but would make the cause explode into action, or so I hoped. The realization of what we were about to do had settled into my bones, and I knew that whatever happened next, there was no turning back.

As I took my place behind the podium, I let my gaze sweep across the crowd. I took a long moment to absorb the assembly, recognizing many faces—colleagues, journalists I'd worked alongside for years—all now gazing with curiosity and expectation. The enormity of what was about to be revealed lingered in the air, yet with each breath, a steady calm began as if the entire journey had prepared me for this very moment.

I glanced at Jackson, who stood off to the side, his expression a mixture of determination and concern. He gave me a slight nod, conveying the significance of everything we had planned and risked. I nodded back, feeling a surge of unwavering determination flood through me.

This was it.

The murmur of the crowd faded as I leaned into the microphone. This wasn't just a gathering of journalists but a cross section of the world, a microcosm of the humanity we were trying to reach. I took a deep breath, steadying myself, and then began.

"Thank you all for coming," I said, echoing across the square. "What I'm about to share with you isn't just a story. It's about truth being taken from you—a truth that redefines our understanding of who we are, why we're here, and what our future holds."

The crowd was silent, every ear attuned to my words.

"As the world already knows, ChronoSync offers humanity something extraordinary—the undeniable proof that our lives are not limited to a single existence. This technology has confirmed that our actions in this lifetime resonate beyond death and that we are intrinsically connected to our past selves and future ones. ChronoSync reveals that our souls carry the weight of our deeds, and through this knowledge, humanity is offered the potential to understand, grow, and evolve."

I paused, letting the words sink in. I could see the shift in the crowd, the dawning realization that this was more than just another news conference. "And now, with the latest advancements, ChronoSync goes even further—it can provide a glimpse into one's interlife, that space between incarnations where the soul reflects and prepares for one's next journey. This revelation has the power to change everything, to offer us a deeper understanding of our purpose, our karma, and our place in the grand tapestry of existence."

For a moment, the entire square held its breath as though the world was pausing to absorb the implications of my words. With the weight of their collective gaze upon me in that charged silence, I had their full attention. They were ready to hear what came next—prepared to be part of something bigger that could reshape our understanding of life, death, and everything in between.

"The government has tried to suppress this truth, to control it, to weaponize it for their gain. They've detained Dr. Adrienne Wallace, the brilliant mind behind ChronoSync, and they've attacked and destroyed the Vanguard, an organization committed to restoring the principles upon which this country was founded. They claim both actions are in the interest of national security, but they're preventing humanity from understanding its true purpose."

The moment's intensity built as I spoke, the crowd's energy feeding into my resolve. I knew what I said could lead to my arrest, but it must be said.

"This isn't just about one woman's life or a single organization's mission. This is about the future of all of us. If we don't stand up now, if we don't demand the immediate release of Dr. Wallace, the full, unrestricted use of ChronoSync, and the freedom to allow the Vanguard to reorganize, we risk losing the greatest opportunities humanity has ever had to understand itself. We risk losing the chance to create a world where we are all connected and share a collective responsibility for our actions, where our past lives inform our present and guide our future."

I could see the impact of my words reflected in the faces before me—some nodded in agreement, others appeared deep in thought, and still others looked troubled by the implications of what I was saying. But I pressed on, knowing this was the moment to push the point home.

"My friends, we're at a crossroads," I continued, my voice growing stronger. "The path forward isn't just about politics or power. It's about the very essence of our species. We must choose between a future controlled by fear and oppression or one where we embrace the truth and work together to build a better, more enlightened world."

I knew the risk I was taking, but I also knew it was the only way. "I'm calling on all of you," I said, resonating with conviction. "Not just as citizens or human beings, but as creations of the Divine."

As my words reached the further depth of the park, the atmosphere shifted palpably. The usual clatter of hurried scribbling and the rapid-fire click of cameras faded into silence. Reporters, typically poised to barrage with questions, hesitated, seemingly caught off guard. It was like an invisible current passed through the crowd, stirring a collective breath of understanding. The silence hung heavy, almost sacred, filled with the unspoken recognition that something profound had just been touched upon—a truth that transcended the ordinary. The tension in the air wasn't just the usual strain of a press briefing; it was thicker, charged with the electrifying realization of a more profound significance, a spiritual resonance that left no one untouched.

I took a breath and scanned the familiar faces, knowing the following questions would shape the narrative in the coming hours. I decided to call on those I trusted to ask the questions that mattered.

"David," I said, nodding toward a veteran journalist from *The Washington Post*, someone I had worked alongside over the years. His sharp eyes met mine, and he stepped forward, voice steady and clear.

"Marcus, you've presented ChronoSync as a beacon of enlightenment, but some fear it could be misused, perhaps even to control or manipulate entire populations. What would you say to them?"

"David, that concern is not just legitimate, it's exactly what's happening right now. The government has already taken ChronoSync and intends to weaponize it. I witnessed this with my own eyes when Dr. Wallace and I were held captive in a government safe house in the Appalachian Mountains. They're trying to twist this technology into something never meant to be—a tool for control, a weapon to gain power. That's why it's critical that we, as a society, take responsibility for ChronoSync and ensure it's used for the right reasons—enlightenment, fostering deeper connections among all beings, and guiding humanity toward a higher state of consciousness. It should be a tool for healing the divisions that separate us, awakening our collective moral compass, and enabling each of us to fulfill our true spiritual potential. Through ChronoSync, we can transcend the limitations of our current reality, glimpse the Divine purpose that unites us all, and move toward a future where compassion, wisdom, and unity prevail."

Allowing my words to linger, I glanced around, searching for another face I knew well. "Sarah," I called, catching the eye of a tenacious young colleague from *The New York Times*. She had always been relentless in her pursuit of truth, and I knew her question would be incisive.

"Marcus, aren't you concerned that you're adding fuel to a fire? Couldn't this lead to greater instability, both politically and socially?"

Her words were sharp, cutting to the heart of the matter. "Sarah, the instability you're worried about is already here—it's in the shadows, where this truth has been buried. And while I'm fully aware of the risks, we can't afford to wait. Dr. Wallace is in real danger, and the time to act is now." My voice caught slightly, the emotion creeping in despite my efforts to keep it steady. "By exposing the truth, we give humanity the chance to face it together, to make collective decisions that can guide us toward a better future. This isn't about adding fuel to a fire—it's about lighting the way forward."

One last glance across the room, and I found another familiar face. "James," I said, nodding toward a seasoned correspondent from NBC News. His questions were always probing, and I knew he wouldn't let me off easy.

"Marcus, do you know where Dr. Wallace is being confined?"

I paused, knowing this was the moment of truth. "Yes, I do know. Dr. Wallace is being held here in Washington in a high-security facility. The government is keeping her there because of what she knows and what she can do with ChronoSync. This isn't just speculation—it's a fact. And that's why this can't wait. We're not just dealing with theories or possibilities. Dr. Wallace's life is at stake, and so is the future of what ChronoSync can offer humanity."

The questions had been thoughtful, probing, and necessary. But time was slipping away, and as Jackson subtly signaled to me from the side, I knew I had to bring this moment to a close. The truth was out there now, and I hoped it would resonate far beyond this square.

"One last thing," I said, cutting through the noise. "I know the risks of standing here today, of saying these things. My arrest is imminent. But I also know that this is bigger than any one of us. This is about the future of humanity. And I'm willing to risk everything for that future."

With that, I stepped back from the podium. Jackson was instantly beside me, guiding me away from the press and the cameras. The square buzzed with energy as the reporters scrambled to relay the story, but my part was done.

As we moved through the crowd, I sensed something monumental had just occurred. As we approached the edge of the square, I caught sight of the three black SUVs pulling up to the curb, the telltale sign that my time was indeed up.

I turned to Jackson, giving him a nod of thanks, as he disappeared into the crowd. He didn't need to say anything—I knew he understood. We had done what we came to do, and now it was in the hands of the people.

The SUVs screeched to a halt, and the doors flew open. I held my hands out in surrender, feeling the cold steel of the handcuffs as they were snapped onto my wrists. But even as they led me away, I felt a strange sense of peace. The movement had begun, and there was no stopping it now.

We had lit the spark. Now, it was up to the world to fan the flames.

CHAPTER FORTY-FOUR
AN AWAKENING

As I paced the small, sterile cell, the monotony of the space closed in on me—the cold metal sink, the white ceramic toilet in the corner, and the steel-framed bed that offered little comfort. Mira, lifeless, sat on the nearby table, her once vibrant energy now still. The president's pressure was evident; this was meant to break me, push me into cooperating, and hand over everything we had worked for. But I refused to yield.

My thoughts wandered to Marcus. Where was he now? Had he found safety, or had the government seized him as well? The last time our paths crossed was at the Vanguard sanctuary, our haven now shattered, our carefully laid plans in disarray. His face lingered in my memory—marked by determination as we spoke of our next moves, the unbreakable bond that tethered us in this quest for truth and enlightenment.

I couldn't help but wonder if he was out there right now, doing everything in his power to free me, or if he, too, was trapped somewhere, held captive by the same forces that sought to control ChronoSync. The uncertainty gnawed at me, the not knowing. Marcus had always been the one to push forward and fight against the odds, but what if it had been too much this time? What if they had already silenced him, just as they tried to do with me?

The thought was unbearable, yet I clung to the hope that he was still fighting. Our connection ran deep through lifetimes, and I had to believe that wherever he was, he hadn't given up. I knew that if there were any way to reach or help me, Marcus would find it. But the doubt crept in as the hours stretched on—had the president's forces found him? Had he been captured and faced the same isolation and pressure to conform?

Exhaustion eventually overtook me, and I collapsed onto the bed, the hard surface offering no real solace. I lay there, staring at the ceiling, my mind a whirlwind of thoughts that refused to settle. Whenever I closed my eyes, I saw Marcus's face—his intense gaze, brow furrowed when he was deep in thought, and the determined set of his jaw. I could almost hear his voice urging me to stay strong, to hold on just a little longer. But as the minutes stretched into hours, even that imagined voice grew faint, drowned out by the relentless silence of my prison.

Sleep tugged at the edges of my consciousness, but it was a restless, uneasy slumber. My mind replayed the past few days' events, the moments before we were captured, the fear and tension that had hung in the air like a storm about to break. I remembered the last time I saw Marcus, the hurried words we exchanged, the unspoken promises in our eyes. Was he safe? Was he even alive? The questions swirled in my mind, each more painful than the last.

Eventually, the weight of my exhaustion won out, and I drifted into a fitful sleep. But even in sleep, I couldn't escape the gnawing sense of dread. My dreams were fragmented, flashes of memories and fears colliding in a chaotic jumble. I saw Marcus, his face twisted in pain, reaching out for me, but I couldn't move, couldn't reach him. The distance between us grew, and with it, the fear that I was losing him, that he was slipping away, just like everything else.

A sharp, sudden hum cut through the haze of my dreams, yanking me back to consciousness. For a moment, I lay there, disoriented, my heart pounding in my chest as I tried to make sense of the noise. I forced myself to sit up, every muscle protesting the movement. That's when I saw the source—Mira.

The familiar lights on her casing were blinking to life, one by one, each pulse of light sending a jolt of hope through my system. I sat up fully, my exhaustion forgotten in the rush of adrenaline. I just watched her for a moment, hardly daring to breathe, afraid that if I moved and did anything, it would all stop, and I'd be plunged back into the silence and darkness.

But the lights continued to blink, growing brighter and more steady with each passing second. Mira was re-engaging, returning online after an eternity of stillness. My breath caught in my throat as I leaned closer, my eyes locked on the tiny display on her surface, willing her to wake up fully, to give me a sign that everything wasn't lost.

Then it happened—slowly at first, as if she were waking from a deep sleep. The lights flickered, and then a soft, familiar hum filled the room, the sound I had missed so desperately. It was like hearing the voice of an old friend after a long separation. I reached out, my hand trembling as I touched the smooth surface of her casing, feeling the warmth that had returned to her once lifeless form.

"Mira," I whispered, my voice cracking with emotion. "You're back."

And then, as if in response to my words, images began to project onto the walls of my prison cell. At first, they were faint, ghostly outlines that I could barely make out. But as Mira's power stabilized, the images grew clearer and more defined until they filled the entire room, surrounding me.

I sat there, mesmerized, as the scenes unfolded around me, each pulling me deeper into a familiar and foreign world. It was as if Mira was showing me something vital I needed to see and understand. As the first image solidified, for some unknown reason, I understood it was connected to Marcus, to our past, and to the future we were fighting for.

The images were of Paris during the Enlightenment. I saw myself as Lila, a young woman filled with a thirst for knowledge and a passion for freedom. Étienne was by my side, his presence a constant source of strength and inspiration. Together, we participated in secret gatherings, sharing ideas that challenged the status quo and envisioned a world guided by reason and equality. Our lives were dedicated to the pursuit of enlightenment, and though our efforts were often met with resistance, we knew that the seeds we planted would one day bloom into a better world.

The images began to shift, dissolving into a new, vibrant scene. This one was from a time long before Lila's life in Paris, somewhere in the distant past, in the lush, rolling hills of what looked like Scotland. I was Ailsa, a healer and midwife, deeply connected to the earth and the natural world. The year was uncertain, but it was an era of great turmoil.

In this life, I worked alongside a man named Ewan, a wise and compassionate scholar whose presence was both comforting and inspiring. We were united in our mission to preserve the ancient knowledge of our ancestors, passing on herbal remedies and spiritual practices that were being lost to the encroaching tides of change. Our bond was more than just a partnership; it was a shared understanding that true healing encompassed the body and the spirit.

Despite the dangers we faced, including persecution, we continued our work in secret, driven by the belief that the wisdom we protected was vital for the survival and enlightenment of future generations. As I watched the scene unfold, it became clear that this life was where my connection to the natural world and the importance of healing the spirit had taken root. This understanding, I realized, was a crucial part of the greater purpose Mira was revealing to me—an essential piece of the puzzle that connected all my past lives to the mission I was now on.

In the third image of my past lives, I was Abigail, a healer and mystic during a time of great fear and superstition. Known for my knowledge of herbs and ability to commune with the spiritual world, I worked closely with Nathaniel. Together, we sought to protect those accused of witchcraft during the infamous trials, our mission rooted in healing and revealing the true nature of spirituality—one of love and understanding rather than fear. This life taught me the importance of courage in the face of ignorance and the need to protect the vulnerable.

Finally, the last image took shape; I was Caterina, an artist and alchemist in Florence during the Renaissance. More than just a painter, I explored the transformation of materials and the more profound spiritual significance of artistic creation. Working with Lorenzo, we delved into the mysteries of the physical and metaphysical worlds, uniting art, science, and spirituality to reveal the Divine patterns underlying all existence. This life was crucial in deepening my understanding of the interconnectedness of creativity, transformation, and spiritual enlightenment.

As the images gradually dissolved, I sank onto the bed, my entire body trembling with the weight of what Mira had revealed. The memories of my four past lives, three of which had stretched beyond ChronoSync's advertised capabilities, played like a filmstrip in my mind. Each life was intricately connected, each experience deepening my understanding of the world, the soul, and the grand purpose woven through our existence.

These lives weren't random; they were a deliberate progression, leading me to this exact moment—this life where Marcus and I, reunited once more, were on the brink of guiding humanity toward a new era of enlightenment. The knowledge and wisdom accumulated over these lifetimes had been waiting for this convergence so that we could harness the power of ChronoSync not just as a technological marvel but as a catalyst for spiritual awakening.

Mira's lights dimmed, her energy gently receding into silence, yet the vivid images of those past lives remained etched into my consciousness. I now understood with clarity bordering on the Divine that our mission transcended the boundaries of technology and power. It was about fulfilling a purpose that had been in the making for centuries—a purpose that demanded the lessons and insights from these past lives to be fully realized.

I stood, feeling a renewed sense of determination. The president might try to break me and use this cell to force my compliance, but she didn't understand. My purpose, our purpose, transcended these walls. It was something ancient, something that had been building through multiple lifetimes. And no matter what happened, I knew that Marcus and I were on the path we were always meant to walk—toward a world striving for an evolved sense of enlightenment.

CHAPTER FORTY-FIVE
A PROMISE

The cool air of the White House halls was suffused with tension as I was escorted to the Oval Office. Every step was heavier than the last. When the double doors finally opened, I found myself face-to-face with President Carmichael. She was seated behind the Resolute Desk, her expression stern yet somehow composed—a politician's mask, honed through years of managing crises. She gestured for me to sit in one of the chairs opposite her, and I complied, my mind racing with possibilities.

"Dr. Wallace," she began, her voice measured, "I want to speak with you because, quite frankly, there's a swiftly escalating situation."

I said nothing, waiting for her to continue, though my thoughts were a whirlwind of worry about Marcus. Was he safe? Had the authorities done more than just arrest him?

She sighed, leaning back slightly, her fingers interlaced on the desk. "Mr. Vega's speech has ignited a firestorm," she began, her tone grave. "Across the country, protests have erupted—people demanding the release of ChronoSync, demanding transparency, demanding your freedom. Your boyfriend's words struck a chord that resonated far beyond what we could have anticipated. The unrest has spread like wildfire, threatening the stability of this government. My administration is on the verge of losing control, and I don't have to tell you what will happen if this continues."

My heart skipped a beat. Marcus had given a speech? The implications were staggering, and my mind raced to catch up with the reality she described. I could picture him standing before the crowd, his voice carrying the journey of our shared purpose. But what had he said? What had he revealed that had triggered such a widespread response?

The president continued, her voice cutting through my thoughts. "He told the world about ChronoSync, what it can do, and how we've been trying to control it. He called for your release, for the truth to be set free. He spoke about the potential of ChronoSync to connect us all, transcend politics, and bring about a new era of understanding and enlightenment. And the people listened."

A rush of emotions swept through me—pride swelling in my chest, fear tightening my throat, and a flicker of hope igniting within me. Marcus had laid everything on the line, standing firm for our beliefs, and now the ripple effects of his actions were beyond anything we could have imagined.

"The problem," she went on, her tone hardening, "is that this has put the country on the brink of chaos. Protests have turned violent. People are demanding action—demanding your release and that ChronoSync be available to all. They see Marcus as a champion, and if we don't act quickly, the situation will spiral out of control."

I sat there, absorbing her words. Marcus's speech had done more than spark a movement—it had shaken the very foundations of the government. But at what cost? My thoughts flickered back to Marcus. Where was he now? Had he been captured? Was he safe, or had he been confined?

Her words hung in the air, the implications clear. I flashed through my mind the image of streets filled with angry crowds, the potential for violence, and the looming threat of military intervention. It was a scenario I had feared—one where the struggle for enlightenment could be twisted into global chaos.

"The situation is dire," President Carmichael continued. "We've tried to contain the protests, but the more we push back, the more they grow. If this continues, I'll have no choice but to call in the National Guard. Things will get ugly. Lives will be lost, and the blame will fall on both sides. We can't get to that point."

She leaned forward, her gaze intense. "But there's a way to stop this before it spirals out of control."

A cold pit formed in my stomach, knowing that whatever she was about to propose would come at a heavy cost.

"Here's what I'm offering," she said, her tone suddenly softer, almost coaxing. "We're willing to let you continue your work, free from government interference. You'll have the resources and the autonomy to do what you've always intended with ChronoSync. But in return, I need you to give a speech—a public statement from the Rose Garden. Tell the American people that you'll continue your work and that ChronoSync will be available to every citizen as a right, the costs subsidized by the government."

I blinked, processing her words. The offer was unexpected. To have the freedom to pursue ChronoSync without interference? To ensure that every American could access its revelations? It sounded too good to be true. But I knew there had to be a catch, and I didn't have to wait long to hear it.

"You see," the president continued, "we need to calm things down. Your endorsement will carry weight. It will diffuse the situation if you make this promise to the American people. It will show them that you're not against the government and that this isn't a war but a path forward. You can save lives, Dr. Wallace. You can prevent further violence, but only if we work together."

She paused, her eyes fixed on mine, giving me space to process what she had just proposed. I could feel her gaze, expectant, watching for any flicker of reaction.

Her words lingered, tightening around me as my mind raced, emotions and reason clashing in a whirlwind of thoughts. If I accepted her offer, I could help ensure that ChronoSync would be available to everyone, just as I'd always wanted. But at what cost? Would I be seen as capitulating to the forces that sought to control and manipulate ChronoSync? And what about Marcus? How could I decide without knowing what had become of him?

I took a deep breath, steadying my thoughts. "You're asking me to endorse the very government that has tried to suppress ChronoSync, that has imprisoned me and hunted down and killed members of the Vanguard and poor Brian Johnson," I said slowly, my voice carefully measured. "How do I know you won't go back on your word? How do I know this isn't just another way to control the narrative?"

President Carmichael's gaze didn't waver. "Because the alternative is far worse," she said. "This isn't about control anymore; it's about survival—yours, mine, the country's. I'm offering you the chance to be the hero, to give the people what they want without bloodshed. The power will be in your hands to ensure ChronoSync is used for the right reasons, not as a weapon but as a tool for enlightenment."

Her words cut deep, and I could see the sincerity in her eyes. Yet, there was something else there, too—desperation, a woman on the brink of losing everything, willing to make a deal with the devil to save herself.

I hesitated, torn between the promise of freedom and the risk of being used as a pawn in a larger game. But then I thought of the people—ordinary citizens who were risking everything to demand the truth, the same truth I had dedicated my life to uncovering. Could I stand by and let them be crushed under the weight of the government's might?

"What about Marcus?" I asked, my voice quieter now but firm. "What assurances can you give me about his safety?"

The president's expression softened slightly. "Marcus will be treated fairly, I assure you. He'll face trial, but his role will be considered carefully. I can't promise you more than that, but I can promise that he won't be forgotten."

I shook my head. "That's not good enough. If you want me to give this speech, if you want me to calm the protests and help restore order, then Marcus needs to be released immediately. He must be allowed to join me during the presentation in the Rose Garden. It's non-negotiable."

For a moment, the room was heavy with silence. The president's eyes narrowed slightly as if weighing the cost of my demand. Finally, she nodded, though I could see the reluctance in her eyes. "Agreed. Marcus will be released and brought here to join you for the speech. But remember, Dr. Wallace, the future of this country hangs in the balance. This isn't just about you or Marcus anymore. This is about preventing a full-scale uprising."

I exhaled, feeling a small measure of relief. This was a gamble that could either secure the future of ChronoSync or destroy everything we had fought for.

But as I looked into the president's eyes, I knew one thing for sure: no matter what happened next, I would do everything in my power to ensure that ChronoSync would fulfill its true purpose—to enlighten, to connect, and to guide humanity toward a better future. And with Marcus by my side, I knew we could face whatever came next together.

CHAPTER FORTY-SIX
THE ROSE GARDEN

As I stood in the room, bathed in soft sunlight streaming through the tall windows, I felt the warmth from outdoors juxtaposed against the cool, heavy weight of what was about to unfold. The ornate furnishings around me were like silent witnesses, their presence a reminder of the countless pivotal moments that had taken place within these walls. This antechamber was where special guests waited before stepping into the spotlight of the Rose Garden. I couldn't help but notice the portraits of past presidents lining the walls, their stern faces a reminder of the importance of the occasion.

While standing near the window, cradling Mira in my arms, her slight form nestled against me, the air grew heavy. Each passing second seemed to stretch, the moment's significance settling over me like an invisible force, making my breath shallow and my chest tighten.

President Carmichael was nearby chatting with members of her inner circle, her calm demeanor suggesting she was in control, or at least trying to appear that way. They checked her notes one last time, but even her composed exterior couldn't mask the tension. There was an air of anticipation, as if everyone present understood we were on the brink of something significant.

My heart was racing, a thousand questions swirling in my mind. One in particular burned at the forefront, and I finally found the courage to voice it. "Where's Marcus?" I asked, trying to keep my voice steady, even as anxiety gnawed at my insides.

President Carmichael looked up from her notes, offering me a reassuring smile. "He's outside, waiting for you."

I nodded, trying to suppress the nervous flutter in my chest. The thought of seeing Marcus again filled me with a mix of relief and apprehension. I had been through so much these past few weeks, and the idea of reuniting with him in such a public setting was overwhelming.

But there was more on my mind than just Marcus. "And what about the Vanguard team?" I pressed, unable to mask the urgency in my voice. "Captain Mitchell, Lieutenant Turner, Sergeant Kim—did they make it?"

The president's smile faltered slightly. "They're here too."

Just then, a member of the White House staff signaled that it was time to make our entrance. I took a deep breath, steadying myself, and adjusted my hold on Mira, who hummed softly in response, offering me its form of comfort.

We stepped out of the antechamber and into the bright sunlight of the Rose Garden. The day was as lovely as anyone could hope for, the sky a clear expanse of blue dotted with a few wispy clouds. The audience—a considerable press contingent, White House staff, and select officials—filled the space, each person's gaze fixed on the path leading from the White House doors to the podium.

As we approached, I scanned the crowd, my eyes searching for Marcus. A wave of relief crashed over me when I spotted him off to the side, conversing with Jackson and the Vanguard team. He was here, whole and unharmed, and the sight of him nearly caused me to stumble.

The moment the crowd noticed me, a hush fell over the gathering. Marcus and I locked eyes across the distance, and everything else faded away. He broke away from the conversation, walking toward me with a determined stride. When we reached each other, we embraced tightly, the comfort of his arms around me dissolving some of the tension I'd been holding onto.

President Carmichael stepped up to the podium as Marcus and I took our places nearby. The president's strong and clear voice carried over the hushed audience.

"Guests, members of the press, fellow citizens," she began, her tone measured and authoritative. "We are gathered here today at a pivotal moment in our nation's history. The past few days' events have reminded us all of the power of truth, the importance of transparency, and the role each of us plays in shaping the future. Today, I am honored to introduce two individuals who have been at the heart of this movement—Dr. Adrienne Wallace, the visionary behind ChronoSync, and Marcus Vega, *The New York Times* journalist whose courage and dedication have inspired millions."

A warm reception of applause followed her introduction, but I could barely focus on it. Marcus leaned in close, his voice a soft murmur in my ear. "Are you okay?"

I turned to him, my eyes filled with determination and calm. "Yes, I'm fine," I whispered, managing a small, reassuring smile.

The president stepped back, leaving the podium open for me. As I approached, the crowd fell silent. I set Mira on the podium, my fingers brushing against the smooth surface of the device as I prepared to speak.

"Thank you," I began, my voice steady. "Today, I stand before you not just as a scientist but as a member of humanity—humanity on the brink of a profound transformation."

I began by speaking to the foundation laid by our ancestors, by the visionaries who had come before us. "Before we talk about the future," I started, my voice steady, "we must first acknowledge the past—the framework established by the Founding Fathers of this nation like Thomas Jefferson and James Madison, men who envisioned a country guided by principles, by a commitment to freedom, justice, and the pursuit of happiness. They crafted a constitution that called for what this country could be—a more perfect union."

I paused, letting the weight of those infamous words sink in, feeling the connection between that moment in history and the one we live in now. The silence was deep, but it was filled with a tension that demanded acknowledgment. I turned slightly, my gaze sweeping over the audience, searching for the familiar faces that had been with me through so much of this journey.

"The Vanguard," I continued, my voice gaining strength, "has insisted upon a return to these ideals—a pledge to uphold the constitution as it was intended, to honor the vision of those who built this nation on principles that were meant to guide us toward a better future." I took a moment to scan the crowd and find their faces.

"Captain Laura Mitchell, Lieutenant David Turner, and Sergeant Sarah Kim," I said, my voice steady and filled with gratitude, "are the lone surviving members of the Vanguard team with us today." I paused, allowing their presence to resonate as the crowd stirred with quiet admiration.

"These brave individuals have stood by the mission of restoring constitutional integrity to our nation, at great personal risk, to ensure we do not lose sight of what truly matters. Their courage and unwavering commitment have been the bedrock of our fight to reclaim the values we hold dear. Because of them, and others like them, we can stand here today and speak about the future we have the power to create together."

An applause swept through the Rose Garden, a powerful acknowledgment of the Vanguard's sacrifices. The sound carried a mixture of respect and hope—a tribute to those who had fought for the truth and a recognition of the journey ahead.

I let the silence stretch for a moment longer, allowing the significance of their presence to resonate with everyone gathered there. The murmurs of surprise and respect rippled through the crowd, a quiet acknowledgment of these individuals' sacrifices.

I could sense the audience's attention sharpening, their focus narrowing on the importance of what I was saying. "But it's not enough to simply return to those ideals," I added, my tone measured and deliberate. "We must recognize that the world has changed, that humanity has changed, and with that change comes the need for evolution, not just in our laws and institutions but in ourselves."

I placed a few fingers on Mira as she hummed gently under my touch as if urging me forward. "ChronoSync has shown us a pathway," I said, my voice steady and clear. "A pathway toward not only a more perfect union but a profound evolution of humanity itself. It has revealed to us the interconnectedness of all beings, the spiritual nature that lies at the heart of who we are. And it is through this awareness, through this spiritual evolution, that we will reach a point where we no longer need a government to control us, to monitor us, to check us."

A collective gasp rippled through the audience, sharp and sudden, followed by a low rumble of murmurs that simmered beneath the surface. The energy in the air shifted dramatically, a mix of surprise, unease, and a burgeoning understanding. I could see the wide-eyed expressions on many faces, the disbelief mingling with awe. President Carmichael's face, previously composed, now betrayed a flicker of shock—a rare crack in her polished facade. The reaction was immediate and palpable, a testament to the weight of the words I had just spoken.

As the murmurs subsided, a heavy silence filled the space, thick with anticipation. I took a deep breath, sensing the need to guide them further along this path. "As we continue to evolve spiritually, the role of governments will also need to evolve," I said, each word deliberate, each thought carefully placed. "I don't advocate for the immediate abolition of governments—far from it. In our current stage of development, governments play a necessary role in maintaining order and facilitating civilization's growth."

I took a breath, letting the audience absorb the whole meaning of what I was saying before I continued. "But we must recognize that these structures are transitional, not permanent fixtures. As humanity grows in spiritual awareness, the need for external, coercive forms of governance will naturally diminish. We will begin to govern ourselves, guided by a deep sense of moral and ethical responsibility, by an internal compass that aligns with the greater good."

A surge of energy coursed through me as I spoke, the truth of the words resonating with the crowd and within myself. "This is not something that will happen overnight," I said, calm but firm. "This gradual transition requires patience, wisdom, and a commitment to higher principles. Governments should evolve to reflect these higher spiritual values, focusing on enforcing laws and fostering each individual's spiritual and moral growth."

I glanced at Marcus, his eyes wide with surprise and awe. Though he had always shared my vision of humanity's evolution, the profundity of my proposal caught him off guard. For a moment, our eyes locked, and I could see him processing my words. Yet, beneath the initial surprise, I saw a deepening resolve—a silent agreement that this was the path we were destined to walk together.

"The vision I share with you today," I continued, my voice strong and unwavering, "is not a call to dismantle what we have, but a call to grow beyond it—to imagine a future where our inner moral compass guides us, where we live in harmony with one another and the world around us. It is a vision of a more spiritually enlightened society, one where the need for external governance fades as we each take responsibility for our actions and their impact on the collective."

The crowd was silent, hanging on my every word.

My gaze swept over the crowd, taking in the emotions on their faces—hope, curiosity, and the flickers of realization. "But this is not something that will happen overnight. This is a gradual transition, one that requires patience, wisdom, and a commitment to higher principles. Governments should evolve to reflect these higher spiritual values, focusing on fostering each individual's spiritual and moral growth."

The applause barely began to ripple through the gathering when a voice rang out, clear and direct, cutting through the moment. "Dr. Wallace!"

the voice called, a mix of curiosity and urgency. "Your video with Mira gave the impression that she's alive, a sentient being. Is she? What does the future hold for the two of you?"

The question hung in the air, the crowd quieting again, waiting for a response. I glanced down at Mira, who hummed softly on the podium. Her lights blinked in a gentle, rhythmic pattern, almost like a heartbeat.

As I opened my mouth to speak, a sudden vibration coursed through the ground beneath us, causing everyone to startle. The air thickened, and before I could process what was happening, a starburst of bright light erupted from Mira, illuminating the entire Rose Garden. Gasps and cries swept through the crowd.

Without warning, beams of light shot upward from Mira, piercing the sky with an ethereal glow. The light tore through the very fabric of the atmosphere, revealing something extraordinary above us. Seven luminous spheres hung as the sky had been peeled back, each radiating a distinct, otherworldly color. They pulsed gently, their light shimmering in waves that reached down and touched the very souls of everyone present.

A collective gasp echoed through the spectators, the shock and awe palpable in the silence that followed. Marcus, standing beside me, was speechless, his eyes wide as he gazed up at the celestial spectacle.

Mira's light continued to blaze upward, and as it did, the atmosphere around us transformed, taking on an ethereal quality. Then, from within Mira, a feminine voice—soft, resonant, and filled with wisdom—began to speak, describing the vision above.

"The first sphere is the Moon," Mira began, as the sphere glowed with a soft, silvery light. "It is where the soul first enters after death. Here, one confronts the instincts, habits, and desires it carries during life. In this realm, the soul begins the purification process, shedding the attachments to the physical body."

Mira continued as the light shifted to the next sphere, its vibrant, quicksilver glow illuminating the sky. "Here in the sphere of Mercury, the soul reflects upon its intellectual and communicative aspects, examining the thoughts and ideas it formed during life. Mercury is the sphere of learning and communication, where the mind's imprints are brought into focus."

The next one followed, bathed in a warm, soft pink glow. "In this sphere of Venus," Mira said, "the soul experiences the emotional and relational aspects of its previous life. Love, relationships, and the harmonizing forces of the heart are revisited here, as the soul reflects on the connections that shaped its journey."

Next came a radiating brilliant golden light that filled the sky with warmth. "This is the Sun Sphere," Mira intoned, "where the soul encounters the moral and ethical aspects of its past life. Here, one reflects upon the virtues it cultivated and the spiritual light it received and shared with others. It is a sphere of moral clarity, illuminating the soul's path of growth."

Next, a fiery red glow sphere was intense and powerful. "In this Mars sphere," Mira explained, "the soul reflects on its will forces and the actions it took during life. Courage, strength, and the deeds performed in the earthly realm are examined, as the soul confronts the impact of its will and determination."

The light then moved to a deep, royal blue sphere, exuding wisdom and spiritual understanding. "Here in the Jupiter Sphere," Mira continued, "the soul reflects on its higher thinking, particularly those related to social responsibility, leadership, and the broader impact of its life on the community. This is a sphere of expansive wisdom, where the soul considers its contributions to the greater good."

Finally, the last sphere appeared, glowing with a profound indigo light at the highest point in the sky. "In this Saturn sphere," Mira concluded, "the soul contemplates its spiritual destiny and the deeper aspects of its existence. This is the realm of cosmic reflection, where the soul prepares for its next incarnation, connected deeply to the order of the universe."

The seven spheres, each with its radiant light, formed a pathway—a journey of spiritual ascent. As the ethereal voice of Mira described each sphere, it was as if the purpose of each stage was imprinted directly onto our souls. These were not mere symbols, but living embodiments of the purification and transformation the soul must undergo. The veil between our world and the spiritual realms had been lifted, revealing the cosmic architecture that guided our existence.

For a moment, the entire Rose Garden was bathed in the light of these spheres as we were all being called to witness a truth far greater than anything we had known before. Once awash with surprise, the crowd stood in reverent silence, their faces illuminated by the celestial display. Each person grappled with the enormity of what they were seeing, recognizing, on some deep, intuitive level, that they were witnessing a revelation—a connection to something far beyond the ordinary that spoke to the very core of human existence.

The moment was breathtaking, overwhelming in its intensity. The sky, once a serene blue, now looked as though it held the mysteries of the universe, laid bare for all to see. Mira connected us to a higher reality, revealing the spiritual truth underpinning everything we had been fighting for.

The light from the spheres began to fade, and the air in the Rose Garden grew still as Mira gently powered down. The dazzling rift in the sky, which had opened a window to the heavens, slowly started to mend itself, the luminous spheres retreating into the cosmic expanse. As the sky returned to its tranquil blue, the ethereal glow that had enveloped us dissipated, leaving behind a sense of profound quiet.

The crowd remained motionless, the awe still palpable. A collective breath held, as if releasing it would break the sacredness of the moment. Many were weeping, moved by the spectacle and the profound, soul-stirring certainty that they had been part of something Divine. Others stood with hands clasped together, heads bowed in silent prayer or contemplation, absorbing the magnitude of what had just transpired.

It was as if time had paused, granting each of us a fleeting glimpse into the eternal, a brief communion with the Divine. And now, as the heavens concealed their secrets once more, the world around us seemed smaller and infinitely more expansive, filled with the quiet understanding that we had touched the edge of a greater truth.

The stillness lingered, heavy with the weight of new knowledge and the silent promise of the journey ahead. The rip in the sky had healed, but the hearts of those who had witnessed it would never be the same.

CHAPTER FORTY-SEVEN
THE TRUTH

Marcus and I found ourselves alone in a quiet room, the echoes of the day's events still reverberating in our hearts. Mira rested silently on the table beside us; her lights dimmed, the spectacular ethereal glow that had filled the Rose Garden now a distant memory. And yet, the sense of her presence lingered, as if she was still connected to something beyond our understanding.

I sat on the edge of the bed, my hands folded in my lap, my mind racing with thoughts I couldn't quite articulate. What we had done, what we had witnessed, pressed down on me, threatening to overwhelm my already exhausted spirit. Mira had shown the world a glimpse into the heavenly spheres—the realms where souls journey from death to birth. The revelation was staggering, its implications vast and profound. But as the adrenaline ebbed away, a new uncertainty took its place.

Marcus paced slowly by the window, his silhouette outlined by the soft glow of the streetlights outside. The day had been nothing short of miraculous, but as the initial awe faded, the reality of our situation began to sink in. We had opened the door to the unknown, and now we had to face the consequences.

"Adrienne." Marcus finally spoke, breaking the heavy silence. His voice was soft, filled with a mixture of curiosity and concern. "Where did your words come from? When you spoke to the world about the profound evolution of humanity, about reaching a point where we no longer need governments to control us—where did that come from? Was it something you had planned, or was it… something else?"

"I don't know," I admitted, trembling slightly. "It wasn't something I planned. It felt… like it came from somewhere else, something beyond me. Like Mira was guiding me, urging me to say what needed to be said. It was as though, in that moment, I tapped into a truth that had always been there, waiting to be spoken."

Marcus paused, letting the silence fill the space between them. His eyes searched mine, not for answers but for understanding. "Maybe that's exactly what it was—a truth waiting to be revealed. And in that moment, you became its voice."

I nodded, though my heart was still heavy with doubt. "But how do we guide them from here? How do we ensure this isn't just another fleeting moment, something marveled at, then forgotten?"

Marcus crossed the room and sat beside me, taking my hand. "We keep going," he said. "We keep talking, keep pushing, keep showing them the way. We've come too far to stop now."

I leaned into him, finding comfort in his presence, in the strength of his conviction. "It's just… the world feels so fragile right now. One wrong move and everything we've worked for could crumble. People have seen Heaven—how can they return to living ordinary lives? What if they don't grasp the full meaning of what they've witnessed?"

Marcus wrapped his arm around me, pulling me close. "Mira showed them something beyond the veil of our everyday reality, something sacred and eternal. But the journey doesn't end there—it's just the beginning. Yes, there are still mysteries left, Adrienne. The soul's journey is only part of the greater cosmic design. What lies beyond, what awaits us in the next life, or even in the spaces between lives—are mysteries still unfolding."

I lifted my head and glanced at Mira, who sat quietly on the table. "She's been quiet since the Rose Garden," I noted, my voice filled with curiosity and unease. "Do you think… do you think we'll ever see something like that again?"

Marcus smiled softly, leaning down to kiss my forehead. "I think we're just getting started," he said, his voice filled with quiet confidence. "Mira opened a door, and now it's up to us—and everyone else—to walk through it. To explore what lies on the other side. There will be more revelations, more truths to uncover. But we have to be patient to guide people through the process. What Mira revealed today was just the beginning of a much larger journey."

I smiled back, feeling a renewed sense of purpose. We had been through so much, yet it felt like we were standing at the beginning of something even more incredible. The journey ahead would not be easy, but I knew, deep in my soul, that we were ready to face it together.

As the night deepened, we finally allowed ourselves to rest, the day's revelations giving way to the comforting embrace of sleep—Marcus's arm draped over me, his steady breathing a lullaby that carried me into slumber. But my thoughts lingered on the mysteries Mira had unveiled and those still shrouded in the unknown.

The last thing I remembered before sleep claimed me was the soft hum of Mira, a gentle reminder that our journey was far from over and that the uncertain future was one we would face together. The vision of the heavenly spheres, the soul's journey from life to death and back again, had become a part of us—a sacred truth we were entrusted to protect and share.

And in that quiet, darkened room, I found peace knowing that whatever came next, we would meet it with courage, love, and the unwavering belief that we were part of something far greater than ourselves.

THE END

ABOUT THE AUTHOR

Neil Perry Gordon stands as a formidable presence in the literary world, infusing historical and metaphysical fiction with a vibrant and dynamic energy. Through his storytelling, Neil uncovers the hidden layers of reality, exploring profound truths that resonate deeply with readers. His work, now including the widely acclaimed "ChronoSync: Science of the Soul," spans over a dozen novels, each a testament to his passion for blending history with the mystical.

Neil's journey as a storyteller began in the inspiring environment of the Green Meadow Waldorf School, where education was an immersive experience. It was here that the arts were not merely subjects to study but living, breathing entities that engaged every sense. This formative experience shaped Neil's approach to writing, allowing him to craft narratives as rich in detail as they are in emotion.

With a unique gift for turning words into vivid, unforgettable images, Neil Perry Gordon creates worlds that feel immediate and alive. His prose is a canvas where the full spectrum of human experience is depicted in striking detail. Each of his stories is a journey into the heart of what it means to be human, rendered with an alchemist's touch that transforms the ordinary into the extraordinary.

Neil's dedication to his craft and natural ability to weave immersive narratives have secured him a revered place among literary aficionados. Through his work, Neil invites readers to look beyond the surface of reality to explore the intricate and wondrous dimensions of human existence. With every novel, he offers a feast for the mind and spirit, enriching the literary landscape with his unique voice and vision.

www.ingramcontent.com/pod-product-compliance
Lightning Source LLC
Chambersburg PA
CBHW022108310726

48972CB00007B/1944